Demons Within

Demons Within

ISBN 978-0-6151-4218-0

First Edition

10 9 8 7 6 5 4 3 2 1

John is struggling to regain control. His fears, once hidden deep inside, have begun to take control of him, causing vivid dreams and hallucinations. Some of the dreams are merely historical facts about his families' history, while others are meant only to pitch him deeper into a state of insanity.

In his travels, he comes across many clues that can help him understand not only what is happening, but also help him control the thoughts in his head and return his life to a somewhat normal state. But John doesn't know how to best interpret the clues and he finds himself faced with a few people who say they know what he is going through and will gladly help.

However, not all of those he meets mean to help him and it is up to him to find the truth hidden underneath the many layers of defenses that he has put up to keep the truth from coming out. Johns mind takes him on a roller coaster horror ride through his life and the history of his family where he learns of a demon named Chaos whose sole purpose is to take possession of him and return from his exile to rule the minds of all the people in the world.

John is also dealing with conflicting advice from people who often lead him away from the very truth he seeks to find. In the end, the question is; will John find the truth and overcome the demon who seeks to due him harm, or will his mind prove too weak causing him to lose everything he cares about to the

Demons Within

A Novel By

William Hartnett

For my wife Terinna

And my children
Allyson, Liam, Brayden!

You keep me going every day.

"To dream is to dare to go where others fear to tread."

Anonymous

"A little fear is a good thing, but only if it's someone else fearing you."

Fat Tony Marachino

The Darkness Begins

I saw him again today. It seems that no matter where I go or what I happen to be doing, he is there. It wasn't always this way. Time was I could go about my daily routine and he would not be there, but not now. It hasn't been that way for what seems like an eternity. In fact, I can't remember what it was like when he was not around.

I started my day today the same way that I always did. Maybe that was part of the problem. You should never start the day analyzing a dream from the night before because you only remember pieces at a time, and never in any kind of right order. Why was I thinking that? What could this mean? What's with the dancing dog? I don't know. Anyway, after my morning bathroom ritual I headed out to the same café that I found myself frequenting lately. The coffee was good and I could be there for as long as I felt I needed to be to catch up on the day's events.

He was sitting right there in the corner. I don't know why I didn't spot him when I walked in but there he was, dressed as he always did in a full-length black coat, black hat, black shirt, you get the picture. He was an imposing figure, his long legs sticking way out from underneath the table. His face had cut features and his eyes gave me a cold, hard stare. I found myself staring back at him, not so much staring back as not able to look away. He tipped his sunglasses down with his finger and met my stare with his deep black eyes. I felt my feet go numb and my muscles didn't respond to my demand that they move to look away. He raised his arm towards his head and extended his index finger and thumb, bringing them back down until they were pointing at me. He made a gesture of a gun going off and spoke the same words, make that the only words that he had ever spoken to me, "What's up kid?" Seeing him there, I remembered the first time that he made himself known in my life.

I was visiting my grandfather in the hospital because he had been diagnosed with multiple types of cancer and the prognosis was not good. I had seen him only six or so weeks earlier at his house. At that time he was fine, outwardly so. He had cancer for a while and had quite a few legions removed from his skin over the past couple of years. Being only the grandson, I was not privy to all of the health problems of my grandparents. This probably did a lot to increase the shock when I saw him for the last time.

My grandfather was an extremely social man. Always the politician, he knew someone almost everywhere we went. He was old, as were all members of my family, but not too old. He loved sports and was die-hard Red Sox fan even in the worst times. I remember growing up taking the 'T' into the city every summer to see the games with him. On summer nights, we would sit out on the porch and just talk. He could carry on a conversation about anything, but he had strong beliefs and would argue them anytime the need arose. The memories I had of him were part of who I

The Darkness Begins

was. The lessons he taught stay with me to this day. That day in the hospital changed everything forever.

My father wanted me to go see him in the hospital. Let me first say that I don't do hospitals period. Something about their sterilized environment freaks me out. I think that a hospital is by far the scariest place that you can be. I knew he was sick, but I figured that when I saw him he would be the same person that I remembered. I could not have been more wrong.

We got to the hospital around one o'clock or so; my parents, my brother and myself. I figured we would spend about an hour here and then make the trip back home. We took the elevator up to his floor and made our way to his room. Hospitals are always too bright and this one seemed even more so than normal. All around us there were families visiting relatives, doctors seeing patients, and little kids running around as if this were a playground or something. There was also a strong smell of ammonia in the air. This was probably to hide the stench of all of the sick people. I started to feel sick.

I don't know why but all of a sudden my palms began to sweat. I know I don't like hospitals, but I've never really had any type of reaction to being in one. We reached his room just as someone was coming out. It was him. The man from the café. The man from my dreams. He was dressed in all black, to which I have since become accustomed, and he rushing out of the room. He cocked his head to me and said, "What's up kid?" Then he was gone.

As soon as I turned the corner into the room my world turned upside down. Lying on the bed was not my grandfather but someone, something, with all of these growths all over its skin. There were I.V. tubes hooked up to both of his arms and he looked as if he had lost 100 pounds. He was frail. I had never seen him like this. He had always been strong in both appearance and presence. He was bitter and when I started to talk to him, his responses were vicious, swearing at me about the doctor's, my father, his life. I knew at that moment that he was dying and it was too much for me to handle. This was not him. This person was not my grandfather.

I began to feel closed in and I couldn't breathe. My feet were going numb and my hands began shaking. I had to leave, run away from this place as fast as I could. What was happening? Why was I feeling this way? I felt my head begin to split open. It felt like someone was prying it apart. My eye began to flicker wildly as I gasped for air. I couldn't speak, but needed to scream. I wanted to leave but couldn't move. My legs were locked to the floor. I started to sweat profusely and I fought with all I had to turn around and leave.

Once outside the room I staggered. A nurse came rushing up to me and said, "Honey are you o.k.?" She put her hand on my shoulder to brace me up and I turned towards her, "I'm o.k., I just need some air." I said. She sat me down and went to get some water. I felt my heart racing and still couldn't breathe. I got up and staggered towards the elevator. I started jamming the down button with my thumb for what seemed like a thousand times before the doors finally opened and I stepped inside. With the last ounce of strength I could muster, I pressed the button for the ground floor just as everything went white.

Demons Within

The next thing I was aware of was my body floating through what felt like a very thick liquid which was making it almost impossible for me to control my movements. I opened my eyes and could see nothing but darkness all around. Sounds from the outside fought to penetrate the thick force surrounding me, but they were unable to break through and I was trapped in a shield of silence floating out of control. I tried to shout but no sounds came out of my mouth. My heart was racing and I began to hear its maddening thump ringing through my ears.

Other sounds began to make their way into the darkness. The screech was the first thing that I heard. It was like the brakes on a train, only 100 times louder. The sound echoed through the darkness and its volume kept increasing. I felt the pulse in my ears growing faster and faster. My head, my god the pain in my head! My left eardrum popped with a deafening roar and I screamed out in pain. But my cries were drowned out by the deafening roar. The screech grew louder as a shrill cry joined in, threatening to burst my other eardrum and I was helpless to stop the noises piercing through my head. The space that I occupied began spinning and I felt my whole body tearing itself apart, limbs flailing wildly in all directions as they began to snap away from my body. The brightness of the white grew in intensity until I felt my mind shut down.

I came to with a start in the lobby of the hospital. I did a quick check of the vitals, arms still attached, fingers moving, and vision good. I realized that I wasn't breathing so I drew a quick breath and coughed it out before it could be completed. My heart rate started to slow and I started walking to the door. What the hell was that?

When I got outside the first thing that I noticed was the breeze. There wasn't one. Then why was I getting a chill? I felt a coldness more intense then I had ever felt before. Looking around everything appeared off a little. I can't really explain but something about everything was off, wrong somehow. I saw people walking to the hospital and others going to their cars but I couldn't feel their presence. It's like they weren't really there.

I knew then that it was only a matter of time until my grandfather would no longer be around. I began to wish that I had spent more time with him. You know how it is when you're young. There's plenty of time for everything and nothing bad will ever happen to anyone close to you. You don't think about the bad things. Your whole life is ahead of you and there's nothing or no one that can stop you. Talk about a reality check.

My family came out of the hospital as all of this was going on and asked if I was alright. What am I going to say to that? We were never close in the feeling-sharing department. Emotional displays of a personal nature were never shared. That's just the way we were. We had gone through a lot as a family but had never really grown that bond that you see on Lifetime. To me, that was a foreign concept best left for poor actors who had gone past their prime, if they ever really had a prime.

We all got into the car and as we were pulling away, I saw him again. He was standing on the curb by the entrance looking at me. Looking through me, I should say. He gave me a nod and walked out of my line of sight.

The Darkness Begins

I began to wonder about the feelings that I was having. As I said before, everything was a little off. But was that because of the realization that I wasn't invincible and neither was my family, or something else? Had my memories of my grandfather, once such a strong part of my personality and my existence, been corrupted forever based on only two minutes of visiting, or was there something else at work here?

In bed that night, I felt as if I had aged many years in one day. My perception of life was altered in a way that I had never expected, and I wanted no part of this new phase.

Three weeks later my grandfather finally succumbed to the evil known as cancer. I had lost people before but it never really hit me until now. At the wake, there were many people he had known throughout his life. They all had stories to tell about the kind of person that he was, how much he helped them out, and how much they would miss him. I wondered what the point of all of this was. Some say that it's part of the grieving process to help people cope, but I felt nothing. How could it be that this event would stir up no feelings in me? Was I in denial? Did I choose just not to deal with this? That's precisely what happened. I took all of the feelings that I had and just made them disappear. To me, he was now just a memory. It would be the same as if I had never met him.

The funeral was held, of course, on a cold rainy day. We went through the process of going to the funeral parlor, getting all of the cars lined up behind the hearse, turning all of our headlights on and following in a long procession to the church. When we arrived, we all got out and made our way inside.

I remember the church fairly well. It full of Catholic history with ornate fixtures and pane glass windows depicting various characters of the bible doing whatever it is that they did to justify the homage paid to them. I consider myself a Catholic, but a lapsed one at best. While I grew up going to church every Sunday, going to c.c.d. classes, and attending various church functions, I couldn't seem to remember any of the teachings. The priest stood over the casket and said a lot of really nice things about my grandfather. He had been going to the same church for so many years I would hope that there were good things to say about him.

The mass ended and we went to the cemetery. There were more prayers and a song, I think, followed by an invitation to someone's house afterwards for a reception. A reception? After this loss, we should all be expected to go drink coffee, eat little sandwiches, and start deciding where all of his things were going to go? This to me was unreal.

As I started back to the car, I noticed someone standing behind a tree watching the funeral. It was him again! Why was he there? Did he know my grandfather? Did he have other business at a cemetery on a rainy day? I turned to my brother and asked him if he recognized the man standing behind the tree. When he looked over, there was no one there. I didn't understand it; he was there just a minute before. As I was getting into the car, I started to get that same feeling of impending doom that I had in the hospital. You couldn't get me away from there fast enough and I haven't been back since.

Demons Within

Now you know the first time that I met him. Why he came into my life at that point is unknown to me, but it's a question that I find myself asking a lot nowadays. Perhaps his arrival marks my promotion into full-fledged adulthood from adolescence. Maybe it marks the opening of a new part of my life which will be marked by situations meant to test my mettle as a moral person and a good Catholic. Maybe it's a sign that I shouldn't take anything for granted. Maybe he's all in my head and I should just get over it. I hoped it wasn't something that I needed to get over because I was afraid that I wouldn't have the mental strength to take on that task.

Now here he was again and I was once more powerless against him.

I wanted to leave but couldn't move, my legs refused to obey the commands coming from my brain, and I was trapped in his stare. He pushed his glasses back up and returned to his paper. Why was he here? Why could I not move? What power did he hold over me? My mind began to race and I felt another migraine coming on. These too had become part of my daily life. I had so many now that I almost didn't notice when they were happening.

I finished my fourth cup of coffee and put my money on the table. I had to get out of there, now. I had never felt urgency like this before. I felt my adrenaline pulsing through my veins, flowing rapidly, and I couldn't get out of there fast enough. I rose to my feet and started towards the door but my progress was slowed by my weakened leg muscles. It felt as if I were walking through tar, my leg muscles tearing at each step. The room started to get hot and I felt sweat running down my back as I struggled to reach the door that would let me out of what I perceived as a dangerous situation.

The inwards rush of air from the door took my breath away and I felt myself going faint. I staggered to my car, scratching the paint with my key as I tried to open the door. My hands were shaking violently as I turned the key in the lock. I opened the door and fell into the car, bumping my head into the rear view mirror. It crashed to the floor leaving a glue mark on the windshield. I closed the door and immediately felt normal, well, as normal as I have felt lately. There was no more fear and my shaking had ceased. There was only calm. What was that all about? I felt my heart rate returning to normal as I pulled out of the lot.

The Key

After I got out of the café, I couldn't wait to get home. The way my life had been going lately, it seemed I always couldn't wait to get home. Everywhere I went things just weren't the same. New experiences felt distant as if I were watching them on TV. I didn't _feel_ part of them. I didn't _feel_ anything. The feeling in the café today was by far the worst I had experienced with him so far. It was sheer terror.

Over the years, I have always expected him to show up. Even so, I am never really prepared for when he does. He always seems to catch me totally off guard. I didn't know how much more of this I could take. Why couldn't I confront him? I wanted to go up to him and tell him to leave me alone, go pick on somebody else! Every time I have a thought, he worked his way into it. My feelings have become a twisted pile of rubble that I can't seem to sort through. I keep sifting through them, picking up a scrap of a memory here, an emotion there, but nothing of any substantive value.

I walked into my house and threw my keys on the table. There were no messages on my machine, although that was nothing new since I had lost contact with anyone that you would remotely call a friend long ago. With the way I had become, it was no wonder. Well there was one good thing remaining in my life. I still had my dog.

I went upstairs to take another shower because I felt extremely dirty all of a sudden. It felt like something was crawling all over me. I stripped off my clothes, turned the hot water on high, and jumped into the shower. The room quickly filled with steam and I looked around for something to help me scrub off the eerie feeling that was making my skin tingle. I found a loofah on the edge of the tub and started to work it over my body, pressing down hard with all of my strength as I scrubbed. The more I worked the loofah, the dirtier I felt. I scrubbed harder until I had removed all of the dead skin from my body leaving only a new, pink layer. I continued the maddening scrubbing and the new skin became raw and cracked from the abuse I was unfairly inflicting upon it. By the time that I finished, my whole body was pink and bleeding from the torture. The loofah was full of dead skin and clumps of hair. I threw it down into the tub and stepped out of the shower, not feeling any cleaner than when I had entered. That was odd. I went into the bedroom and checked the clock. It had been three hours since I returned home from the café. How did so much time pass by so quickly? What the hell was I doing for three hours in a shower? I looked into the mirror and saw my skin for the first time. It was all torn up with a few ragged pieces clinging on for dear life, hoping that they would be spared from another wrath. I grabbed some lotion from the dresser and started to work it into my damaged skin. The pain was almost intolerable as the cream worked its way into the many cracks on my skin, trying to heal the wounds.

I got dressed, taking care to choose a shirt that wouldn't further irritate my skin, and decided that I needed some fresh air. Feeling generous, I decided to take the dog with

The Key

me. As usual, he was twenty different kinds of excited when he realized that he would be going out. He had the same routine every time. First, as though in disbelief, he cocked his head and perked up his ears. Then the dance began. He jumped around on all fours, spinning his body around in a curling type motion with his paws extended outward in a raise the roof dance style. Then he pounded the floor with his front legs giving a deep bark each time his feet hit the floor. I put the leash on and off we went.

I love to drive and the dog loves to drool. What a perfect combination. We got into the car and took off. Driving is the only thing that clears my head nowadays. The road is your only worry. I have always loved driving because it is the only time that I feel totally in control. Every start, stop, or turn is entirely up to me. If I want to go faster, I do. Nothing bothers me. This is my domain. <u>He</u> can't find me if I don't stop. Up the road there's a store that I frequent because they stock all of my chosen vices. I pulled up to the curb and jumped out, leaving the dog patiently waiting for me to return with a treat.

I felt like a soda. A huge, cold soda. Ever since I first laid eyes on <u>him</u>, I have been unable to quench my thirst. I must pee thirty to forty times a day. I decided on a grape soda from the fountain and I grabbed the largest cup they had, filling it to the top with ice. The sound of the carbonation hitting the ice triggered something buried deep inside of me and I found myself thrown into another dream.

I'm five years old and back in my old house in a town just outside of Chicago. Its late autumn and the leaves are off all of the trees except for a few diehards who cling to their branches. The wind has picked up and the leaves are flapping wildly; their sound startling the birds that have nested in the tree, causing them to fly off to wherever birds go when they are spooked. There's a brook behind the house about 50 yards or so. I decide to go exploring as I do so often and I'm looking for a good tree to climb. There's nothing better for a 5 year old boy than an old tree with lots of branches. The sun has started its rapid decent to the other side of the world and the wind is bitter cold. I begin to wish that I had brought my jacket. My mother would kill me if she knew I was exploring without one.

I spot what looks like a good climbing challenge on the other side of the brook, a place where I'm not supposed to go because our land ends at the brook and my mother forbids me from going past the imaginary line. However, as I look around I don't see anyone so I decide that I'll just go for a quick climb. I start up the tree at a fairly brisk pace, and before long I have made it as far as I can without breaking any of the branches. When I look downstream, I see an old shack tucked in some dense undergrowth. That would make a perfect fort! It is getting somewhat late, but the shack is only about twenty-five yards from here. Besides, I can run really fast so it shouldn't take long at all.

I repel down the tree and start running towards the shack. My shoes have become covered in mud, slowing my progress a little. Finally, I make it to the shack. It looks old, I mean really old. The roof has started to come apart from being exposed to the elements and the boards that make up the walls have started to fall apart. I decide that rather than going in right away, I should just peek in through the slats. I can't see very much, as it has started to get pretty dark. I make my way to the other side of the shack and peer inside. There, on the ground next to an old soda can, is a shiny silver key.

No kid can resist picking up a piece of treasure on an exploration, especially not this kid. I get on my belly and crawl through a small opening. The ground is cold and wet and my clothes will surely tell my mom that I was off exploring again. I decide that the cost of getting the treasure far outweighs any repercussions that will befall me. Inside the shack, there are a lot of cobwebs and spiders. I don't like spiders, or any bugs for that matter. I reach down and pick up both the can and the key. I think that this will make an excellent instrument. I put the key inside the can and shake it rapidly.

Apparently, I am not alone in this shack, a fact that becomes very obvious when I shake the can. Out of the dark corner of the shack comes the biggest dog that I have ever seen. He is not too happy that I have invited myself into his house and he begins to growl, softly at first, then with more authority upon seeing my size. His hair is standing on end and his large teeth are showing through his lips.

I want no part of angering this dog anymore and need to leave right away but there is a problem. He is in front of the door and if I go out the same way that I came in, he would pounce on my back. For the first time in my life, I feel fear. I don't see anyway out of my present situation and it has grown completely dark. Even if I manage to get out of the shack, I still have to make it all the way back to my house. There is no way I can do that before the dog gets me. I could climb back up that tree. Dogs can't climb trees. However, this dog isn't like any other dog that I have seen before. This dog is now standing on two legs. I feel someone's hand on my shoulder. I start to turn around and....

"Sir are you alright?"

I opened my eyes and saw that it was the clerk at the store. He was looking at me with what seems a high level of concern.

"Sir, do you need some help?"

I realized then that my hand was extremely cold. I looked down and saw that soda was pouring all over it. I jerked my hand away from the machine and it stopped, leaving me standing in a pool of soda that had spilled all over the floor. I turned back towards the clerk but he had already gone to get a mop.

I started to feel a great pressure on my head as though it was being squeezed like a sponge, twisting back and forth. My pores opened up and I began to sweat profusely as my hands started to shake. An all too familiar feeling of dread began to take over my emotions. It was a feeling I have felt all too often. I ran out of the store, knocking over a display rack and a surprised clerk on my way out. I ran to my car, which I left running with the dog in the back seat, and threw it into drive. When I cut out into traffic, a car screeched sideways onto the sidewalk to avoid hitting me and crashed into the store. As I sped off, I heard the man release a stream of profanity, the likes of which haven't been heard since Archie Bunker ruled the airwaves years ago. I needed to get away faster. The car accelerated through an intersection and I jammed the wheel to the right. The tires squealed in protest as I took the sharp corner of the highway onramp.

What the hell was happening to me? Why did I blank out in the store? There didn't seem to be any good answers to these pressing questions. There was only one thing for which I was sure, I needed to get away. There was something at work here, something that's not keeping with the normal spectrum of things. Today my emotions were all gone except for fear. Fear is all I know and because of that, I can only react with panic.

I needed to know the significance of that dream. I have had them before but never that real. I could swear that I was there, staring into the face of the dog. All of the feelings were still fresh in my mind. The dreams have never lasted as long before and have never really caused me to black out. In addition, I have never felt such a strong feeling of fear afterwards. There must be something in that dream that would tell me what's been going on for so many years. Is it the dog? Could that be a connection somehow? Or how about the key? The dream did seem to be centered on my getting that key. What could the key signify? Maybe it unlocks something, but what? A memory of some sort is the likely answer, but nothing has ever followed the likely path with me before. I couldn't analyze the dream while I was still driving, so I decided to go somewhere to sort it all out.

I decided on the resort. It's one of the few things that I have left from my first marriage, a timeshare that we acquired when condominiums where the hottest thing since sliced bread and people were buying them before they were even being built. It is located up in ski country, which was kind of funny considering the fact that I don't ski. Never have. She was into skiing, the bitch that is. That is not exactly a mean thing to say when you know actually know who she is. She'll even tell you herself that she's a bitch. I guess that's something to be proud of these days. At least she knows what she is. I on the other hand am starting to have serious doubts as to whom or even what I am.

She left me many years ago because to use her own words, I was holding her back from reaching her dreams. Based on what she has done since the divorce was final, the only dreams she had were seeing how many different men she could screw, and then screw over. The timeshare was the only thing that we both retained control of together; she wanted it for a getaway spot; I wanted it so she couldn't have it. We developed a system for deciding who would get to use it and when. I would call her and ask permission. Some system.

My son was the only thing from our relationship that I truly missed. During our final years together, she did everything in her power to convince him that I was no good. When it came time for the custody hearing, he wanted nothing to do with me. She and her lawyer even managed to convince the judge that my mere presence would have a negative affect on his ability to lead a normal, healthy life. I was denied shared custody and all visitation rights. When I left the courthouse that day, I remember waving to my son as he got into the car with his mother. He didn't wave back. I haven't seen him since.

Demons Within

I didn't think that there was anyone scheduled to be at the resort but if there was, I needed to find a hotel that would take in the dog. He's not exactly good when it comes to change and after this car ride was finally over he would in for a big one. I noticed that he was still whimpering in the back, even more than he was before, so I pulled over to let him out.

This part of the highway was never very busy this time of year as there's not a lot of snow that usually fell in October, so the trip upstate would be fairly non eventful. I pulled the car over at a rest area and opened the seat so that the dog could get out. It was only then that I saw what was causing him to whimper. On the seat next to him was a black hat, the same black hat that the man was wearing in the cafe this morning. When I lifted up the hat, an old soda can rolled onto the floor. A grape soda can. I felt a cold shiver go down my spine and then everything turned white.

When I woke up, I noticed that my dog was lying down beside me with his head resting on my leg. The sky was dark and the air had a distinct chill. I looked around to get my bearings and saw that the car was still there. I tried to remember exactly what had happened to me before I passed out. I went out for a drive to get a soda. Ah yes, I blanked out again and spilled soda everywhere. Wait a minute there was a dream. I was five years old again and there was a key inside of a can and a dog. The can. It was in the car under the hat! I got to my feet and ran to the car. The dog woke up and, as if sensing my state of excitement, started barking nervously.

I made it to the car and looked into the backseat. There was nothing there. There was no black hat. There was no grape soda can. There was nothing. Period. How could that be? That couldn't have been a dream because my hand was still sticky from the soda that had spilled all over it. Those items were in the car I was sure of it. I saw that the dog was upset and was whimpering with his head hung low to the ground. Someone had been in the car. That was why the items were missing. Had the man from the cafe been in my car while I was passed out? If so, what the hell did he want? Where was the damn hat? What was the deal with the can? I didn't want to find out what would happen if I stayed there any longer so I got the dog, put him back into the car, and headed back out for the resort.

The Stain of Blood on my Eggs

When I got to the resort, my thirst had returned even more overwhelming than before. I knew that the bitch kept the downstairs fridge full of beer year round in case she decided to steal away with one of her many boy toys, so I grabbed a couple and called for a pizza. The beer went down smoothly and by the time the pizza arrived, I had put a significant dent in the beer supply and realized that I would need to make a run to the liquor store if I were going to be here for any length of time. I decided to see what was on pay per view and settled in for what I hoped would be a peaceful and uneventful evening.

I heard a faint beeping but chose to ignore it because there were so many different kinds of electronic devices and gadgets here. However, the beeping continued as I was trying my best to teach my liver a lesson it would not soon forget and it seemed to be getting louder. There was no way that I was going to get any peace as long as it continued. I looked around in a sort of half-assed manner, trying to determine which one of these elitist yuppie gadgets was about to make the acquaintance of a wall while traveling at an extremely high velocity, when I noticed a flashing red light that was coinciding with the beeping. It was the answering machine. No one knew I was up here. Maybe someone had left the bitch a message wanting to use the place for a while. Well whoever it was, I would enjoy disappointing them.

I walked over to the machine and saw that there were 20 messages waiting to be retrieved. Whoever had left the messages must have thought it was really important so I reached down and pressed the play button. The first message was that of a man and he spoke only one word.

"Sleep."

Just then my finger went numb as a jolt of electricity shot up through my arm and into my head. There was a loud screeching sound followed by a wailing scream that pierced through my ear, shattering the drum. The noise made my head feel like it was being pried apart. My left eye began to flicker and I lost all feeling in my legs. I fell to the floor in a lifeless heap, my mind again slipping away into the dream.

I am cold and scared. The dog grows taller as I watch in mortal fear. His head, once actually resembling that of a dog, stretches and twists until it is no longer that of a dog. Its fur grows out at an alarming rate, running down onto the floor and slithering towards me. His fangs grow longer and more pointed with saliva pouring down their length, dripping onto the cold earth. I feel my knees lock together and I find myself shaking uncontrollably. The last thing I should be doing right now is standing here while it does whatever it's planning on doing, but my fear holds me in place.

The ground beneath me begins to shake, causing me to lose my balance and fall backwards in a panicked twisted motion. The dog thing begins to walk towards me as

The Stain of Blood on my Eggs

I struggle to regain my footing. I feel a scream forming in my throat and it erupts from my mouth, making the creature more excited. The dog thing leans down over me with its saliva dripping from its extended fangs and coating me in its stench. It no longer resembles a dog at all, but rather a demonic boogieman of nightmarish proportions.

The dog thing cocks its head to the side and its mouth begins to open, revealing the darkness that until now had been concealed behind its fangs. I see what could have been a tongue, but not in the normal sense of the word, as it is throbbing and sores cover the surface, each one oozing a thick, black liquid. Its teeth were receding into its gums, which are turning black and oozing the same dark liquid. As I look up to meet hits stare, I see that its eyes are protruding from its head, growing wider and more pronounced. The color in the pupils turns darker until becoming as black as the ooze dripping from its fangs.

I struggle towards the small opening that I had crawled through, more than willing to risk turning my back to the dog thing just to get away. The wooden slats of the shack start to reform and grow together, covering all openings and leaving no way out. My only hope now is the door that it is blocking. I feel something grab my leg and I turn to see that the dog thing is right on top of me wrapping its claws around my ankle. I feel the ooze pouring from the creatures mouth spread over my foot and begin to crawl up my leg. With all of my might, I pull my foot away from its grasp and run through its legs towards the door.

The dog thing screeches and turns to give chase. I have to get home. The ground begins to soften and each step becomes a struggle as it turns into the same black ooze that is coming from the dog things mouth. I see that the door is within my reach and as I extend my arm to open it, I sink deeper into the ooze. I flail my arms, fighting for my life to get to the door, but the ooze is beginning to envelope my torso and I realize that there is no hope. I turn to face the dog thing just as his mouth is closing over my head, shutting off the precious sliver of light that I was using to escape. The last thing that I see is a shiny key sliding down its throat.

I awakened from my latest dream and immediately noticed the dog. He was sitting on the couch, which was a big no-no, and had something dripping from the corner of its mouth. I shook my head to clear my clouded vision and saw that whatever was dripping had begun to stain the couch and sink deeper into the fabric of the cushion. I got to my feet and started to walk over to the dog but before I could get there, he jumped off the couch and ran out into the yard.

I looked down at the ink-like stain that had now fully soaked through the cushion and realized that there was nothing made that would get it out of the fabric. Moving closer, I saw that it was also dripping onto the floor creating another stain on the new carpet. I reached out to touch it and pulled my finger back to my nose. It stank. It stank like the breath of the dog thing in the dream. I sat down on the coffee table and attempted to piece the latest development into the puzzle that had become my life. The answering machine. It had all started when I went to check the messages on the machine. I walked over to it and a chill made its way down my spine when I saw that there were no messages waiting. None. There had been twenty waiting in the queue when I passed out. Perplexed, I turned back towards the couch and saw the stain had vanished. I inspected the fabric of the couch that only a moment before was soaked and dripping onto the floor and it appeared new, as if nothing had ever spilled on it.

The Shop

There had to be some simple explanation to the things that were going on inside of my head. Somehow they have to make sense or I'll go mad trying to figure them out. I felt fatigued and decided that I needed to take yet another shower and get some sleep. I went into the bathroom and turned on the light. It was blindingly bright and I squinted until my eyes became used to it. I turned on the water and saw that there was definitely no shortage of bath products from which to choose. Various soaps, lotions, gels, and tablets lined the side of the tub, all with varying degrees of floral scents. I didn't want to use any of them. The stench would remind me of the other person who sometimes occupied this place.

I found an unopened bar of regular man-type soap underneath the sink. I unwrapped it and stepped out of my clothes and into the welcoming hot shower. The water from the shower head was hard and stung my skin like a thousand tiny needles. I took deep breaths to let the steam work into my sinuses and clear my head. I could no longer avoid what was happening, but I still needed to know what, if anything, I could do about it. It seemed that regardless of what I did, I wouldn't be in full control. This could become very dangerous for others as well as for me. I wondered how that poor bastard who crashed into the store was doing. That was probably not the worst thing that could happen. What would happen if I blanked out while I was driving? I could have killed somebody. Maybe I already had. I didn't want to live with that for the rest of my life, but what choice did I have?

I couldn't very well stay at the resort forever, and going back home seemed to pose too many risks. I had some flexibility with my job, so getting some time to sort through the events wouldn't prove too big of a problem. That only left one thing, which was what to do next. I got out of the shower and toweled myself off. I threw on some shorts that I found in one of the drawers and went into the kitchen to see if there was anything left there to drink. The thirst was getting worse and I noticed that my lips were extremely chapped. I got a large glass of water and headed to bed for the night, hoping to have a peaceful sleep.

I woke up the next morning rather late and called work to tell them that I would be taking some time off for personal reasons. It was late morning, so I decided to go out for a jog. I called out for the dog and we left on our morning ritual. The air was clean up there, not like in the city where you almost have to wear a mask to keep out all of the poisons that are floating around. It was still before peak time so there weren't that many people in the area yet. Those who were either lived in one of the remote houses reserved for the upper crust of society, or they were getting their shops ready for the busy time.

There was a café, just off the main drag of shops, which is open year round. I had eaten breakfast there on many occasions and the quality was far superior to that of any in the city. An old couple that had come up here years before it had become the place to go ran it and they made everything on site. They even had chickens out back to get the eggs fresh daily. The wife managed the entire front of the house operations including waiting tables, cashiering, and bookkeeping. The husband was the cook and always made sure to come out and greet every customer after their meal was finished. When the season was in its peak, they took on one of the local girls to help but then it was just the two of them.

I arrived just as the wife had begun to beat out the rugs. We exchanged pleasantries and then proceeded inside. The place had not changed much since I first came here many years earlier. It had fifteen booths, which seated up to six people each, and a long breakfast bar with twenty or so stools around it. I've always been partial to the booths because they give you plenty of space to spread out a paper and relax. Sitting at the bar involved a lot of hunching over and unless you were over 6 feet tall, your legs dangled helplessly over the side of the stools. You also had to make small talk with any moron that decided to sit down next to you. I liked to be left alone to my thoughts. Along the wall hung various old pictures depicting of the original people of the area. The town had been founded in the early 1800's as a fishing town with five large lakes and twenty or so smaller ones dotting the landscape. Access to the ocean was provided by a river that connected the larger lakes. A variety of people had come and gone through this area and each left their own little mark.

Two large windows overlooked the shopping district and the seats next to them were prime choices during the busy time for those who want to be seen. I looked at the menu and decided on the fat mans platter, which consisted of three eggs, three pieces of bacon, three pieces of sausage, a heaping pile of homemade hash browns, three pieces of toast, a large blueberry muffin, a large glass of orange juice and unlimited coffee. They should have called it the coronary instead of the fat man but I suppose that by being one of those, you eventually got the other.

I picked up a copy of the local paper from the basket by the bar and flipped through it as my coffee arrived. The classified section was always the largest, as there really wasn't that much in the way of news in the small town. My breakfast arrived along with a bowl of food for the dog. They always made sure that every guest gets great service regardless of race, color, creed, or breed. I started in on the pile of food while my dog hungrily wolfed down his unexpected meal.

We finished up and then left to explore the rest of the town. The temperature hadn't risen very much and there was a definite smell of snow in the air. In the distance, I could see the peaks of the mountains jutting through the low flying clouds. The leaves had fallen off all of the trees except for the pines, which gave off a very pleasant aroma. The dog slowed my progress as he reacquainted himself with each and every tree along the way. Just up the road on the left, I spotted a new shop. Looking at it closely, I got the impression that the owner has a somewhat dark sided demeanor. In the window, there were statues of demons and old books arranged like an alter and I got the feeling that this was just a small taste of the strange things that I would see inside.

Demons Within

There was a no pet's sign on the door, so I tied the dog to the hydrant and made my way inside the strange, new shop. I opened the door and a little bell rang to announce my presence. I looked around and attempted to adjust to the new surroundings. There were six or seven display cases full of trinkets of a medieval cultish type nature. Long swords, blades, and maces were suspended from the ceiling, their tips dangling only a few inches from my head. It didn't seem like the type of place that you would find in a resort town. I wonder what the shopkeeper was thinking when he decided to open this shop in the family friendly resort town.

On the counter, there were a few token souvenir shirts and key chains along with a stack of guidebooks for the area. The wall behind the counter was covered with shelves that contain more statuettes of demons and knights and a shelf of books. From where I stood, they appeared very old and dusty. I would think that you would want to clean them up a little before you put them on display. I scanned the titles; *Book of dreams, Signs of the Coming, Book of Deeds, and Book of Revelations.* These were definitely on the darker side. Now I really began to wonder why this shop would exist anywhere, not just here.

After being in there a while, I noticed that there appeared to be no one working. I wandered around some more, noticing even stranger items in the display cases. There were no prices on any of the items in the shop. Not for nothing, but if I did want to purchase something it would make sense to know what it would cost.

I came to another set of shelves full of old pictures that appeared to have been taken quite some time ago. They also had a dark edge to them, portraying events like tortures, slayings, and open graves. What kind of person would want to buy something like that? Certainly not me. I decided that I would take my leave of the shop of horrors and began to wonder where the owner of the shop was hiding. I really didn't want to call out, for fear of what type of person he might actually be. On the way out I noticed another book, one that affected me more than anything else in the store. On the cover of the book there was a picture of a demon that I had actually seen before, and the sight of it made my blood run cold. It was the dog thing.

I ran out of there as fast as I could, so fast that my dog was having a hard time keeping up with me. I kept going at full speed until I got back to the resort. My mind was an absolute wreck. I had lost all control over myself and I was scared to death. Up in the sanctity of the mountains, I thought that I would have time to collect my thoughts. It was proving not to be the case. I grabbed some water from the tap and sat down at the kitchen table. That shop has no business being in town. I felt that whatever was happening to me was building up to a climax, and I didn't know if I wanted to stay until the final curtain.

Inside my head, there was total chaos. Thoughts once buried deep in my subconscious mind bubbled up to the surface. I had buried a lot of memories and emotions over the years and now they were teaming up to take control over my mind. I have done some things that I am not particularly proud of, but the things that I regret doing aren't that big when weighed against all of the things that happen in the world every day. People do horrible things to each other now that would have been totally unheard of a few decades ago. Murder; rape; mutilation. Now that I think about it, I suppose that we as a species haven't changed all that much since the good old days of the bible. Why we haven't evolved past these and other horrendous acts is well beyond my understanding.

There has always been evil. Something has been handed down generation after generation that causes people to do things that others would find reprehensible. There is no one thing that these types of people have in common either. Some "experts" on human behavior and development claim that there are certain social and biological things that cause people to behave differently than the norm. I tend to disagree with all of them. For instance, there have been cases of childhood abuse both physical and mental to which public defenders get people acquitted of the crimes that they commit. If they truly are "driven" to commit these crimes by events that are forced on them why then do their siblings not behave in a similar fashion? If evil is in a gene, then why do the children of 'normal' parents with proper upbringing sometimes commit heinous crimes?

There is no reasonable explanation of what constitutes evil. It is not a thing that can be identified prior to an action taking place. Who would have thought that cute little Adolph Hitler would grow up into the monster that he became? Surely, his parents never believed that their child would ever be anything but a good little boy. Watch the news when there's a story about a killing. They always interview the neighbors who say what a nice person he or she was and they never thought they were capable of doing such a horrible thing. Even their own families can't believe what they did. How then can we identify evil if it doesn't show itself until it's too late?

I had reached the conclusion that whatever was happening to me was evil, plain and simple, and if I didn't do anything to stop it, there would be serious consequences. In order to stop it, I needed to understand it. In order to understand it, I needed to confront it. I hoped that I have the strength to see it through 'till the end.

Baseball, Hotdogs, Apple Pie and Books of the Dead

I felt that the only way to beat this was to come at it head on. In my opinion, under-standing the dream was the key to solving the mystery. I needed to understand that before I returned to the shop for that book. The picture on the book gave me hope that I wasn't really losing my mind. By seeing the dog thing on the cover, I had hard evidence that something was behind the mental torture I had been enduring. Until now I couldn't understand anything, but the book was the first piece in solving the puzzle. I hate puzzles.

I went into the bathroom to get something to help me sleep. Just like all of the soaps that I saw arranged on the tub, there were no shortages of aids to assist me in my quest. I didn't want to sleep for days on end, but I did need an uninterrupted sleep. I took two pills and headed off to the bedroom. Lying on the bed, I began to relax as I prepared for what I thought will be the toughest night of my life. My mind was full of many different thoughts, and I found myself struggling to concentrate on something that would allow me to sleep. What I wanted to accomplish tonight was to continue the dream from where I had left off, if that were in any way possible. The air in the room began to cool and thanks to the pills, I started slipping into a deep state of sleep.

"Get your hotdogs here! Peanuts, popcorn, crackerjacks here!"

"Excuse me, is this seat taken?" a voice from behind asks me.

My vision is very cloudy, but beginning to clear up as I begin to hear more voices around me. I see that I am at a baseball game. It looks like Fenway Park in late August.

"Boy, it sure is a great day for a game dad!"

"Peanuts, popcorn crackerjacks here! Hey fella, get outta the isle will ya? I'm workin here! Get your fresh roasted peanuts here!"

"Excuse me sir, but is anyone sitting here?" the voice asks again.

I turn to see who is asking me the question and a tall man of enormous proportions stared at me with an aggravated look on his face. He was balancing a tray containing two beers, a pretzel, three hot dogs, an order of nachos, and a bag of peanuts. His belly protruded from the waistband of his pants, and his rode up towards his chest. I looked down at his legs that are so big he can barely get into the isle. He was wearing a Yankees hat that had seen many, many better days. The blue color had long since faded into a dull grey, and the stitching on the logo was brown and stained. I found myself staring and he asked the question again, more agitated this time,

"You gonna move so I can sit or what!" he screamed.

"Sorry," I said "didn't hear you the first time."

Baseball, Hotdogs, Apple Pie and Books of the Dead

"Freakin Red Sox fans! And you people say that we're rude?! Jus' get outta my way."

I stood up and he squeezed his way past me, spilling half of his beer on me in the process. He sat down, or I should say he crouched down until it almost looked as if he were sitting. Looking around, I saw that this was indeed Fenway Park. The green monster loomed right there in left field where it had always stood. The game appeared to have been a sell out, and I couldn't spot an empty seat as I scanned all of the sections. I looked at the scoreboard and saw that the Sox are playing their rivals, the dreaded Yankees of New York. There is no score on the board, as the game had not yet started. The sky was clear and there was a strong breeze coming in from left field. There would be a lot of pulled hits today. I wondered who was getting the start.

"Get your programs here!" a voice bellows out from behind me.

"Excuse me, may I have a program," I ask.

"Dat'll be half a buck," the kid replies and reaches for my money.

I reached into my pocket and realized that I didn't seem to have any money. I checked all of my pockets and nothing doing. The hawker became disinterested in me as a potential customer and moved on to someone feverishly waving a dollar in the air.

"How could I have gotten into a game with no money?" I wondered aloud.

"Hey, down in front!" a voice screamed from right behind my head.

I left my seat and started walking up the stairs towards the entrance to the section. I was feeling very parched and wanted an ice-cold beer to quench my thirst. I smacked myself in the head, remembering that I didn't have any money and wondered how I was going to satisfy the craving. I made my way through the crowd and search out the beer line, smelling all of the scents of Fenway in August. It was a mix of piss, garbage and sweaty old men with just the right amount of stale cigar smoke mixed in for flavor. As I got closer to the line, I saw a pair of kids leaning up against one of the trashcans. They couldn't have been more than six or seven years old, and as I passed by them, I caught the eye of the taller of the two. I was looking at my little brother and myself. I stopped and stared in disbelief. An older man stepped in front of the two boys, blocking my vision for a moment. He handed each of the two boys a soda and they turned and began walking away from me. I recognize the frame of the older man with the two boys. It was my grandfather.

I turned around and began to walk away when I bumped into someone. Beer splashes all over me and I cried out," Oh shit!" as the man began to fall backwards. The contents of the tray that he was holding flew up into the air, a hot dog flying off to the left and a pretzel to the right. I reached out to grab his arm to prevent him from falling completely over and he grabbed onto my sleeve to pull himself back onto his feet. He stood up straight and began to brush himself off. I noticed that he was a fairly large man and hoped that he would view this incident for what it was, an accident, rather than a drunk who had staggered into him.

I raise my hands to him and say, "Sorry about that, I didn't see you there."

Demons Within

He looked around in disbelief and said, "Well that's all fine and good, but look at my food!"

"Listen," I said, "I'm really sorry about your food. I would be happy to replace it for you but I don't have any money."

"Well I suppose you could work it off," he said and with that, he handed me a key that was dangling from a chain. "Go down to the field house and get me a change of clothes from my locker. I can't very well enjoy this game if I'm covered in beer."

I took the key from his hand. It was a new key, very shiny, and it was attached to a small figurine of some sort with a long black leather strap. There was a number seven inscribed on the key. "I'll meet you in section four, third row back. Don't take forever either," he ordered and reached down to retrieve his hat.

I started down the corridor towards the field house, feeling extremely bad about ruining the man's shirt. I wanted to get this done as soon as possible and then enjoy what should be a great game. As I kept walking, things began to change around me. The lines of people thinned out and the smell, once pungent and overbearing, subsided leaving nothing but clean air for me to breathe. I need to hurry up or I would end up missing the first pitch. I started running and felt the wind slapping me in the face as the field house came into view. There was a man standing at the entrance and upon seeing me, moved his body to block my path. He put his right hand out to stop me while reaching for his back pocket with his left. I slowed my pace until coming to a stop a few feet from where he stood.

"Whoa there fella, this here's restricted access," he said, pointing to a sign to further emphasize his point, "no unauthorized personnel."

I held up the key the man had given me and extended it towards him.

"I need to get into this locker and get something," I said.

He examined the figurine dangling from the key and began moving his hand towards it. Suddenly, there was a loud clapping sound as a bolt of electricity shot from the figurine and into the guards' hand. I watched him fall to the ground as his body began to convulse and he started to foam at the mouth. I stood there in shock and a voice came into my head,

"Hurry! They're coming for you!"

I felt a wave of panic come over me and I hurried past the fallen guard. I ran towards the row of lockers and came to number seven. I put the key into the lock and tried to turn it. It wouldn't budge. I took the key out and examined it, only to find that the grooves on the key had smoothed out. Had it always looked like this? I hadn't really looked at it when it was given to me.

"Hurry, hurry," the voice continued, "They know who you are."

I tried the key in the lock again and this time it wouldn't even fit inside. The figurine swung around hitting my arm as I continued to struggle to make the key fit into the lock. I began to hear voices coming from behind me. They had found the guard. Someone was yelling frantically for an ambulance. I looked down the row of lockers

Baseball, Hotdogs, Apple Pie and Books of the Dead

to see if there was anything that I could use to get this locker open. I don't know why I was feeling nervous; all that I was doing was getting clothes out of a locker for someone. The feeling of nervousness was growing stronger. I had to get into this locker. This had become the most important thing I could ever do. I ran behind the row of lockers and found a toolbox. I opened it and pulled out a screwdriver, and then I returned to the locker. Standing there, right before my eyes, was the one person that I didn't want to see. He stood there in his long, black coat, looking more imposing than ever before. He was leaning against the locker and removed his dark glasses so that he could stare at me with his cold, black eyes. He put his glasses around his shirt and grabbed a Zippo out of his shirt pocket.

"What's up kid?" he said as he lit himself a cigar. The smoke began to waft from the end of it and swirled up around his head. He took a few long puffs from the cigar and opened his mouth in an elongated stretch. His chin moved upwards and from his mouth came a series of smoke rings, thick and blue, and they grew larger as they made there way towards there I stood, frozen with fear. The first of the rings made it to me and my feet went numb. The smoke rings settled around my head and my vision became extremely clouded. Slowly, they made there way down the length of my body until I was covered by the blue haze. My head began to spin and I saw the man lean over to place something on the ground. The smoke around me thickened and I found myself struggling to breathe. The sound of my gagging on the smoke drowned out the sounds of the people I heard before.

Suddenly, the air around me began to clear, and my breath returned to my lungs. The stench of smoke had receded from my nose, and I saw that the man was no longer standing in front of me. I looked around and he was nowhere to be found. I checked the spot where he was standing and noticed that there was something there on the ground. It was a shiny object, and the sunlight was reflecting strongly off its surface. I walked towards the spot and reached down to retrieve it. It was a key, the same key that I had seen in my car underneath the black hat, the same key that was in the dream.

I picked up the key to study it and saw that there was nothing strange or unusual about its appearance. It was just like any other. I was standing in front of the locker and suddenly remembered why I was there. The screwdriver was on the ground and I was still holding the ineffective key that the man had given me. I decided that I would try to open the locker with the new key. I didn't have anything to lose, and it would be better to try it before resorting to breaking open the locker. I reached for the lock and the key slid right in, turning with no resistance. The locker popped open before me and I opened the door to peek inside.

Inside of the locker, there were various items of clothing and a few toiletries. I looked through them and didn't notice a shirt. I was sent here to retrieve a shirt so there must be one there. There was also a small duffle bag on the top shelf of the locker. I reached up and pulled it down. It was heavy. I hadn't expected it to have so much weight to it and for this reason it slammed to the ground, pulling me down with it. What could be inside? I reached for the zipper and opened it. Inside there was only one item. It was a book. The book looked very familiar to me so I picked it up out of the bag, and I noticed that it wasn't as heavy as I thought it would be. It was an old, worn out book with many pages and a dusty blue cover with some sort of illustration on it. I brushed off some of the dust with my hand and the picture on the cover began to appear. It was some sort of thing with wild looking eyes and drooling fangs, its body covered with a thick matted coat of hair. Its mouth was open and there was a long black tongue coming out of it, covered with pus and sores. I realized that I had seen this book before in that freaky store in town. The thing on the cover was also beginning to stir up a memory in my head. I know that I had seen this too before.

It was the dog thing.

The sound of my alarm clock jolted me from the latest dream. I gathered myself together and grabbed the pad and pen from the bedside table. I wanted to write everything that I remembered down while it was still fresh inside of my head. I wrote for what seemed like hours, recording every detail no matter how irrelevant it seemed. When I had finished, I put on some pants and a shirt and headed to the kitchen for some coffee.

The dog was awake and patiently waiting by the door to be let out. It had gotten very bright outside for this time of day. I opened the door and he barked to me as he raced out into the yard. I set up the coffee and went to grab the paper. Small towns could be very strange at times. Although nobody lived here on a full time basis, there was always a copy of the local paper waiting at the door each morning when someone was here. I grabbed the paper and waved to the neighbor who was watering his lawn. He waived back and we exchanged some small talk about what was happening in town, the weather, and various other inconsequential items. I left his all too pleasant company and went back inside, where I hoped my notes would provide me with something that I could use to understand the events of late.

So far I had experienced many strange things and with some effort, I hoped to piece them together into a neat, little pill that was easy to swallow. My plan sounded simple enough, at least in my mind it anyway. I wanted to find out how I could get a handle on things so if I thought through each thing that happened with a calm, rational mind, I would eventually reach a feasible explanation. I grabbed a cup from the cabinet and poured myself some coffee. I placed the notes from the dream I had on the table and put a bagel in the toaster. I needed a full stomach before I tackled this imposing task. The bagel popped out of the toaster and I sat down to read the paper.

As was the usual case with small town papers, the content left a lot to be desired. The front-page story was about the expected rush of traffic that would be arriving in a matter of weeks. There were interviews with a few of the local shop owners about how they expected this season to be compared to past seasons. The paper also mentioned that a few of the roads leading into town would be closed so that repairs could be completed before the busy season hit in full force. Below the fold, there was a story on a dinner that was being held in honor of a resident who had helped put the town on the national map. It went on to list the people who were expected to attend and what would be served for the main course. Tickets were available at the library on a first come first served basis for $7.00. This was the front page.

Baseball, Hotdogs, Apple Pie and Books of the Dead

I opened up to the "Arts and Entertainment" section and saw an ad for the grand opening of the shop I had visited. The ad was meant to look like a flyer for one of those old sideshows that traveled from town to town, promising people spectacular sights and sounds for those who dared attend. The background of the ad showed a group of people gathered around a man speaking from a soapbox with children running by with small trinkets designed to amuse them. Above the crowd there was a woman suspended from a wire while balancing a large pole with her feet. The dress of the people in the picture was 19th century garb and they all appeared to hang on every word that the man spoke. The man standing on the soapbox apparently was the head of the show. He was wearing a long coat and a top hat and his arm was extended towards the tent with his animated face hawking the show inside. The front flap of the tent was open and there was a small child peeking inside.

I still wondered what kind of person would open a shop like that in a small town like this one. It was definitely something that would stand out like a sore thumb. I thumbed through the rest of the paper and then decided that it was time to tackle my problem. I put the paper aside and got a fresh sheet of paper from my notepad. On the left side, I wrote the word 'TRIGGER'. On the right side, I wrote 'ACTION.' I had to figure out if anything that I was doing caused one or more of the actions to happen to me. The first thing I wrote was 'hospital'. Across from that, I wrote 'appearance'. That was the first time that I had seen the man I have come to fear. I also wrote 'grandfather' because I had gone to the hospital to see him and maybe that was a connection somehow. I also wrote 'lost emotions' as this was also the time that I started not to care about things.

The next trigger I wrote was 'Cafe'. The action for that was 'appearance', for when I again remembered seeing him. 'Panic' was another action for this trigger as well. The words were coming more rapidly now, 'Soda' went with 'dream', 'key', 'dog thing', and 'panic'. On and on it went until I had compiled quite a list of triggers and actions. I quickly scanned the list looking for common denominators and there was definitely a common theme at work here. The key had appeared often, as did the man and the dog-thing. I still could not come up with a common trigger that could tie all or some of these things together. The actions struck me regardless of whether or not I was asleep. I decided to concentrate on only the things that appeared frequently. Since the dog-thing was one of them, I was due to pay the shop of horrors a little visit during its grand opening extravaganza.

The dog barked at the door and I opened it to let him inside. I went back to the ad to see when the shop was due to open so that I could plan accordingly. The grand opening was set for today at noon. There was a coupon for a free resort t-shirt with any purchase over five dollars. Another shirt I didn't need, but ripped it out anyway. I gave the dog some food and checked the clock. It was eleven thirty. I would have to hurry up if I wanted to beat the rush. I went upstairs to change before I headed out for what was sure to be an interesting day.

Halloween Comes Early

I arrived at the shop at 12:05. I had wanted to be here when the doors had opened to see the man who owned the shop. This was not the case. I walked through the door as a group of kids darted past me. There had to be fifty people in here! The shop was crowded as it was before you factored in the addition of all of these people. There were men and women of all ages, along with about ten to fifteen kids, crowded into the dark shop. People were grouping together and pointing to various objects in the display cases. I overheard a group of senior women talking in front of me as they commented about the dark nature of the figurines that they were seeing.

The counter was crowded with young kids who wanted to see the strange figurines on the wall. A woman, apparently a mother to one of them, was yelling for her son to get down from the glass case. There was a person in costume working the crowd, handing out coupons for some of the local shops. She was dressed in appropriate attire for the nature of this shop with a long, poofed out dress that was torn and tattered in various places. Her hair was a mess with cobwebs and dirt strewn throughout its mangled shape. She had no shoes on and had lash marks in her forearms. I stopped her as she approached.

"Excuse me miss, is the owner available?" I asked.

"Certainly my lord," she replied, "he is with some patrons in the book section."

"Thank you for your help," I said as she handed me one of the sheets of coupons from her waistband.

"Enjoy your stay and do tell your friends about us," she responded. With that said she was off.

I made my way through the throngs of people and eventually came across a group of men who were being helped by a tall man dressed in garb of the time as well. He had his back to me and was explaining the contents of a particular book to the group of middle aged men. As I waited for him to finish I scanned the rest of the store and saw that there was another section that I hadn't seen on my previous visit. A small doorway led to an even smaller set of stairs that connected the room to the rest of the store. I decided that I should explore this new discovery before meeting the shop's owner in case I had any other questions for him about his peculiar place of business.

Excusing myself past a small fat man, I made my way through the door and down the stairs. It was darker in here than the rest of the store and the stairs creaked with each step, adding to the lure of the shop. There were no people in this room which was set up to make you travel in one direction all the way to the end like a display in a museum. On the walls were items of torture covered in what seemed to be dried blood. They consisted of long blades with curved spikes coming out of their tips. I saw a few pictures like the ones up front, scenes of tortures and witch burnings. The floor was dirt and there were areas of it that were wet causing muddy pools that made clean passage virtually impossible.

I looked up towards the ceiling and was instantly repulsed by what I saw. Severed heads and body parts were strewn across the length of the ceiling, suspended by what looked like bloody strings, almost intestine like in their appearance. I felt vomit making its way up my chest into my throat, and a bitter taste filled my mouth. I swallowed hard and paused to take several deep breaths. 'This guy was a sick bastard', I thought to myself. I regained my composure and continued through the maze of small hallways. It was set up to be an homage of death, and I didn't think that this shop would last in such a conservative little town like this.

I turned the first corner and was thrown back by a sickening breeze that shot into my face from an unseen vent. It smelled as if something had died in here a long time ago and someone was keeping it on low heat to bring out the most pungent, nasty smells that could be released. I gagged and turned my head back away from the smell and I could only imagine how many people would soon be puking all over the floor if they weren't already after seeing the many grotesque items in the shop. With that thought, I checked the bottoms of my shoes and the floor around me to see if I had stepped into anything. Nope, all clear. I took a few more calming breaths and placing my hand over my nose and mouth, turned to go back down the smelly hallway.

I turned the corner and began to walk towards a display case that hung on the far wall. The smell seemed to have disappeared so I lowered my hand from my face. Strange sounds began to come from the walls, sounds of sheer terror with high pitched screams and painful moaning. I assumed that there were speakers set up in the walls to add this effect so it didn't bother me too much. I got to the case and tried to see what was inside, but the glass was very dirty and there was no light shining on it, making viewing what was inside difficult at best. I leaned towards it and cupped my hands over my eyes to see it a little better. I was almost touching the glass when I felt a cold hand rest itself on the nape of my neck. A chill went all over my body and I jumped up in surprise, releasing a small squeak from my throat.

"I understand that you wanted to see me," the voice in the dark said to me.

I turned around and was face to face with the owner of the sick shop of horrors.

"Sorry," he said, "did I startle you?"

"Uh, yea, just a little." I sarcastically replied.

"No blood, no foul," he said. "How can I be of service today?"

"Well for starters, you can tell me what the hell this room is supposed to be. I almost lost my breakfast on the floor!"

"This room is not yet open," he said, "One of the children must have opened the door. I have yet to fix all of the locks and am sorry if you were discomforted in any way."

Demons Within

"I can only imagine the nightmares that kid will be having for the rest of his life if he was as spooked as I am now. So what is this place, a haunted house of some sort?"

"No, not really." He said. "This is merely a collection of things that I have accumulated over the years. A lot of the items that you see here are from an old side show that used to travel throughout eastern Canada in the latter part of the nineteenth century. They came into my possession through an estate of a distant relative of mine. I have always been fascinated by the darker periods of man's existence so I was extremely pleased to acquire them. When I finish this section, I hope to educate people into the dark side of man's nature so that they can see everything that they're truly capable of doing."

"Well people are capable of much more than this," I replied, " Our existence has not always been marred with the evils that I am seeing in this room, and although people are capable of doing some really nasty things, I would think that one wouldn't want to dwell on them as a matter of study."

"People who are interested in things of this nature will be fascinated by the collection," he said, "but my aim is to show people what happens when mob rule is the only rule. Take the Salem witches for example. Innocent people including young girls were burned alive on the words of only a few small children. There is no justifiable excuse for what these people did to their fellow townspeople. Panic set in and when all was said and done, innocent people lost their lives. We as a people need to understand the demons that live in all of us so that we can protect ourselves from events like that."

"Your words are ringing true in my ears." I said. "I often find myself trying to understand my own demons and lately it seems that there can be no peace within my head until I do."

"We all have demons that we need to deal with in our own ways. In ancient times and even today, there are people who believe that demons cannot be totally controlled, but rather need to be placated. They worship them and sometimes even attempt to summon more evil demons to do some type of evil bidding for them. Sometimes these people go mad, but on rare occasions the demons do decide to work for them, albeit on a temporary basis, and only to further their own agendas"

His last statement troubled me greatly, as I reflected on the things that were happening to me lately. "Surely you don't believe that people can conjure up evil spirits to do their bidding like they were calling for a pizza or something," I said sarcastically.

"On the contrary," he replied with authority, "I believe that demons are already here, and the people who sometimes attempt to summon them merely give them an excuse to wreak havoc on the masses."

"Well, my initial impression of you based on my first visit here proved correct. You're a kook. And I don't think that this shop will last the week in this place."

"Something brought you here my friend." He replied with a condescending tone.

"Yea. Your full page freak show ad in the local paper. By the way, I want my free t-shirt for almost losing my breakfast due to the extremely graphic nature of your so-called 'collection'."

Halloween Comes Early

"The ad may have brought you into my shop, but something in your head brought you to my private room. No one can walk through walls you know." He reached out and pointed behind me. I turned around and saw that the walls had disappeared. Instead of a maze of hallways, it was now just one small room with no visible way out. I turned my head back towards him in disbelief.

"This has to be some kind of cheap ass parlor trick," I said as he began walking towards the wall where the door had once been.

"On the contrary," he replied, "this is the original construction." He emphasized his point by knocking loudly on the walls in various places. I felt my stomach drop to my feet and struggled to make sense of this latest addition to my ever shrinking sense of control. This could not be real. I must be having another dream. I slapped myself on the face, hard. Let me say that it hurt like hell. Somehow this was real and now I was trapped in the room with a raving lunatic.

"Don't overanalyze this too much or you'll drive yourself crazy," he said to me. Out of no where a chair appeared in front of me. "Take a seat and I will try to explain it to you." I sat down and he pulled another chair down directly across from me. I took this opportunity to give him a once over.

He had an imposing frame; I guess he was about six feet four or so, with large tough hands. His hair was grayish white and he had a good deal of razor stubble on his face. Looking into his eyes I could see that he generally didn't sleep too well, as they were loaded down with layers of bags. His skin had a leathery appearance and there were many wrinkles on his forehead. He had broad shoulders and extremely long legs. His clothes were ragged, as were the clothes the woman in the store wore and they fit him as if they were his own every day wear. He had a rather large nose that came to a small point at the tip. I guessed his age to be early to mid seventies.

He sat down in the chair and placed his dry hand on my shoulder, sending another chill down my spine. "I can help you if you trust me," he said. "I have helped many people with their demons over the years. This is not the first town that I have chosen to set up shop in and you are not even close to the first person to walk through that imaginary door. I know that you are going through some emotional turmoil now and nothing you do seems to make it better. That is precisely why I'm here. I can help you come to terms with your demons, if you are willing to take some risks."

I took a cigarette from my pocket and went to light it. My hand was shaking badly and I couldn't get the flint to spark. He reached out with his finger and touched my hand. The shaking stopped immediately. I lit the cigarette and took a long, hard drag. I exhaled and blew a thick cloud of smoke into the air. I had tried everything I could think of to help myself come to grips with the things that had been happening, but so far nothing had seemed to work. I didn't know this guy from a hole in the ground but I felt totally out of control at this point. I needed to do something and here was a guy who claimed to understand what I was going through. Should I put my life into the hands of a self proclaimed freak or attempt to deal with this on my own? This was not something to be taken lightly. I took another drag from my cigarette and looked into the strange man's eyes.

Demons Within

"Look, I don't know who you are or even more if I should trust you," I said. "Even though what happened here so far today has scared the shit out of me, it's still nothing compared to the larger scheme of things in my life right now. I will promise for now to listen to what you have to say and nothing more."

"That's understandable," he said, "but I am confident that very soon you will come around to my way of thinking on how best to deal with this situation. I am going to ask you one question, and from there we can proceed. What is the one item that you came back to the shop for?"

I thought about that for a moment before responding. Surely this man couldn't read mind as well.

"What difference does that make?" I asked.

"Each item in the shop represents something to someone that needs my assistance," he replied. "None of the people currently in the shop will purchase anything that is on display, as they cannot see things as you do. For them, they see various items that peak no interest other than to get them out of their quaint little houses for a while. They will browse around at all of the items in the cases and thumb through some of the books on the shelves, but none of them will have any desire to purchase anything. You see things that represent something that is hidden deep within your mind. You find the items scary and grotesque. This room also represents something to you. Even though you had a hard time going through the maze, you still chose to take on the challenge of seeing what was waiting for you on the other side. But there is one item in particular that after seeing yesterday; you could not get out of your head. This is the item that will tell me where to begin with you, and it is the item that if you walk out of here without, you will die."

The last three words that he spoke made me white with fear. 'You will die', he said. Surely he could not propose to know how I would die. He did say a lot of things that were true. I did find the items in his shop both scary and grotesque and I also could not get the book out of my head. I had come down here today not only to find out what kind of person owned this shop, but to walk away with that book no matter what the cost, be it monetary or physical. Had I really been willing to do anything for the book? What if it was not for sale? Would I have snuck back here to steal it or something worse, something evil? 'You will die.' Those are the words he had used and I suddenly agreed with him.

"There's a book in a case by the door," I said, my body quivering, "it is rather old and has a picture of..."

"Chaos, demon of dreams," he interrupted, "I am very familiar with that one. Today you will take this book home with you. Do not stop anywhere on the way and do not put it down. When you get home, put it somewhere safe. Whatever you do, don't open it until I see you again. The contents of that book are very powerful and to someone who is still coming to grips with their own demons, they could easily take over your weakened mind. If that happened in your present state, you would not survive."

Halloween Comes Early

There he went again talking about my death. All of this talk of demons and dying had taken all of my energy away. I felt my eyes getting heavy and had an urgent need for a drink. This all sounded like something out of a sci-fi movie, the only thing missing was a leprechaun with an evil cackling laugh to complete the cast. I decided that I had nothing to lose if I listened to what he had to say. I still felt as if I could back out if I didn't like that way that things were going. I couldn't have been more wrong.

"I will be by your house at exactly 10:45, not a minute earlier, not a minute later," he said. "Until then, keep it safe and do not open it. If anyone comes by do not answer the door for once this book leaves the safety of the case that holds it, he will know that you are aware of him and he will do everything in his power to stop you from continuing on your chosen course of action." With that said he rose from his chair and led me out through the door which had somehow reappeared. We made our way through the crowd of people and came to the case. He removed one of the glass panels from the side and handed the book to me. It was very light for a book this size. I guessed it at 10,000 pages and after handing me the book, he had one last thing to say

. "The key should be kept close." He touched his hand to my shirt pocket and then walked back into the shop. I looked down at my pocket, which was now weighted down, and noticed that something was inside. I reached my hand down into my pocket and pulled the item into the light for further examination. It was a key. A figurine was attached to it with a long, black leather strap. I turned it over and stared in disbelief. It was that same figurine that had shocked the guard in my dream. It was the dog-thing.

Just how much this guy knew about me remained to be seen, but he was somehow connected to my dream. This was the key that found the book in the dream, and now the keeper of that book had given me the very same key. Slowly things were getting connected, but I still couldn't see how.

I returned to the resort around two or so, feeling extremely tired. Today's events had taken a lot of my energy and I could definitely use a nap. I went upstairs and put the book on the bedside table, shooed the dog off the bed, and went back downstairs to let him out. The sun was getting brighter as the day wore on and it felt like mid summer rather than late autumn. The suns rays shone strongly on my face and I saw people return from their trip to the shop empty handed, just as the man predicted. He was right, no one had bought anything. I wondered how many of the free t-shirts he was going to be stuck with, if there ever were any t-shirts.

The dog finished his business on a section of the neighbors' lawn. I would have to clean that up or surely face a fine from the strict co-op board. I went over to the shed and got the pooper scooper and a baggie. As I was picking it up, the dog seemed to laugh at me. Little bastard. Sometimes I wished the roles were reversed between man and dog. It is we who are owned by them and not the other way around. He gets free room and board, a personal trainer to walk with, and a maid to clean up his poop and whatever else he decides to spill on the floor. He even has a pimp. Once a year, I take

Demons Within

him to stud. He's a purebred so I get a nice little check and the pick of the litter. He gets his rocks off and no responsibilities. That's the life alright.

I finished the nasty task and threw the treasure into the trash. The dog came up to me with an old raggedy looking ball and placed it at my feet. We played for a while in an old, familiar routine; I threw it, he returned it full of slobber, I shook it off and threw it again. That's the only thing I don't envy about dogs. They have no control over the drool. After a few more tosses I decided that it had been enough for one day. I took the ball and threw it high in the air. The poor dog ran at full speed to intercept it, but he was closing in on the fence very quickly. I wondered if he would realize it in time. Nope. He hit the fence at a good clip causing his legs to flail out and his body twisted towards the sky. I laughed as he got back to his feet and shook it off, sending slobber flying all over the yard like a sprinkler. "That's for the poop," I said to him.

We went back inside and I got him some water which he drank down like I was never going to give him another bowl. The doorbell rang and the dog stopped drinking and raced towards the door, leaving a trail of drool that dangled momentarily in the air before crashing back down to the ground. He loved people, sometimes a little too much. He had a bad habit of getting overexcited if they didn't pet him fast enough and he would jump on them. He's a big boy and if you didn't know him, you'd freak out. I walked over and opened the door but there was no one there. The dog was still in a heightened state of excitement, his tail furiously waving back and forth. Usually he would race out if someone was standing far enough away from the door, but he stood in place as if there was someone standing right in front of us. I stepped forward and peeked to both sides of the door. No one appeared. I know I didn't imagine the bell, the dogs reaction told me that much. I closed the door and went back into the kitchen.

I got a cup of coffee from the machine and looked towards the door. The dog had not moved and was still rather excited. Usually he walked away whenever the door was closed. I thought that to be rather odd and took a long swallow from my cup. I remembered what the freak from the shop had said to me as I was leaving, "If anyone comes by do not answer the door, for once this book leaves the safety of the case that holds it, he will know that you are aware of him and he will do everything in his power to stop you from continuing on your chosen course of action."

Surely this had nothing to do with that at all. It was probably some kid playing ring and run. I had done that a lot when I was younger. Sometimes it had gotten rather interesting. I got up to top off my cup and sat down to reminisce with myself. I was remembering one time in particular when I was around seven or so...

It was raining pretty hard that day. It was Halloween and all day in school we had been doing crafts and playing games. They had a party where cupcakes and candy corn were seemingly everywhere. Todd and I were inseparable that year. Our teachers called us the terrible twosome as we were always pulling some kind of prank. We were making slingshots out of rubber bands and popsicle sticks. We thought these would make excellent weapons against the older kids tonight who were surely plotting to steal all of our candy. I was dressed as a cowboy and Todd was playing my sidekick deputy. I was the mastermind of the team. Todd made an excellent assistant as it was easy to talk him into trying anything.

Also at our craft table were Kenny and Paul. I had known Kenny for many years. He lived with his parents on a house overlooking the whole neighborhood. He had a big dog named Chuck who always smelled your feet. He was big and hairy and you couldn't see his eyes because off all of the hair. Kenny's house was pretty big. When I went over there to play we would often hide out on one of the many hidden hallways that connected the rooms to each other. It was an old house and everywhere you went you would find someplace that would be excellent to hide in. He had a sister named Karen with ponytails and buckteeth. She was ten and very mean. We would always steal her dolls and she would chase us all over the house.

Paul had just moved in to the house next door two months ago. He didn't have a dog but he had a bird that squawked all of the time. The bird lived in a big cage and whenever I went near it he would squawk at me. Once I put my finger into the cage and he bit me. He was not a good pet to have. Paul had a little sister named Bernadette and an older brother named Phil. Phil was sixteen and always picked in his little brother sometimes tormenting him the whole time I was there. Bernadette never played with us. She had a sickness that made her tired all of the time so mostly she laid on the couch watching cartoons on TV.

Todd finished his slingshot first and loaded it up with a napkin he had dipped into his Kool-Aid. He pulled back on the band and let it fly. It caught a breeze coming from one of the vents in the ceiling and flew all the way to the other side of the room. It hit poor Sally Bopkins just as she was turning around. The Kool-Aid in the napkin exploded all over her costume and she began to cry. Todd threw his weapon in front of Paul and I shoved mine underneath my shirt. Our teacher, Ms. Cooper, looked up from the table where she was helping someone with their project and saw Sally covered in Kool-Aid. Without missing a beat she came right over to our table and stared at Todd. It seems that Todd was the only one who had decided on the Kool-Aid as everyone else wanted soda. She grabbed him by the arm and dragged him over to Sally to apologize.

We laughed about that all day. After school we raced home to get ready to go out. We were only allowed to go to the houses in our own neighborhood but we still planned on getting more candy than anyone else. Todd came over just as my parents were getting home from work. My mother was always the one who greeted the trick or treaters at the door. My father couldn't be bothered with such drivel. Before we went out she gave us the same lecture we always heard, don't go to houses with the lights out, don't get into anyone's car, always have your flashlight ready, and never eat any of the candy until we got home so that she could check it. She said that there were a lot of sick people in the world who put tings like razors into kid's candy.

After listening to her for what was surely an eternity, we grabbed up our gear and ran out the door. We had a pattern that we followed every year. While other kids went in groups, we raced past them and always were the first ones to get to the door. Sometimes we would get lucky and the people were not home but had left a bowl of candy at the door. There would always be a note, 'only take one please'. We never paid that

Demons Within

any attention and would dump the whole bowl into our bags. Some of the old lady's gave out caramel apples and others gave out pennies. We knew who they were and never went to those houses.

After hitting most of the houses our bags became rather heavy. The rain was still coming down pretty hard and that was making parents stop their children sooner, leaving more booty for us. We decided that we were done collecting and now it was time for phase two. We found a large bush to hide our bags behind and started off. The plan was simple. We would go to the houses of some of the kids we knew and ring the bell. When the door opened we would let 'em have it with our slingshots. Todd had gotten some plastic baggies from his kitchen and we filled them with mud. Whoever was on the receiving end would certainly have a mess on their hands when we were through with them. After we released our initial volley we would run off as fast as we could. I didn't think anyone would give chase in this weather.

The first house we picked was Kenny's. I wanted to get a good shot at his sister. We had worked this out with him beforehand so I knew that she would be the one answering the door. Karen didn't believe in trick or treating. She always stayed home and gave out the candy while her parents worked in their basement. We rang the bell and ran behind the bushes by the porch. We cocked our arms back and waited for the precise moment when the door opened to unleash our wrath on Karen the Mean. The door opened and just as we released the muddy bullets, Chuck bounded out from behind the door. He covered the distance to us in only four steps. He jumped and tackled us knocking us down into the mud. Our missiles struck the exact area that we had planned, but not the intended target. Karen had found out about our little plan when she overheard Kenny on the phone with me. She was in the doorway holding poor Kenny in front of her. The mudpacks struck him dead in the face and he was soon covered with the thick, wet dirt.

Todd and I got to our feet just as the mudpacks exploded onto poor Kenny's face. We laughed as the dog began to shake off the mud from his coat all over us.

...that was a good memory. I was glad that occasionally the good ones made their way through the muck of my thoughts. I got another cup of coffee and decided to watch some TV. We had a satellite dish with over five hundred channels to choose from. I had a friend who knew a thing or two about electronics and he had hooked me up with everything for free. There were the local channels, sports channels, news channels, and about a hundred pay-per-view channels. I decided that I would check out the news since I had seemingly lost touch with the civilized world when I arrived.

The first story that I saw caused my heart to skip a beat. On the screen, there was a shot of my house surrounded by fire trucks, police cars, and ambulances. The caption on the bottom of the screen read, 'Suspicious fire destroys home.' I stared in disbelief as I watched the only place that I called home burn to the ground. I turned up the volume to hear the commentary. The reporter on the scene was covered by a big blue poncho and rain was pouring down. Apparently neighbors had seen a strange man running away from the house moments before it had exploded into flames. It was then that I remembered what the man had said, 'he will do everything in his power to stop you from continuing on your chosen course of action.' It was beginning.

River of Chaos and Shattered Dreams

I went to the wet bar, poured myself a tall glass of gin, and drank it down in three gulps. I repeated this process two more times. I couldn't believe that my house was gone. Everything that I owned was in there; my collection of antique candy dispensers, various paintings and sketches given to me by my father, irreplaceable memorabilia from Red Sox teams of the past, my baseball card collection, and so many other things that could never be replaced. The fish. I had forgotten all about my two fish when I left! They were surely boiled by now. I wonder what there last thoughts were. Did they see who had set the fire? I would give anything to see what they saw in their final moments.

The man in the shop had told me that the 'demon' who was stalking me would do something, but surely this was just a coincidence. I wasn't one to believe in all of that hocus pocus. I reached into my pocket and pulled out the key the man had given me. 'The key must be kept close', he had said. I looked down at the figurine dangling from the key and its eyes seemed to be mocking me. I felt a strong wave of anger and resentment welling up from the pit of my stomach, directed at the small figure dangling from the key. I wanted to destroy it, throw it into a fire and watch it slowly melt down, its features melting into one another until it became an indiscernible blob of bubbling plastic.

I grabbed it and squeezed down as hard as I could, feeling its points poking through the skin on my palm. My hand became warm from the blood that was trapped by my grip and a burning sensation began to travel to my wrist and forearm, extending all the way to my elbow. My grip tightened even further until my body shook from the pressure that was building inside of me. I was using all of the strength that I could muster, and the shaking intensified. I screamed out in rage and, raising the keychain up over my head, I reared back and threw it against the mirror over the bar. The instant it hit the mirror, there was a loud shatter as the mirror exploded into thousands of small shards of deadly glass. The cloud of broken glass blew out away from the wall and rained down over my head. I was still screaming when my vision once again went white.

I could see the key sliding down the dog-things throat, just out of reach. Its mouth was closing over my head and I didn't want to let the key out of my sight. I grabbed onto one of the dog-things teeth and pulled myself out of the ooze on the ground, feeling the light disappear from behind me. I stretched out and grabbed hold of the end of the key with my fingertips and it pulled me along as we descended down the creatures long, dark, ooze filled throat.

Sounds were coming from all around me, shrill cries and blood curdling screams overlapping each other and permeating my head. My body twisted and spun down the dark, slimy cave and I pulled myself towards the key. I opened my hand and saw that

River of Chaos and Shattered Dreams

the key was giving off a faint glow, illuminating the area I was falling through. Around me, I could see a river of ooze that was filled with scraps of memories and bits of emotions floating rapidly by. I held the key out in front of me, using it to light the way ahead. My body twisted and turned as I tried to dodge the various feelings and emotions shooting past me at ludicrous speeds.

Inside the river of ooze, I saw a memory of my father working on his paintings, as he had done on so many occasions during my youth. Another scene flew past me, this one of my parents yelling at each other when I had been caught cheating at school. My emotions were all in the river beneath me, leaving nothing in my conciseness except fear. I didn't know where the tunnel would lead or what was waiting for me at its end. The key glowed brighter and I became aware that I wasn't alone. Voices from deep inside my head began to surface with their accusatory tones cutting deep into me. I felt the same way that I had before, when I was bad. The voices were almost incomprehensible, as they all struggled to get my attention. I heard bits and pieces but without the rest of the sentence, they made no sense.

The air in the creatures' throat grew cold around me and I came across yet another scene in the river of ooze, this one harder for me to see than the last. It was my house, burning in front of my eyes and all around me I saw flames licking the walls and making their way up the curtains to the ceiling. I watched my couch explode in a black, smoky cloud. Along the wall, the paint melted off the pictures my father had given me, catching fire as it fell onto the ground and spread over the carpet. The flames made their way to the closet and I watched in horror as the door burst off its' hinges, its contents quickly becoming engulfed by the searing heat of the flames.

I felt the heat from the fire, my body temperature rising and when I breathed in, a searing heat shot down my windpipe and into my lungs. I saw the key in my hand in front of me move to the right so I shifted my focus to see the front door of my house was open and a man run through it with great speed. He was going very fast so I could only catch a glimpse of him. He was dressed all in black and holding a gas can in his right hand. Just before he disappeared from sight he turned his head toward me and I saw his deep, black eyes.

I turned my head away and something pulled me forward with increasing speed. The air was drying my eyes out making it difficult to blink. I screamed and kicked at the air, trying to slow my progress, when I slammed up against a wall. The impact knocked the key from my grasp and I watched it fall down a large precipice. I fell back away from the wall and my body went go numb, as I hit the ground hard, bouncing onto my side. I landed beside the key and reached out to grab it, as the scene around me began to change. My eyes were now adjusted to the darkness and they focused on the wall directly ahead. It was an old, wooden wall with spaces between the slats and a small opening on the bottom. I was back in the old shack in the woods. I grabbed the key and got to my feet. Thankfully, I was in one piece, even though I was a little sore.

I ran towards the door, kicking an old soda can out of my way. Outside the shack it was pitch black and the woods had an ominous look to them. The trees overhead loomed over me and I ran as fast and as hard as I could back towards my old house. I

Demons Within

put the key in my pocket, jumped over a pile of fallen trees and heard something running after me, gaining ground. I sped up my pace and changed course, hoping to outmaneuver whatever was coming. I had a sinking feeling that I knew what it was.

I ran past a large tree and looked behind my shoulder. I could just make out the outline of the thing in pursuit. It looked like a bear, running with its paws hitting the ground and crushing the underlying growth. I heard the wood on the ground snapping as it got closer. Up ahead, I saw a log that had fallen over the brook. If I could make it over that before I was overcome, I could catch the bike trail. Once there, I could gain better footing and run at twice the speed I was currently doing. There was only one problem with that plan; by doing that I would be running away from my house. On the other hand, if I ran up the hill to my house, it would surely overtake me. I decided to take the trail.

I got to the log and crossed it in three strides seeing that the bike trail was only a few steps away. I ran up a small incline and hit the trail at full speed, feeling the wind whipping my hair back from my face as I ran faster. I didn't want to look back; for fear that it would be right behind me waiting for just the right moment to chomp down on my head. The only sound that I heard was my heart pounding in my head. I rounded the first corner of the trail and headed down the long hill that would lead me to my friend Kenny's house. I hoped I could make it that far before it got me.

The trail up ahead had a small incline, and just on the other side of it there was a large branch that had fallen off of one of the trees during a storm. I didn't see it there as I approached. I hit the incline and two steps later noticed the branch but it was too late for me to stop. My right leg hit the branch and I fell towards the ground, my sneaker flying off of my foot and soaring into the night air. My head dropped and I flipped onto my back, landing hard on the ground. I saw my sneaker spin around at the peak of its arch and begin its decent back to earth. I heard footsteps approaching quickly and tried to get up, but I couldn't move my legs. I could only lay there and watch as my sneaker continued to fall.

I tried to scream out, but no sound came from my throat, which had begun to close. The footsteps were growing louder and my heart still pounded in my head. My breath became very shallow as I tried to move with no success. The sneaker became my hope, falling more and more rapidly towards the earth. My legs grew cold and I could no longer feel my hands. This was it for sure. I began to regret ever going on that exploration. I started to cry and I wanted my mom to come to my rescue.

The clouds moved in front of the moon overhead and the night air was getting crisper, with a cold breeze making its way down the hill, enveloping my body with hopeless-ness. I heard the distant howl of a dog and prepared myself for the end. The footsteps were louder now, almost on top of me and I wondered how long it would take until I could feel no more. I hoped it wouldn't be a painful process, but very quick. I noticed a smell making its way down the hill. The footsteps were louder than ever before and I wished it would hurry up and get here so I wouldn't have to feel the fear anymore. Why did I go after that damn key anyway? The sneaker was almost to me now. I closed my eyes and waited for it to arrive.

River of Chaos and Shattered Dreams

My vision began to come back as the scene slowly faded away. In front of me there was nothing left of the mirror except for a few shards of glass dangling from the supports on the wall. All around me, there was broken glass and pieces of plaster that had come loose from the wall. I looked around and saw my dog staring at me from the doorway. The keychain had landed in front of him and I saw that he was reaching down to pick it up. I yelled for him to stop and ran through the piles of broken glass towards him. I reached down, snatched it away from his mouth, and squatted beside him to reassure him that everything was alright.

I looked at the keychain and noticed that its mouth had become black and its eyes were a deeper, darker black than before. I touched its mouth with my thumb and picked off some of the black substance. My hand jerked away from it and I felt like I had been bitten. I looked at my thumb and noticed a small trickle of blood beginning to run down towards my wrist. The teeth on the figurine had become sharper. I got up and went into the bathroom to rinse off my hand, the dog following closely at my heals. I had a feeling he wouldn't be going that far from me anytime soon. I got to the bathroom and turned on the water, shoving my hand in the sink to wash the blood away. After I dried my hands, I went to put on a Band-Aid and noticed the puncture marks in my palm from when I held the figurine in my grip. I put on the Band-Aid and went back to the room to clean up the glass.

I vacuumed up all of the glass that I could while my dog stood his watchful guard in the corner. I no longer felt the same rage that I had when I threw the keychain into the mirror. A sense of calm was taking over my body and mind. Perhaps I just needed to vent out my rage, and the keychain was just the outlet I needed. I could do nothing about the mirror now, so I would have to call someone to replace it tomorrow, if there was to be a tomorrow.

I still had quite a few hours until the man from the shop was due to visit me. So far, I had done two things that he distinctly warned me against doing. I answered a ring at the door, and I had also thrown the key, thereby not keeping it close. According to his line of thought, each one of those actions triggered an appropriate event. Answering the door led to my seeing my house burn down on TV, and throwing the key led to the dream. I went back into the kitchen to write these newest additions to the list that was now becoming quite lengthy.

After I added the newest events, I felt extremely hungry. I looked through the cabinets and saw that there was nothing there to eat. Well, the man didn't mention not to leave the house, so I decided to go back into town to grab a sandwich. The dog, probably sensing what I was planning on doing, became extremely agitated and I did my best to calm him down, even offering to take him in the car. That was usually is an instant obedience tool for him, as it was his favorite thing in the world; I got no happy dance from him. Instead, he lay down and started to whimper at my feet. I couldn't go out with him like that and I didn't think it would be a good idea to leave him there alone after seeing me rage out. I grabbed the yellow pages and called the local sandwich shop to get something delivered.

The food arrived in about forty minutes. I ordered a bowl of the cheddar broccoli soup, a chicken parmesan sandwich, and an order of cheese fries. I also got a hamburger for the dog. He had been through a lot and could probably use a treat. I went to the fridge to get a beer and settled into the living room to scarf down my meal. The TV was still tuned into the all-news, all the time channel, but I really needed to lighten my mood. I turned on the comedy channel and they were showing a Three Stooges marathon. I'm not a huge stooge fan but as soon as I stopped on that channel, the dog perked up his ears so I left it there.

I finished my meal and threw the trash away as I got another beer. I hoped the meeting with this guy tonight would prove helpful. I went back to the list and decided to write some more details down in case they would be helpful. I checked the time on the wall, four o'clock, still had time for that nap before he arrived. I let the dog out one last time before I headed upstairs to sleep.

The alarm went off at ten o'clock and, for the first time in recent memory, I was granted an uneventful sleep. I hoped that there were a lot more of those in the near future. I went to the bathroom for a shower and a shave before my company arrived. Even though my sleep was uneventful, I still felt fatigued, almost as if I hadn't slept at all. Maybe I would feel like this until the mystery of the events was solved. I got out of the shower, toweled myself off, and headed to the bedroom to change.

Twist to the Left

I had just finished changing and was putting on my shoes when the phone rang. There was only the one phone downstairs, so I had to hurry before I missed the call. The dog was in the kitchen whining at the door. I assumed that he needed to go out so I opened it for him. No sooner had I opened the door when the dog became spooked and yelped as he ran upstairs to the bedroom. That was odd. I closed the door and picked up the receiver on the fifth ring.

"Hello," I said. There was no response.

"Hello who is this please?" I repeated. There was a faint sound on the other end of the line and I could hear something moving around in the background. "Who's calling please?" I asked yet again, becoming more agitated at having my time wasted by the silent caller. No voice answered so I put the phone back into its cradle, only to have it ring again as soon as it was hung up. I jerked the phone up and said, "Hello, who is this," in a firm, demanding voice. Again there was no response. The sound of movement had grown louder since last time, and I strained to make out anything else that was in the background. It sounded like something was scratching on the receiver, scratching to dig through the phone. There was still no voice on the line so I hung up the phone and reached down to tie my shoes.

Suddenly, there was a loud knock at the front door, causing me to jump back. I looked at the clock, 10:40, not a minute sooner, not a minute later he had said. I finished tying my shoes and called for the dog. He didn't respond. Usually a knock at the door would turn him into a blithering idiot, but not this time. I walked to the door and called for him again, this time in a firmer tone but he still did not respond from wherever he was hiding. Maybe he was scared of something, as I was starting to get a little freaked out as well. Still, he never failed to respond to my commands even if he was spooked. I got to the door and peeked through the small hole to see who was there.

It was really dark outside so I couldn't quite make out the figure that was standing in the doorway. I reached for the light switch and flipped it on. There was a momentary flash of light and a pop, followed by darkness. Damn, I blew the bulb. I strained my eye against the glass again, but still couldn't see who was there.

"Who is it?" I asked. The person on the other end said something that I couldn't quite make out. I unlatched the chain on the door, still looking through the peephole, and turned the lock to disengage the dead bolt. I grabbed the handle and turned it slowly to open the door and as the handle reached the end of its cycle I asked again, "who's there?" This time there was no response at all. I opened the door slightly to greet my mysterious guest.

Twist to the Left

I felt a whoosh of air and something brush against my leg as my dog went bounding out the small opening in the door. I jerked it open the rest of the way and looked out, but there was no one there. I walked through the front opening and looked around. It was getting damn cold outside. There was no one in sight. Where was the dog? I called out to him repeatedly, but got no response. There must have been someone at the door. I definitely heard a knock, and the dog was going after someone. I walked out into the yard still calling after him but he was no where to be seen. I walked the entire perimeter of the house and even looked up and down the street. Whoever it was had scared the shit out of my dog and now he was gone.

I turned around and headed back towards the house. I was sure the dog would come back soon enough. I gave the yard one last glance and headed inside. Just before the door closed, another whoosh of air raced past me giving me a chill and causing the door to slam shut.

I went back into the living room and reached for the light switch. I flipped it on and off, but the light wasn't working. I went to the hallway and tried that switch, but got the same result. There was probably a power outage of some sort in the neighborhood. I looked outside and noticed the neighbors lights were working just fine. I walked around the condo and tried a few more switches before finally giving up. I must have blown some sort of fuse when I turned on the porch light. I walked back into the living room and suddenly felt a presence. I wasn't alone. I looked around, but my eyes had still not become accustomed to the darkness so I saw nothing.

"What's up kid?" a voice called out from the dark corner of the room.

The voice stopped me dead in my tracks. I was not alone. In the corner of the room, I could make out the shape of someone sitting in a chair. The figure rose up from where he was sitting and I saw that the man was quite tall. I started to get a queasy feeling and felt myself grow weak. The man sparked something in his hand and I detected the familiar smell of cigar smoke in the air. My eyes adjusted to the darkness and I could make out some of his features in the dull glow of the cigars head. He was tall. I couldn't see his clothes, but I could see that he was wearing a hat. His facial features became clear and I saw that he was a very muscular man, chiseled and cut. I knew him all too well.

"Have a seat," he said to me as he took another long haul from his stogie, "we have some things to discuss."

That was the moment I had waited for so long to arrive. Finally, I would be able to confront him and find out his purpose. Finally, I would know the answers to the questions that had plagued my every thought.

"What do you want," I asked the man with the cigar. He took another haul and blew the smoke out in my direction. He took a step forward and stated his demand again, this time more firmly.

"Have a seat. Now."

Demons Within

An unseen force pushed me down onto the couch. I guessed we were going to do it the way he wanted. I sat up straight and looked to where he stood, about four or five feet away. I looked over at the front door. It was at least ten to twelve feet away. I didn't think I could make it out before he reached me.

"What is it that you want from me," I asked in a panicked voice.

"You have something that I want and I came here to retrieve it." He said, and moved away back over to the chair he had been sitting in. He sat down and I heard the leather of the seat crack. I wanted to confront him, but the fear was too strong.

"I don't know what you want," I said, "but take whatever it is and leave me alone."

"I can't do that without you," he said. "I know what I'm here for but I need you get it for me." He took another haul from the cigar and flicked a long ash to the floor. The tip of the cigar glowed brighter and he lowered his arm beside the chair.

"Tell me what it is and it's yours," I replied. "I'll get whatever you want, but you need to leave me alone after that." My voice sounded weak. I wasn't doing a very convincing job of being tough with this guy. He already had my mind, what else could he possibly need? I started to get up, but the unseen force pushed me back down.

"You went to his shop today," he said. "I saw you there. How'd you like it? Did it give you what you needed?"

"I didn't notice you there," I said. "Usually I don't have a problem seeing you." My confidence was beginning to return, my words flowing more freely.

"Sure you did," he replied, blowing more acrid smoke into the already clouded room. "I saw you check out my ass after you got your coupon book."

He was talking about the woman in the shop. How could he have seen that? She was at least two feet smaller than he was. Had he somehow managed to change his appearance to hide from me? I was face to face with him in the shop and didn't even know it. I wondered how many other times he was right on front of me without my knowing.

"I would've thought you a tit man myself," he said, "but you were gawking there with your mouth all open looking like a chump. Funny, I didn't think there was anything else to learn about you."

"What do you mean?" I said. Panic returned to my voice causing it to crack as I spoke. I took some deep breaths, trying to calm myself down, and wondered what else he knew.

"I thought I had you all covered," he said. "You know likes, dislikes, sexual preferences, favorite food. I see what you see when you dream. I liked the baseball game, by the way. I only wished you stayed through to the end. I wanted to see who won."

I remembered that dream. He had appeared to me while I was at the row of lockers. It was he who had given me the key that opened the locker, revealing the book. The book. That's what he wanted. Was Cigar Man actually Chaos, the demon that I was facing? If so, was the book the secret to understanding and defeating him? I couldn't let him have that book, but how could I stop him? I felt inside my pocket and felt the key. Why didn't he mention that? Maybe he wasn't aware of its existence because after all he hadn't given it to me, the man in the shop had. Speaking of the freak, where was he now? He was due here at 10:45. I had expected him to be the one at the door when I answered it earlier. Maybe he was he the same person as the one sitting in the chair across the room. No, he had mentioned the shop before. I checked my watch and noticed that no time had passed since the arrival of my uninvited guest.

"Yes it's true," he said, "I have a certain influence over time as well. Don't worry; you'll get it back and then some when we finish our business here. Now, as I was saying before, I need you to get it for me. I assume its close so you shouldn't have to go very far."

The book was upstairs, not exactly close to where we were now, but not that far away either. I needed to stall him for some time until I could figure out what else to do.

"Why are you in my dreams?" I asked, "What purpose does it serve for you to torment me?" I hoped he would go into some detail on these questions.

"I don't think it would be prudent to disclose that at this time," he replied. "Why don't you get the item and I'll be on my way."

"You still haven't told me what it is that you are looking for," I said. If we were gonna dance, I wanted to lead. "I think you need to give up some information before I consider whether or not to help you now. Answer my questions, or find it yourself." With that said, I summoned all of my strength and shot to my feet. My sudden move of defiance must have surprised him and he quickly got to his feet to meet my stare.

"You stupid asshole," he said, walking towards me. "You have no idea who you're messing with." He raised his right arm towards me and extended his index finger. I felt heat coming from the pocket where the keychain was and it was starting to burn my thigh. He continued to come forward and with each step, the burning intensified. The key. It didn't want him near. I reached into my pocket and pulled it out. He was almost upon me and the room began to shake. There was a noticeable change in the temperature. It had gotten hot, really hot, like I was being broiled over a fire. I continued to raise the key towards him as he approached. It came into contact with his finger and then there was a blinding light that filled the room, followed by a hot blast of air that threw me back into the wall. I heard my joints all crack at the same time and I fell forward, my head bouncing off the floor. I took a breath and blacked out.

I woke up to the feeling of something wet on my face. I raised my head and tried to open my eyes. Something was licking me, and it just got me on the mouth. I put my hand in front of my face to block the wet tongue and turned my head away. I squinted open my eyes and saw that I was on the floor in the living room. I felt something pawing at my head and I whipped around and saw my dog. I lowered my hand and opened my eyes fully to make sure that what I was seeing was real. My stare was met by the ugly face of the dog and as soon as he saw me look him in the eye, he barked and started to dance around my fallen body. I struggled to get to my feet, tripping over him a few times as I did. I got to my feet and noticed that it was very bright. The lights had come back on and my eyes weren't quite used to it yet. There was something else that had changed. The man I had been speaking to was no longer there. I looked around the room and there was no sign of him.

I began to wonder if I had dreamed the whole thing up. It would make sense, considering that he had made his presence known in a few other dreams of mine. It was then that I noticed the smell, which was unmistakable evidence that he had indeed been there in the room with me. I continued walking around the room, looking for the source of the foul odor, but I found nothing. As I started to leave the living room for the kitchen I spotted the source of the foul odor. It had fallen off of the table and rolled underneath the chair. The carpet around the area where it had stopped had begun to turn black, its edges beginning to take on an orange glow. I reached down and picked it up while I stomped the burnt area with my foot, snuffing out the oxygen it so desperately needed to survive. The tip of the cigar that once had glowed brightly in the darkened room, ceased to shine as soon as I raised it from its hiding place.

I took the foul smelling object from the room and opened the front door. I walked outside, went to the trash cans that were lining the driveway, and threw the cigar away. The air was crisp and I took in as much of it as my lungs could handle. I exhaled and watched as my breath was carried away into the night. The dog came up behind me and sat quietly at my feet. I turned and patted him on the head, happy that he was safe again with me and wondered where he had gone off to in such a hurry. I examined him and at first glance he appeared to be alright, as there were no visible abrasions on his skin and nothing noticeable on any part of his body. I looked down at his paws and then saw something lying on the ground in front of him.

It looked like a mangled baseball cap. I reached down and picked it up. Yep, that's what it was. It was an old, worn Yankees hat. The color had faded to a dull grey and the logo, once proudly white, was stained and brown. I continued examining it and suddenly I remembered that I had seen it before. It was in that dream that cigar man had spoke of with the baseball game. I felt a warm feeling come over my body as I realized that I had a tangible piece of evidence that the dreams were in fact real and not just some figment of my overactive imagination. I was not letting this cap out of my sight even for a moment; for it was the only thing I had to prove that I was not going mad.

I put the cap on my head and went back into the house and it suddenly occurred to me that I was still waiting for a visit from my 'friend' from the freak shop. I walked to the kitchen to check the time. It was half past eleven. He hadn't shown up. Either that or I hadn't seen him when he arrived as I was occupied with cigar man. I rushed upstairs with the dog right at my heals and darted into the bedroom to get the book. It was gone. I was supposed to keep it safe and now it had disappeared. Frantically, I rifled through the drawers of the table, thinking that I might have put it there. No such luck. I went over to the dresser and tore open all of the drawers. I tore through all of the items, throwing them on the floor all around me. The dog jumped onto the bed and laid down putting his head between his paws. It wasn't there.

Twist to the Left

I ran over to the closet and threw open the doors as panic began to set in. I continued to tear through all of the various drawers and cabinets looking for the book but it was no where to be found. I stopped my fit and went over to the bed and sat down. I put my head down in my hands and began to cry, the events of late finally taking their toll on my weakened emotional state. The dog crawled over and placed his head on my lap, his eyes looking up at me in the typical sad puppy dog fashion. My face was flush and my nose began to run. I reached over and scratched the dog behind the ears. Where had the damn book gone? Why didn't the man from the shop come to see me as he said he would? The dog got up and left the room as I struggled to come up with answers to the unwelcome questions.

After thinking about those things for a while I knew that I still had no control over anything and went downstairs to find the dog. He was sitting on a chair in the living room so I went over to join him. I sat down and gazed out the window into the night, watching the clouds move slowly to cover the light of the moon. There were so many things going on and I needed someone to talk to about them besides the dog. Although he was a great companion, he was a lousy therapist. I took off the cap and placed in my lap. It was then that I noticed something was sticking out of the inside of the cap so I pulled it out. It was a business card. I turned it over and read it taking in each word slowly.

Fat Tony's Cigar Shop

Specializing in hard to find makes for the finicky connoisseur.

Home delivery and 24-hour service available.

Try our new selections of Cubans.

20% off for new customers.

There was no phone number listed, just an address downtown. Did this card have any significance to me? The shop didn't sound familiar. I had been down there only today and I would've noticed another new store. The card said 24-hour service available. Surely they weren't open at this time of night. Maybe they had an on call service for their existing customers. That would fit in for the upscale, yuppie type of people that you found in the upper part of town. I know of one guy who had called a restaurant in Mexico City to have them deliver a container of guacamole because he couldn't find anything palatable up here. The owner had originally balked at the idea, until the guy offered to pay him one thousand dollars to have it sent overnight. That is a lot of money, especially in Mexico. The restaurant owner probably closed up shop for a week to vacation after that.

I took the card with me and went into the kitchen to get a beer. I wasn't a big cigar fan but I needed to find out if the shop had anything to do with what was going on. I grabbed my coat and leached the dog and headed out meet Fat Tony.

I Wish I Were A Gangsta Baby

The temperature continued its decent to the bottom end of the thermometer and the cloud cover overhead increased, threatening to block out all of the moonlight pouring down from the sky. The dog was happy to be out of the house, as was I. The streets were empty except for the occasional car trying to find an all night deli. The people of the city would never totally come to grips with a place that didn't have anything you wanted, at anytime you wanted. There had to always be a place to go for coffee, a place to eat, a place to go when you needed laundry done at two in the morning. All night dry cleaners were a must, as one couldn't possibly be expected to get a good night sleep if their pants didn't have a razor sharp crease at all times. These days it was all about 'me'. People had lost all feeling of empathy towards others and replaced it with pure, selfish greed. If something wasn't available, they would complain and demand compensation for their inconvenience. My ex was like that, which was precisely why she was an ex instead of an is.

I don't remember when exactly the change happened in the world. One day we were all going around doing our jobs and raising our families the best we could, and the next day we were blaming teachers because little Johnny had issues with authority. We stopped holding ourselves accountable for child rearing and instead relied on new drugs designed to turn our kids into mindless drones. Television had long since replaced conversation as we were inundated with show after show of worthless dribble. Educational programs, once a staple of Saturday morning viewing, were replaced with cartoons featuring robot squads fighting each other to the death, and kids raising imaginary creatures designed to do nothing other than battle.

Standardized tests were developed to show where schools were failing their students, while the money used for education was being slashed in favor of more popular programs, such as futuristic missile defense systems and increased aid to our countries sworn enemies. The world was descending into an open grave, and all the while we were working on shoveling the dirt over our heads. People were getting away with murder while we focused on building up our net worth at any cost.

Over the past few years I began to retreat from the world of television, as I feared I was becoming immune to the evils of everyday life in America. I spent less time worrying about money and more time working on things that would make a difference. I had recently taken up reading to young kids at the local youth center. They were always grateful to have someone take the time for them and I received smiles every time I was there.

I stopped at the bank to grab some cash from the ATM because if I was going into a store, it would make sense to have some money. I took out a twenty and headed to the main strip. There was a couple on a bench in the park at the top of the hill. The lights of most of the stores were off, so the main source of light was the

I Wish I Were A Gangsta Baby

moon that was slowly disappearing behind the ever thickening clouds filling the sky. I didn't see the cigar store anywhere. There were only twenty or so stores on this street and they were all closed. I past the place where I had eaten breakfast and continued up the hill to where the shop of horrors was located.

A sudden burst of wind hit me as soon as I past the restaurant, so strong that I almost fell over. The dog growled softly and came to an abrupt stop at a dumpster next to a ski shop. I pulled on the leash but his body stiffened in defiant resistance. His growl became more intense and he lowered his head until it was almost touching the ground. I looked in the direction that he was growling, but all that I saw was the dumpster. The dog was now in full attack stance. I had never seen him that upset before. I walked closer to the dumpster, the dog was still a little ahead of me, when another burst of wind hit us blowing the cover off the dumpster, and it crashed with a loud bang against the wall of the building. I jumped back from the noise and acciden-tally released the dogs leach from my grip. The dog darted towards the source of the noise like a greyhound chasing a rabbit. I saw something jump from the dumpster and run behind the row of closed stores. I ran after the dog, calling out to him as he disappeared around the dark corner.

I rounded the corner of the ski shop and into the darkness of the alley. It was much darker on this side of the store and I squinted to allow my eyes to adjust, but couldn't see the dog or whatever it was he was chasing. I ran through a puddle and felt water splash up my pants leg as I continued my pursuit of the spooked pooch. I ran and called out for the dog for another 100 yards or so and then stopped. He was too fast and there was no way that I was going to catch him on foot. That was the second time he had run off and I didn't like that. He had been the only constant in my life until recently and now that it was not the case, I had nothing left to fall back on.

I turned around and walked back towards the dumpster, my pace a lot slower than before, with my head hung low in defeat. The dog had come back the last time he ran off, even with a clue of sorts, so I had some hope that he would return. I rounded the corner of the shop and approached the dumpster, its lid was still open from the wind, and went over to glance inside. I didn't see anything interesting, as I was not an aficionado of dumpsters, but looked around some more anyway. Inside, there were a few plastic bags on the bottom, along with three broken down boxes, a broken broom handle, and a small purple sack with cloth ties on the top of it. It looked like a Crown Royal bag, but there didn't appear to be any of the good stuff inside. Still, it did have something inside of it, as the bulge in the bag was noticeable. I climbed over the side of the filthy dumpster and jumped inside.

The smell was definitely worse inside than out. I don't know how some people managed to go through dumpsters on a regular basis. I suppose that when you don't have any other choice it makes it easier, but what about that first time? I wonder how long it took for someone to muster up the courage to climb up and over the side, with grime covering their hands and the wretched smell sticking to their clothes, and climb in to retrieve something. Their shoes, as mine were becoming, would certainly be ruined, with a sticky slime on the soles and grease marks running along the sides. Digging around in unknown refuse, with your exposed hands being cut by various objects, must cause a lot of infections. I grabbed the sack and climbed back over the side to the 'safety' of the street.

I checked myself out and saw that my shoes were indeed ruined. My pants once crisp and clean, were covered by an unidentified sticky substance, and there was a smell that was sticking to the air around me. I walked over to the curb in front of the dumpster and sat down to examine the small bag that was heavy for its size. I pulled on the cloth that was closing the top of the bag and it opened, causing a faint mist of powder to shoot from the pouch and hit me in the eyes. My eyes began to sting immediately, and my tear ducts went into overtime trying to cleanse them from the uninvited germ. I closed my eyes and the stinging grew more powerful, as if cutting off the oxygen from the air outside made it worse. I tried to open them but found that my eyelashes were starting to stick together, making my ability to see an impossible task. I dropped the sack and raised my hands to rub the dust out of my eyes. The stinging was unbearable by then and I felt it working its way into my sinuses.

I stood up as my nasal passages opened their dams and released the wave of snot they were struggling to hold back. I opened my mouth to try to draw in a breath, but found myself only breathing in the wretched dumpster air that was surrounding me. I gagged and began to cough, spittle flying from my mouth, and fell to the ground. The stinging had extended to the back of my head and was beginning to travel down my throat towards my chest. I couldn't breathe and my eyes were now completely sealed shut from the mysterious powder. My hands grew cold and had I began to lose feeling in my legs. My heart rate increased tenfold, and the stinging now encompassed my entire body.

A bright light came into my vision and intensified with each beat of my heart. I felt my consciousness slip away as the familiar screeching sound make its way into my world again.

I was on the ground on the bike trail and still could not bring myself to move. Overhead, the clouds were thickening around the moon and my sneaker was falling more rapidly towards me. The footsteps behind me were so loud that they began to drown out all other sounds, and the smell, that horrible smell, grew stronger and more pungent like a pile of rotting garbage. I wanted mom to come and make everything alright like she always did when I was scared.

The sound of the footsteps finally stopped, leaving only the sound of my still pounding heartbeat in my ears. The air around me became silent and still and I felt something breathing on my neck. I could also make out a voice, though not all of the words that it was speaking.

"....ok?.....hear me?"

I laid still and waited for the end to come, as I still felt doomed by the dog-thing that was chasing me through the woods. The voice passed through my conscience again,

"...need help?.....an ambulance, quickly!"

I Wish I Were A Gangsta Baby

I felt brush something against my forehead and a great pressure forced itself down on my chest. It felt like I was being crushed over and over again and my ribs were getting sore. The pressure on my chest stopped and I felt something grab onto the back of my neck and tilt my head up. A sudden rush of air forced its way through my mouth and into my lungs. The pressure started back up again, followed by another sound from the voice,

".....three, four, five, six."

The pattern continued on; a rush of air, chest crushing, counting, "...two, three, four." I heard a loud siren and red flashes appeared in my eyes. There was a lot of commotion around me and then my body was lifted up into the air, coming to rest on a much softer surface than the ground that I had been laying on. Then the pattern began again; a rush of air, chest pressure, counting,

"...five, six, seven, eight."

The sound of a door closing and more loud sirens and red flashing. The sounds faded away and the pattern stopped.

I opened my eyes and looked around. The light was very bright and I had trouble seeing clearly. My head was pounding and a series of painful jolts were ripping through my body. With each jolt, I felt my muscles spasm and my heartbeat quicken and pause. The voices had returned, this time greater in number,

"..charge paddles....needles ready....clear!"

The jolt came again, this time with more oomph. I felt my heart jump in my chest and my toes felt like they were on fire.

"...are here....wait outside."

Something opened my mouth and I felt a hard object being forced down my throat. I wanted to gag, but couldn't move the muscles in my throat. The light, once blindingly bright, began to go dark. The voices continued around me,

"...ok? Wake up pal, you alright?"

I felt a cold splash on my face and came to with a shake. There was a man standing over me with a filthy shirt and in desperate need of a shave. He had a round, hard face and the hair that was left on his head was all over the place. He was holding a paper cup over my head that was still dripping from the contents it once held. I opened my eyes wider as he turned his head away from me.

"He's awake now Joe," he said to his companion, "that water woke him right up." He looked back at me, "We almost ran you over with the truck, didn't see you lying in front of the dumpster. You alright pal? Little too much to drink eh?" He was holding the velvet sack in his hand waving it back and forth. "I can't drink this stuff either, knocks me right on my ass."

I struggled to my feet, bracing myself on his shoulder. The stench was too much for me to take and I fell back to the ground.

"Easy there killer," he said. "Don't go so fast. Here, grab my hand." He reached out and grabbed me by the wrist. He tugged once and I was immediately propelled to my feet. I bumped into him and was falling back again when his companion grabbed me by the shoulders to prop me up. He held me there until I had regained my balance. I turned around and saw that he was just as filthy as the other guy was. He was wearing an orange vest and a dirty yellow cap. His arms were covered with healing cuts and his hands felt rough through my shirt.

"Partying by yourself," he said, "you should never do that. You know there's people you can call and they'll help you out."

"I wasn't partying," I said, "I went out and my dog got away from me. I went after him and tripped on something I think."

"Looks to me like you tripped over the side of that dumpster," the fat one replied. "You got scum all over yourself and you reek." This coming from someone whose odor was so bad it was causing my eyes to tear up. "What time you go out pal?"

"Around eleven or so," I said, "I was looking for a place called Fat Tony's."

"Well its almost six now. You were down for a long time."

"You like to smoke?" the fat one asked me.

"Not really," I said, "I needed to ask the owner some questions, that's all."

"Tony's my cousin," he said. "You a cop? He don't need no trouble from you guys, he's clean now."

"I'm no cop," I said. "I came across his card and wanted to see his place of business, that's all. I think he might be able to help me out with something."

"You make trouble for Tony an' you'll be hearing from me," he said, and emphasized his point by shoving me in the shoulder.

"There's no trouble, I can assure you," I said, staggering backwards from the sudden, unwelcome jab. "If you could tell me where his shop is I would appreciate it."

"Two blocks up on the right. You gotta hurry if you wanna catch him. We just came from there an he was gettin ready to go home for the day."

"I appreciate your help gentlemen," I said, and turned to head towards the shop. "By the way, have you seen a dog running around? I really need to find him."

"Nope," said the thin one, "no dogs tonight. There a reward or something if we find him?"

"Well I don't have much but I'll see what I can do." I replied. I was getting annoyed and wanted to leave.

"One last thing, lay of the sauce buddy," the fatter of the two said. "That stuff will kill ya."

I thanked them again and headed off towards Fat Tony's. While I was thankful to them for not running me over, I couldn't help but sense they would if I gave their cousin any problems. Just what I need, a couple of wise guys after me along with everything else. Maybe I could hire them to go after cigar man. I laughed to myself and continued towards the store. I had been out of it for a long time and still felt a lot of pressure on my chest. I needed to get back home as soon as possible to write down what had happened.

Fat Tony's had a very small storefront. There was a door with a small, barred window inside of it and one main window that was also covered by steel bars. This looked like a store that belonged in the city, not up here where crime was still quite rare. I approached the window and looked at the items on display. There were a few assorted humidors assembled there along with a row of lighters and other smoking paraphernalia. There was a neon 'Lottery' sign flashing in the window that looked like it hadn't seen the clean side of a sponge in years. The door was reinforced steel and had tags all over it from various gangs. There was a pull down gate just below the roofline and a giant padlock on the bottom of the frame. This store, like the shop of horrors, did not belong here. There was a sign on the door listing the hours of operation, which were all left blank. Above the door, there was a small camera with a little red light flashing on top of it. Well, whoever was in there knew that I had arrived. I paused to collect my thoughts and get myself together. I looked down and realized that I was filthy, the gunk from the dumpster and the street were clinging to me, and I still had a smell following me around like a shadow. I picked off some of the trash from my shirt and brushed off my pants legs the best I could. I thought to myself that my appearance, no matter how bad it night look, didn't really matter all that much.

I took a deep breath and opened the door to the sound of a bell ringing over my head. I walked inside and the door slammed shut behind me, trapping me in alone. I looked around at the contents of the store and saw a wrap around display case that also served as a counter. Inside of it there were many shelves full of boxed cigars as well as individually wrapped ones. The bottom two shelves had various other items on them; ashtrays, lighters, cigar cutters, and a few other smoking related things.

On the counter stood two spinning displays that held more lighters that appeared to be less pricey than the ones found in the case below. There was also a rack of imported cigarettes beside the cash register and a shelf containing various cigar related magazines. Behind the counter, I saw a wall that served as a giant humidor with a lot of little drawers filled with cigars with even more displayed on numerous shelves. There was a sign on the wall directly behind the register that said, 'Only the finest people deserve the finest things.' A hidden door on the wall opened and a large man entered the room.

He was huge, around 450lbs. I guessed, wearing a yellow button down shirt and brown polyester pants. His arms were massive with no shortage of hair covering them, leaving no visible skin. His head was also full of thick, black hair that was slicked back by roughly a half gallon of the cheapest grease you could buy. He had a tattoo on his right arm that had become faded over the years and it was hard to make out what it was at this distance. His face was rough and filled with numerous pockmarks and scars. He also had the biggest nose I had ever seen, and I feared if he sneezed in this small place I would be blown back through the door. He was wearing rings on all of his fat fingers and had an earring dangling from his left ear to complete his gangster ensemble.

He waddled towards me, his eyes glaring at me like I had just called his mother a whore or something, and put his hands on the counter. Sweat poured down from his forehead and I could see that he was out of breath. I thought the glass counter would surely give way with all his weight, but it held firm only creaking slightly as he leaned on its surface. He raised a finger at me and said, "you need somethin buddy?"

I weighed what I was about to say very carefully, as I was unsure of what would happen next. Was I about to meet yet another member of the ever growing cast in this twisted play being produced by Chaos? Or was he just a man in desperate need of a bypass, a big bowl of bran, and a personal shopper. I swallowed hard and walked up to the counter, still looking around for something that was preparing to jump from the walls and attack me.

Just One Puff

I reached the counter and met the fat man's cold stare. He didn't look to happy to see me standing there in front of him. He was chewing on a cigar nub while giving me the once over. His shirt was unbuttoned halfway to his naval and there was thick mat of black hair growing out of the opening. I could sense the mistrust in his eyes. He looked like the type of person who didn't trust his own mother.

"Waddya need, pal?" he scowled. "I'm kinda in a hurry, you know."

"Are you Fat Tony?" I asked as I continued scanning the room.

"Depends on who's askin the question," he replied sourly. "If you're a cop I ain't seen him in weeks."

"No, I'm not a cop." I replied and took the business card out of my hat and handed it to him. He looked it over and flung it back on the counter. His eyes came again to meet my stare.

"So," he said, "you need a smoke, or what?"

"Actually I was hoping you could help me out with something. I found this card in an old baseball cap and was looking for the caps owner."

He paused for quite some time after I posed my inquiry. I could almost hear the gears in his head grinding to come up with an answer.

"I don't know anything about anyone with a missing hat," he finally said. "Maybe you should try lost and found or something. Look, as I told you before, I'm in a hurry here so if you got business you'd better bring it up otherwise I'm leaving."

I decided to put everything on the table for him. If this man did have a connection, it would be known to me right away. If he didn't, I would leave.

"Please indulge me for a minute." I pleaded, "The man that I'm looking for has a very unmistakable presence. He's over six feet tall with well defined features and black eyes. He likes to dress in all black and I don't think he talks too much. I believe he has something that belongs to me and I'm looking to get it back. I think he is a customer of yours. Any help you can give me would be appreciated."

He thought about it for a minute before replying. "I've got a lot of customers pal and I don't like to get into their business, cause that would hurt my business you know?" He pounded his fist on the counter, shaking the fragile glass beneath. "Maybe you should talk to a cop, I'm no snitch."

I decided that this conversation wasn't going to yield any positive results unless I did something to earn some measure of respect from him.

Just One Puff

"Well, I appreciate it anyway," I said. "Say, how long have you been here? I don't remember seeing this shop before. It definitely has an urban feel to it."

"I've been here for a while now," he told me. "There's always a need for a place to get a good smoke, ya know? People come here from all over to find that one thing they can't get anywhere else. I specialize in the hard to find models, no Philly Blunts or Swisher Sweets here. I got no use for those punk kids who jus wanna crack 'em open and fill 'em with that shit weed. You wanna get high, go to a gas station or something, not here. You smoke?"

I saw an opening and decided to take advantage of it before it closed up.

"I have been known to enjoy a good smoke on a cool night with a glass of cognac," I said, "but it's so hard to find one that doesn't stink up the whole house, you know?"

I saw his shoulders relax and decided to continue working on him. "I know people who smoke them like cigarettes, one after the other but I think that defeats the purpose of the process. I mean if you're gonna have a smoke, have a smoke, not some mass produced crap you can find at any five and dime."

"I see that you're a connoisseur in taste, but I gotta tell ya your dress leaves a lot to be desired." He pointed to the trash that was still clinging to my shirt. "What is that funk you brought in here with you? You smell like my cousin, that stinky weasel. You never heard of a laundry mat?"

"I had a little too much last night," I said. The lie came a little too easy from my lips. "I ran into your cousin actually. He woke me up with a little shower." I had to go this route in case the two of them got together later to compare notes. The last thing I wanted was to be on this guys bad side.

"Yea that sounds like him" Tony chuckled. "He always did go out of his way to be a prick. I suppose I could shop you around before you go. Then I would definitely recommend hosing yourself off before you go out again. That funk is gonna kill me."

He walked me through various models of cigars that to me all looked the same, describing where and how they were made, and what kind of smoke they gave you. I learned about the importance of a humidor, as well as the correct way to light a cigar. He recommended a few magazines that I should read if I was going to be a serious cigar enthusiast. I ended up purchasing three different models, a small humidor, and a book on good places to go for a smoke. It set me back quite a bit, but I wanted to leave him with a good impression so he wouldn't hesitate to answer any other questions that might come up in the future.

After I had made my purchases, he invited me back later on that evening to join a few of the locals who got together every week to smoke. There was going to be a good mix of people there and he also mentioned the owner of the freak shop. I asked him how long he had known him and he said the guy did him a favor once and the two of them got to know each other. So there was a connection here after all! I thanked him for his time and left to go home and shower, my purchases tucked safely beneath my arm.

Demons Within

I left the shop as the sun was beginning to peak over the horizon. The morning air was cool, and the clouds that had moved in overnight were starting to break up, allowing the sun to make a grand entrance in the sky. I walked past the restaurant just as they were opening up for the day. The wife was bringing in the floor mats from the previous day and the husband was bringing eggs from the chickens out back. I waved as I past and as they waved back, they looked strangely at me, as I must have looked wretched. I continued past the row of still closed stores on my way back and saw the dumpster where I had spent most of the night. I slowed as I past it, trying to remember everything that I could so I could write it down in my notepad.

As the far corner of the dumpster came into view, I saw something lying on the ground. It was my dog. I ran over to him and squatted down to pat his head. Apparently he had been sleeping and he came around very slowly. He looked up at me and his nub began to wiggle rapidly. I scratched his belly and he sneezed at me a few times. Now I knew how badly I smelled if even he couldn't handle it. I checked him out and nothing appeared to be wrong. He had waited here patiently for my return, but where had he gone? The leash was missing, so I had to keep my eye on him so he wouldn't run off again as we went back home.

We got back as the neighbors were leaving for the day. They gave me a half wave and a concerned look as they drove by. I couldn't wait to get in the shower to wash off the nights events. I put my bag on the table in the kitchen, set up a pot of coffee, and jumped into the shower. Tonight should prove quite interesting, as I would finally get to confront the man who said he was there to help me but never showed up. I finished the shower, toweled myself off, and went to get the paper outside.

It was turning into quite a nice morning and the sky was totally cleared from the clouds that had loomed so menacingly just a few hours before. The sun was coming up over the mountains, and there was the gentlest breeze making its way down from the tall peaks above. I actually found myself toying with the idea of living up here full time, away from the hassles of life in the city. I didn't exactly have a house to go home to, and with my experience I could easily get a job up here. I would also be benefiting from a sizeable check from the insurance company for the fire that had consumed my home. I bought it for a song at auction and it was now worth much, much more.

I could have stayed there dreaming all day, but then I remembered what was happening in my world. Frustrated, I came back to reality a little too quickly for my liking. I grabbed the paper and went back into the kitchen. I poured myself a cup from the machine just as it was completing its cycle. Perfect timing. I sat down and checked out the newest happenings around town.

The front page articles were rather boring, nothing new here, so I turned my attention to the opinion page. There were a few letters to the editor about the road closings that were happening to get ready for the season. Even in a place far from the toils of the city people didn't want to be inconvenienced. There was a short letter about some foreign policy decision that had recently been made, and the author both agreed and disagreed with it in the same sentence. The last little piece was from a

Just One Puff

man named John from New York City. Apparently, John was complaining about the lack of 'civilization' in this the area his wife had chosen to vacation. He didn't appreciate those 'people' in the restaurants that treated him like a leper for lighting up his stogie after his meal was finished. From his letter, I got the feeling that he was one of the types that thought the world and everyone it was meant to serve him. I had run into many of those types during my run in life. The last thing that he wrote was what really caught my eye. He mentioned the shopping district and the fact that there was nothing but souvenir shops catering to idiots. He even had to 'settle' for a cheap cigar from the drugstore because there wasn't a proper shop for discerning folks such as him.

I put down the paper and looked at the bag on the table. Yes, it was there alright. I reached over and pulled out its contents; humidor, cigars, book. These things were real and I was holding them right in front of me. Maybe 'John' had just failed to see the shop in his travels through this small town. Well the shop existed, as I had the proof right here and nothing was going to change my opinion on that as long as I had them. I picked up the humidor to examine it further. It had been finely crafted with quality wood and a Swiss quality barometer installed in the lid. I turned it over and couldn't see where the pieces of wood had been joined together. I suppose this was one reason people were so picky about where they stored their newest acquisitions. I put it on the table and opened the lid. Inside, there was a single cigar wrapped in a piece of paper. I picked it up and removed the paper. It looked like any other cigar to me. I checked the paper in my hand and saw that there was writing on it so I unrolled the note and read its contents.

SMOKE ME NOW

I felt like Alice in Wonderland. Eat this, drink me. Was I also expected to follow a harried looking rabbit down a long hole? The cigar sat in the humidor in front of me and I detected a scent coming from it. It started out smelling like a cigar but then began to slowly change. I picked it up and put it to my nose. I smelled faint hints of coffee and vanilla beans. Rolling it between my fingers I began to smell freshly cut grass and chocolate covered cherries. I inhaled the scents deeply and felt my nose swell to take in all of the extra smells; beer and pizza, marshmallow and peanut butter. Every scent was something that I was extremely fond of, and I moved the cigar closer to my nose and took another deep breath. I was overwhelmed by all of the smells that were coming from this little cylinder in my hands.

I no longer detected the smell of a cigar and I wondered if this would indeed taste differently because of the smells that it was releasing. I decided to give it a try; after all one little puff wasn't going to kill me. I took out the cutter that was in the humidor and snapped off the end. It fell to the table without a sound. I grabbed a pack of the matches Fat Tony had given me and took one out. They were the good kind made from wooden sticks. I touched it to the side of the box and struck it. The flame grew slowly from the end of the stick, sparking and twisting as it did. It sucked in more oxygen and shot upward, filling the air with a sweet, sulfur smell. I placed the match underneath the cigar and began twisting it back and forth between my fingers just as Tony had taught me to do. The stogie was slow to catch, and smoke slowly made its way into the air. The room filled with smells of vanilla and Christmas cookies and I put the cigar into my mouth and took my first puff.

Smoke filled the air around my head, as I continued to puff until the cigar could sustain the burn by itself. After a minute or so, I took some of the smoke into my mouth and let it stay. I felt it dance around my teeth and soak into my gums, and my tongue picked up the flavors that were being held by the smoke. A wave of relaxation took over my mind and I decided that this wasn't too bad, so I raised my head back and exhaled, watching the smoke make its way around the room. I took another long haul and repeated the same process. Good. I stood up and felt light headed due to the smoke entering my bloodstream and making its way into my brain. It felt like a good smoke was supposed to feel and although I was no expert, I would think others who were would agree with my evaluation.

I walked around the kitchen as I enjoyed the many different flavors mixing in my mouth. My muscles were becoming relaxed and my mind cleared from all of the thoughts that had been plaguing it for so long. I looked outside and watched as a few wisps of clouds were making their way through an otherwise perfect sky. This felt good, right somehow. I made my way into the living room and sat down in my favorite chair next to the window. Each time I exhaled from the pleasurable cylinder I was smoking, I felt more at peace with the world. The dog came in and sat down at my feet, looking up at me as I continued to slip into a deep state of relaxation.

The cigar was burning slow and sure and the smoke from the tip continued to swirl around the room, making many different shapes and patterns as I moved my hand to my mouth and away again. I began to analyze some of the shapes as I gazed around the room. It was like watching clouds when you were a kid. That was always a good test of one's imagination. There was always someone who didn't see anything but clouds and they inevitably gave up on trying to use their imagination for anything. The smoke was causing the shapes to swirl together and the last thing I saw before I past out was a shape of a dog.

Great American Smokeout

I felt myself floating through the air, my body twisting and turning, and I opened my eyes. Something was wrong, terribly wrong. I was looking down at myself lying on a table and there were people hurrying around me with needles and bags of fluids. A man was standing over my chest pushing down on me, as another one watched while he held two paddles in his hands. The one that was pushing me stopped and the man with the paddles stepped into his place. He shouted 'clear' and I felt a jolt go through my body, causing me to lose my vision temporarily. When I regained it, I saw myself on the table, limbs flailing, as the man with the paddles moved in for another shock. A searing pain shot through my chest and I screamed out but no one seemed to be able to hear me.

Someone was putting a long needle attached to a hanging bag into my arm. I saw the man put down his paddles and a nurse handed him what looked like a knife. He cut my chest open and I could feel the blade slicing through my skin. He handed the knife to a nurse and she then handed him a strange looking instrument of some kind. He took it from her and put it into my chest. I heard a loud crack as I felt my ribs break away from my body. The pain was more intense than anything I have ever felt before.

The man then took a needle and shoved it into my heart, injecting a liquid that stung me like a thousand bee stings. He grabbed the paddles again and put them directly on my heart. Another searing jolt went through my body. I couldn't look at this anymore and turned away. Through a window, I saw my parents clutching each other. They were crying and I wanted to cry with them. A loud voice said, "Clear!" and another jolt went through my body.

I looked back towards where I was laying on the table. There was a machine hooked up to me and an alarm was screeching loudly. I saw a monitor with a straight line going through it, and a long piece of paper spitting out of the front. The paper had gone all the way to the floor and was starting to pile up, creating quite a mess. Something pulled me away from my body and an overwhelming urge to fight came over me, so I struggled in midair against the unseen force that was pulling me away. The room was growing brighter and I looked towards my parents again. They had fallen on the floor in each other's arms, and a woman was leaving the room, taking off the mask she was wearing around her face. The door closed behind her and she turned to face my parents. I could see her motioning with her hands at the room and my mother screamed out and fell flat on the floor. My father went down to hold her while his eyes filled with tears.

I floated away from the room as it became a blur of white. My body was being pulled back towards some source of heat. A feeling of peace came over my mind. The thoughts that were once ravaging in my mind were leaving me, being

Great American Smokeout

replaced with strong feelings of love and affection. I turned towards the force that was pulling me and saw an even brighter light than the one I had left in the room. I squinted my eyes in the light, but they quickly adjusted and I began to see more clearly. There were shapes floating past me slowly. One of them turned to me and touched my hand and I felt immediate warmth. Then it passed right through me, making my whole body warm and tingly.

The shapes began to take form and I could make out the outlines of people streaming by, all of them with the same expression of wonder and amazement on their faces. They were all heading towards the source of light, some more quickly than others. I saw one go racing past me in the other direction and I turned and saw that there were hundreds upon hundreds of others behind me, all heading to the light. I stopped and they began to catch up with me, some of them waving and others grabbing at my hands. I felt other emotions going through me, ones that weren't mine. Each time one of them touched me it set off another round and I soon became overwhelmed by them.

They streamed past me at a record pace and it was getting difficult to make out the people anymore. They became blurred at first, and then changed to shapes that stretched out in front of my eyes. After a moment, they were all just a continuous blur, indiscernible from one another. I no longer felt the force pulling me, so I tried to go back the way I had come. This proved extremely difficult and felt like I was trying to move through molasses. I strained all of my muscles to get through the stream of people and I began to make progress. For every ten or twelve steps I took, I felt myself actually move forward one-step. Voices made themselves heard, telling me to turn around and go towards the light. I began to fear the light and struggled more as other voices urged me to join them.

There was a sudden tug on my shoulder and I stopped struggling against the tide of people to turn and look. I saw my grandfather in front of me and I went still. He reached out and put his hand on my shoulder and I immediately felt his presence as my memories came rushing back to me, exploding into my head. I felt a tear going down the side of my cheek and he pulled me to his chest. I could feel the warmth from his body. It was a feeling I hadn't felt in a long, long time. I looked up into his eyes and saw him starting to change into something else. His face, once a sign of comfort to me, had stretched out, and his mouth began to open. A thick mat of hair was quickly covering his skin and I felt his hands on my back jab into my skin. I looked into his mouth and saw that his teeth had grown tremendously and his tongue was turning black. I shoved myself away from him and turned back to struggle against the stream of people that were increasing in volume with each passing second.

I smelled smoke and another feeling of heat began to come up from inside my body. I started coughing.

"Wake up," a voice called out, "come on now its time to go home. I made your favorite cookies and we want to get some while they're still hot."

I couldn't breathe as my lungs filled with smoke. I felt stinging in my eyes and coughed again, more violently this time. The stream of people slowly began turning

Demons Within

into balls of flame, licking against my face. I kept coughing and my eyes were stinging and watering so much that I couldn't see clearly.

"Come on honey wake up," the voice said again, its tone had become more shaky and panicked, the words cracking as they were spoken, "we need you hear now, please wake up."

I felt the heat of the flames that I could no longer see encompass my entire body, and there was a smell of burning hair. A dog was barking and there was something shaking my shoulders. Something pushed against my head and I could smell my mothers' hair, pleasant at first and then turning to a singed smell like burning rubber.

I fought to breathe, the dog kept barking, and I couldn't see anything for the smoke was thick and I felt myself falling down...

I hit the ground and opened my eyes to see that there was smoke every-where. The dog was barking and my legs felt like they were on fire. The dog started jumping around me and I struggled to see through the thick smoke filling the room. I was coughing and my lungs felt like they were going to explode inside my chest. I got to my feet and saw that my pants were on fire so I ripped them off and threw them to the ground, stomping the flame out with my foot. I looked up and saw that the chair that I was sitting in totally engulfed by flames, the leather melting and the wooden moldings were starting to smolder. I ran into the kitchen to grab the fire extinguisher with the constant blare of the alarm ringing in my ears. I got the extinguisher from beside the sink and went back in to put out the blaze.

The heat was as intense as if the gates of hell were right before me and I pulled out the pin and aimed the extinguisher at the chair. I squeezed the lever and a steady stream of foam rocketed towards the raging fire. It hit with a splat and I moved it around to cover the whole thing. There was a loud crash and I turned to see two firefighters burst through the front door, hose in hand. I moved closer to the chair and expended the last of the foam as they released the water from the pressurized hose. The room filled with acrid smoke as the stream of water sent the chair flying back against the wall.

The chair exploded into many pieces upon impact and the water began to crush the still smoldering wood. After a minute or two, the flames were all out and the firemen stopped the powerful flow of water. One of the men went to the remains of the chair and kicked it around with his foot to make sure that there were no burning embers. He bent down and picked up a small object that was lying on the floor beside the chair. He looked at it and then stood to face me. He held the object up for his partner and I to view, and I saw that it was a soggy cigar.

It took about twenty or so minutes for them to finish cleaning up the mess in my living room. The chief came over and asked me a lot of questions about the fire. I could only say that I must have passed out in the chair. I wasn't a smoker and nothing like this had ever happened to me before. Wait, that wasn't entirely true. My house did burn down not too long ago but I had nothing to do with that. The fire was ruled accidental but preventable, so I received a citation and a fine. He also encouraged me to seek medical attention, as I had inhaled a lot of smoke. They all left and I stared at the ruined room. I would have to get the carpet replaced right away so mildew wouldn't start to grow and the walls had gotten soaked making the paint was flake off in a few places. I would end up shelling out quite a bit of cash to put things back to normal. I thumbed through the yellow pages and called someone who was skilled in disaster recovery. They were there in only half an hour and started working right away.

I took the dog outside while they were working because I didn't want to be in there with them looking at me the way they were, with their pitying eyes and sympathetic words. I had a whole day to kill until I was to meet Fat Tony and his group for the Smokeout. After the fire, I really didn't want to go but felt compelled to so I could gain more insight into the events. I also needed to confront the horror shop owner who hadn't come by the previous night. The day was turning out rather nicely, weather wise I mean, so I grabbed the dog and went for a walk.

More people had arrived in town and the hotel rooms began to fill quickly. I thought it was still rather early in the season for them to be coming up, but who was I to say. After all, I was up here as well. I followed the same path I had on other occasions, down the hill and to the shops. The shops that were open had a few customers in them and the street was becoming crowded with cars, all looking for a place to park. I went to the restaurant, having cleaned myself up since they last saw me, and took my usual booth by the window. I ordered a light meal today as I had lost my appetite and could still taste the acrid smoke on my tongue. I suppose I should get checked out, but I didn't want to do the whole hospital thing.

I grabbed a copy of the paper that I had started reading this morning and thumbed through it as I gulped down a few more cups of coffee. I felt everyone's eyes watching my every move and it seemed somewhat freaky. It was possible that I hadn't gotten all of the funk smell off my skin and maybe I was still rather rancid. I did a quick sniff of my arm, but the smoke had ruined my sense of smell. Maybe the dog was attracting their attention. You rarely saw a dog sitting down in a restaurant enjoying a meal. Regardless of what it was, I didn't appreciate the extra attention after what happened back at my place. I finished my coffee, threw some money on the table, and walked out with the dog trailing behind.

I passed the horror shop and noticed that the door was closed with a note taped on its glass. I walked over and read it.

This store is temporarily closed. We will be open again soon under new

management.

New management? The shop had just opened. I knew that it wouldn't last long but I had expected it to be here for a little while longer. Maybe its usefulness had ended when I met the man the day it opened. Wait a minute; I still needed to see him about the book that had disappeared! Now how was I supposed to find the answers I needed. Tony said that he was going to be at his shop tonight, but he didn't mention the shop closing. I really needed him to be there. I looked into the windows and saw that there was nothing left inside, no statues, no books, not even a shelf. One of the other shopkeepers, I believe it was the man who ran the ski shop, was passing by so I stopped him and asked if he knew how I could reach the man who ran the shop. He looked at me inquisitively and said the shop had been closed for ten years and there was no one who had expressed an interest in buying it. I told him about my visit here and the grand opening flyer in the paper and he knew nothing about it.

I thanked him for his time and walked away. He continued staring at me until I was out of sight. I hadn't imagined the shop, nor had I imagined my conversation with its owner. Yes, it was true that the only real proof I had was the book, but that had somehow disappeared and now I was left with no evidence. There was no way I could have imagined the whole experience. The past few days were centered entirely around my meeting him, getting the book, and working on an explanation. If these things never happened, what was I doing for all that time?

I continued walking towards the smoke shop. I needed to see if it too was gone just as the horror shop was. As I approached, the local sheriff cut me off. He raised his hand up for me to stop.

"Good day," he said. "Hell of a morning you've had so far eh?"

"It hasn't been one of my best, that's for sure." I replied. "I'm just out trying to clear my head. I got a lot of smoke back there."

"I would think that you would want to be checked out at the hospital," he said, looking me over. "I know if I went through what you did I would."

"I appreciate your concern," I said, "but I'll be fine. There are already people fixing the damage." He didn't speak for quite a while, letting the silence become uncomfortable, until I found myself stammering out words just to break the silence between us. "Thanks for your concern. I'll be on my way now."

He placed his hand on my shoulder to stop me from moving. I felt the dog tighten on the leash, straining to get between us. He started to whimper loudly and began to back out of his collar. I reached down to grab him just as the collar slipped over his head. The sheriff spoke again, this time with an authoritative tone in his voice.

"I need you to come with me. A matter has arisen that requires your full cooperation." He placed his hand underneath my armpit and pulled me to my feet.

"What's this about?" I asked, "I've done nothing that warrants this treatment."

"I need to ask you some questions about the fire." He said.

"I thought I had already covered all of this with the Fire Chief," I said. "I got my ticket and will pay my fine."

"No, not that fire," he replied, "the one at your house in the city. A fella down there thinks there's something suspicious about it and he asked me for my help. I do find it kind of strange that you did not report it." There was a condescending tone coming across here that I didn't appreciate. "Just come with us and we'll try not to take up too much of your time." As he spoke, a deputy appeared beside him and took hold of my arm. The dog was going crazy trying to get loose from the leash. He didn't want anything to do with this man and frankly, neither did I.

The deputy took control of my dog and slapped a muzzle on him. The dog began yelping and scratching at him. I tried to calm him but I didn't have much luck. He put me in the back of the patrol car and I saw that the deputy was still struggling to gain control of the dog. Finally, the dogs' will won and the leash snapped away from his collar. He took off with the deputy in hot pursuit.

"Don't worry about the dog," the sheriff said, "he'll get him back."

With that said, we took off towards the station.

"What makes an insane man is not the state of his mind, but the state of the minds of those who see him to be insane."

Anonymous

"Resistance is futile."

The Borg

Date With The Devil

I sat in the cell looking out at the clock on the wall and noticed that time did not seem to change. Days seemed to pass, but the clock drags slowly forward and my sense of time is thrown off. That was the first time I had ever been inside of a police station, never mind being locked up like a common criminal. Only two hours had passed since my arrival and I had still not been allowed to speak to anyone. When they placed me in this small cell, I told them that I wanted an attorney. This did not please them, as it would surely make their job more difficult. And why shouldn't it be difficult? I had done nothing wrong and had nothing to hide. Besides, they had lost my dog. They should be the ones inside of this cage, not me. The deputy came limping back into the station about twenty minutes after I had arrived to say that he had been bitten and the dog got away. He said that he fired off some shots, but the dog was too fast and got away. He shot at my dog. I only wish that he had been maimed more severely.

After being pulled violently off the street in front of a large group of people, I felt nothing but hatred for my captors. I wasn't even home when the fire consumed my every possession. I think that small town police have something to prove. Maybe it's a compensation thing, I don't know. Well they would be made to suffer for what they were doing to me.

The sheriff came in, unlocked the cage, and instructed me towards a closed room. He told me that my lawyer had arrived and I would be meeting with him shortly. The room was plain, consisting only of a long table, three chairs, and a water cooler. Its walls were bare except for a mirror on the far side. I assumed that it was a two-way mirror, just like the ones in the police dramas that saturated every television stations programs. I wondered who would be the mysterious man behind the glass watching every move I made, attempting to profile me based on what I was saying and how I was behaving. I had been cooperative, to a point, since my incarceration began, as I did not want to give them any fuel for the fire being lit under my feet.

The sheriff sat me down in a chair and leaned up against the wall by the mirror. His body language gave away the fact that he felt superior and in total control. His arms were crossed over his chest and a look of disgust glared at me from above his dark glasses. Also, he was chewing on a piece of gum in a very annoying fashion.

"You know," he said, "you don't really need a lawyer for this. I only wanted to ask you some questions so we could get this mess cleared up for you." He walked over and pulled a chair beside me, its legs scratching against the floor in a high-pitched squeal. He turned it around so its back was facing me and straddled it as he sat down. His eyes did not blink and he continued to stare straight at me. I sat there looking straight ahead, not wanting to give away the fact that I was scared and angry. My face was a rock, unmovable.

"Any luck locating my dog?" I asked sarcastically, my annoyance with him evident with each word. "I'm holding you personally responsible for his welfare. If anything happens to him, I assure you it will not be a pleasant experience."

"Are you threatening me son?" He asked, cocking his head to one side and getting into my face. "Because you know, that in itself is a crime."

"There's no threat sheriff," I said, "I'm merely concerned about my dog. You had no reason to pull me in here like you did. The dog was nervous and I could have calmed him down if you and Barney Fife would have given me a minute."

Where was my lawyer? I didn't like enclosed spaces and with the cop in my face, it was becoming more closed by the minute. I stood up from my chair but the sheriff immediately shoved me back down.

"I was just going to get a drink of water." I said, the anger beginning to well up from deep in my chest. "Is there something wrong with that?"

He removed his hands from my shoulders and said, "I don't like sudden movements. I'll get you the water, but don't you move a muscle or I'll put you back in the hole." He got up and went to the cooler. He poured me a cup and returned, placing it on the table in front of me.

"Are you going to remove the cuffs?" I asked, "Or do you intend to hold the cup while I drink?" I held up my hands for him to unlock the chains that were beginning to scuff at my wrists. He reached around and took the large key ring from his belt, purposely fumbling with the keys to make sure that I knew he was still in charge. He removed the cuffs and I took the water down in one gulp. "Can I get another, or is that not included in the price of this room?" I asked.

"Get it yourself," he said gruffly. "This ain't no restaurant." There was a noticeable distain for me in his voice and I wanted to explore that to find out why.

"Sheriff," I said, "why am I being treated in this manner? I have cooperated with you fully and still you treat me like a common criminal."

"You brought the lawyer into this, not me," he said. "I wanted to make this as simple as possible, but you chose to take the hard road." His voice was full of rage and I was worried that he would eventually lose control.

"If I am not being charged with a crime," I said, "then I demand to be released." I was not to convincing with my demand, as my voice cracked as I spoke. I just wanted to get out before he lost control.

"You are being held on suspicion of arson," he said. "The fire marshal is faxing over some documents for me to sign to send you back to face those charges but before I do that, I'm gonna need some more information about the fire that happened in your house here." He came back over and sat down next to me again.

"I already gave a statement at my house about the accident," I said, "and I don't know anything about the fire back at my house in the city. I saw it on the news from up here." I was getting increasingly frustrated with him. I looked at the clock, only ten minutes had passed since we entered this room. "Where is my lawyer?" I demanded. "I'm not saying another word until he gets here."

There was a knock at the door and the sheriff got up from his seat. He opened the door and a tall man in a black suit entered the room. The man winked at me and then turned his attention to the sheriff blocking his path.

"Sheriff," he said, "you will leave now so that I can speak to my client in private." He had a commanding voice that demanded respect. "I want the gentleman behind the glass gone as well. My client and I have the right to a private meeting."

The sheriff left the room in a huff, slamming the door behind him and I was left alone with the strange man who held my immediate fate in his hands. He walked over to me, placed his briefcase on the table, and snapped open the locks. He removed a manila envelope, notepad, and pencil and placed them on the table between us. He also took out a small wooden box and laid it down directly in front of me. He closed his briefcase and placed it on the floor beside his chair.

"Please, take a seat," he said, "We can begin right away." He walked over to the mirror and knocked on it several times. He motioned with his thumb for whoever was behind it to leave. I looked over to him and something familiar immediately struck me. There was a strong smell of smoke coming from this man. It wasn't like smoke from a fire, but more like stale cigar smoke. He turned back towards me and then I saw his eyes. They were black. A shiver ran down my spine and I realized that there before me was the man who had been trailing me through my dreams.

"What's up, kid?" he said. "Long time no see."

He reached into his pocket and removed a cigar and I watched as he bit off the tip and spit it out onto the floor. He sparked his trademark Zippo in his hands and rolled the cigar into the flame, turning it slowly and surely between his fingers. Smoke rose from its tip and swirled up into the ceiling in random patterns. He raised the cigar to his lips and puffed on it, the air around him filling with more of the blue haze. The cherry glowed bright orange and I found myself unable to look away. The blue haze made its way to my nose and I detected the same familiar, comforting scents that I had experienced from my earlier smoking experience.

"Sorry to hear about your troubles lately," he said. His black eyes were impossible to read, and the smoke didn't make it easy to read his body language either. He pulled the chair that the sheriff was sitting in away from me and moved it to the other side of the table. He sat down hard and looked directly into my eyes.

"What are you doing here?" I finally asked, the fear easily identified by my cracking voice. "Where is the book?"

"I don't know anything about a book," he said, "I only came here to finish our discussion from the other night. By the way, did you enjoy your smoke? I knew you wouldn't be able to resist it once you smelled it."

A smirk made its way to his lips. It was the first time I had seen anything remotely resembling a smile from him and to be honest, it kind of freaked me out a little.

Date With The Devil

I recalled the dream that I had when I passed out with the cigar at my house. The feelings were as strong in me then as they were while it was happening. I needed to calm myself down before speaking to him again. Although I knew he must sense my feelings, I didn't want to give him the satisfaction of seeing them displayed. I got another cup of water and gulped it down, taking slow, deep breaths in between. I sensed his eyes looking right through me, trying to anticipate my next move. I drank two more cups of water and pushed all of the feelings that I was having down deep, leaving nothing at all for him to read. I turned to face my tormentor with my new-found feeling of calm. He was sitting in the chair leaning back with his legs resting on the table, rocking back and forth while he continued to enjoy his smoke.

I sat back down, stared into his eyes, and said, "Now I think it's time you came clean as to why you're here." I concentrated on my feelings and allowed one of hatred to show itself through my stare. He immediately sensed the change in me and stopped rocking. The legs of the chair slammed to the floor and he got to his feet. He leaned over to me and put his rough hands on the table.

"Be careful kid," he said, "you don't want to go there. Hatred is not something that you can control yet, and it could prove to be your ultimate downfall."

The feeling was growing stronger inside of me and I struggled to hold it at its present level. "Tell me why you're here." I demanded. I felt a vein in my head beginning to grow with my quickening pulse throbbing throughout its length.

"Relax kid," he said, "you don't want to dance with me because I always lead."

He raised his hand to me and a force threw me back from the chair and sending me crashing into the wall. I struggled not to fall as my muscles began to shut down as they always had before. He walked from behind the table and made his way towards where I stood, his hand still raised.

"I think you need to sit back down," he said and lowered his hand, causing my body to slump to the floor. He turned and walked back to the table. I tried to move but my muscles were useless at that point. He grabbed the small wooden box that he had brought with him from the table and returned to where I was still struggling to get up.

"I don't think we should talk here anymore," he said, pointing to the security camera mounted right above the clock. "The walls have ears." I didn't remember seeing the cameras when I surveyed the room. Why hadn't the sheriff come in when he saw what was going on? There is attorney client privilege, but he was still responsible for my well being while I was in his custody. I continued to struggle to regain my footing as the man placed the box at my feet.

"Our conversation would be more productive if we went somewhere else," he said. "Actually, I think you know the place rather well, although it has been a while since you have been there." He opened the box and a fine powder shot out from it, swirling up around my head. I took a breath and felt the mist go into my mouth and down my throat. My head was spinning and my vision became blurry as the mist worked its way down to my legs and out to my arms, causing me to shiver from the coldness it was releasing.

Demons Within

I watched as he packed up the items from the table into his briefcase, taking extra time to wipe off the table for some reason. He closed the case and walked back to me as my blood began to slow in my veins and I could no longer feel anything at all. He reached down and picked the box up from the floor, taking care to handle it only by its edges. He held it over my head and flipped his wrist and the remaining contents cascaded down over me in a snow globe-like manner.

The last thing I heard was his voice saying, "Sleep now."

I woke up slowly, still groggy from the mist that had taken over my mind and body. My head hurt like hell. It was like I spent a long, hard night of drinking and now I was paying the price. My vision was still quite blurry and I could only see outlines of the things around me. My sense of smell however was intact, and there was a stench of burnt wood and scorched wiring in the air. I staggered to my feet, bracing myself on a table for support, and looked around. Everything had the same blurred look, so I concentrated on a single area until my vision returned to normal. Everything in my line of sight was burnt and there were ruined pieces of furniture all around the room. Smoke had blackened the walls and parts of the ceiling had caved in, exposing the supports of the floor above.

I saw the windows were all broken with the remnants of what could have been of a fish tank at one time lying on the floor. This place was eerily familiar, but it was too dark to tell anything for sure. I walked down a hallway and looked into one of the open rooms. There was a bed in the middle of the room, the mattress completely ruined by water, and a large rocker by the open window. I suddenly felt very queasy and realized that I was in my own house. I turned away from the room, but not before a stream of vomit erupted from my mouth, covering the broken door and the wall surrounding it.

I staggered from the room and made my way to the stairs and when I looked up, I saw him standing at the top of the landing. He motioned for me to come up and then walked towards the office. I walked up the stairs with a strong feeling of sadness coming over me, and went to join him. He was sitting behind my desk that was apparently the only thing spared from the fire. I walked into the room, grabbed a folding chair from the wall, and sat down in front of him. Why had he brought me back here? I remembered the dream of the fire and seeing a man running from the house with a gas can in his hand. It was this man who had torched my house.

My sadness was quickly replaced by anger and I rose from my chair with every intention of pounding the man to a bloody pulp. He motioned for me to sit back down and said, "Don't get up, it won't do you any good. If you really want answers, you'll shut up and listen." The anger inside of me was turning to rage and I clenched my fists until my nails poked through my skin.

"Why did you burn down my house?" I demanded, "Thanks to you I'm now the prime suspect" My face stiffened and I felt a low growl coming from my throat.

"I didn't do this." He said.

"I saw you," I screamed out. "I saw you in the dream running out the front door with a gas can. I saw all of my possessions burn in front of my eyes and there was nothing I could do to stop it."

He motioned me down again and this time, it worked. The unseen force pushed me down into the chair and my muscles went limp.

"Here's how it's going to work," he said, "I'm going to talk, you're going to listen. I will answer any questions that you have but you will obey me when I tell you to do something." He paused for a moment to let me absorb everything that he was saying. When he was convinced that he had my undivided attention, he continued.

"I will not be accountable for anything that happens as a result of your non-compliance. This is a one shot deal kid, take it, or leave it."

I shouldn't trust him. So far he had done nothing to show me that I should believe anything that he said, so why should this be any different? I knew it was him in my dream of the fire. I knew that he stole the book from my bedside and although I was sure of these things, I still had many things that I still questioned. What else could go wrong? After everything that I've been through, I deserved answers and here was a man who proposed to give me them. There was no use trying to escape from him, as the force was still holding me down in the chair, so I might as well see if he would say anything that would help me defeat him once and for all.

"How do you want to proceed?" I asked.

"How about some background first," he replied. He got up from the chair and sat down on the edge of the desk in front of me. "I know you must have a thousand questions and I'm sure that they're all very good, but if you'll indulge me for a while most of them will probably be answered by the time I finish. Is that acceptable to you?"

"I don't see any other way so let's here what you have to say. Who are you and why did you choose this place to talk to me?"

"I'm not going to get into who I am just yet," he said as he waved the question off with his hand. "I've been around for a while, long before you came along, and I'll be here long after you leave as well. I took you here because this is a place you used to feel safe and I can guarantee that safety for the moment. However, if you don't follow my rules, all bets are off.

I want to tell you about a kid I used to know. His name was John and he was the oldest of the O'Malley clan, a family that lived in a small town in Ireland, and they were extremely poor. His uncle was Thomas Kelley, who owned most of the land and thus had control over most of the people of the town as well. John had a quick temper and snapped at the slightest thing. He was also a good-looking kid, and the girls of the town were all infatuated with him. He was fifteen and like other kids his age, got into the usual scraps.

He started working for his uncle when he was twelve, first in the field and then in the factory. Everyone worked for Mr. Kelley at some time or another in their lives from field hands to factory girls. John was a hard worker, but occasionally he needed a swift kick in the ass, as he often stood at the machines flirting with the girls. His father had taught him little growing up and most of what he learned was from the other boys his age. He was brought many times before his uncle for punishment after stealing food from the small market in town. His uncle had ruined many switches on the boys' backside and moved up to a stronger leather strap. John's back was full of deep scars and the skin had developed a callous feel to it.

It wasn't unusual for Mr. Kelley to seek out John to administer his brand of corporal punishment when there was a report of something wrong. He was an evil man and I think he actually took pleasure in whipping his nephew. Thomas Kelley didn't stand for anything that would challenge his authority, relation or not.

John was secretly seeing Mr. Kelley's daughter Megan, who was due to be married to another young man on the night of the harvest festival. The marriage had been arranged when both of the kids were born. However, Megan didn't like her soon to be husband at all. She found him to be cruel and unloving. She dared not to speak up, for fear of what that would do to her family. She was madly in love with young John and they had been secretly seeing each other for years behind the backs of their families. John stood no chance of marrying Megan due to his families place in the social order of the town. It didn't matter that his sister was Mr. Kelley's sister, only that his family was poor.

The festival happened every year when the last of the harvest was sold and everyone received their pay. There was music and dancing all night long and the women of the town made all sorts of food, enough to feed the townsfolk for a week. The local distiller supplied bottles of potato vodka, whisky, and kegs of beer and wine and there were games for kids young and old to play. The wedding was going to be the finale of the celebration.

On the day of the festival, John returned home after a fifteen-hour day at the factory. He plan was too meet up with his friends and steal Megan away from her family so that they could be together. John knew that by doing this, he could never go home again, and his family would surely be made to pay for his crime. He had been saving up his money for three seasons and had purchased two tickets on a ship bound to America. Once there, he and his true love Megan could make a new life for themselves.

John got ready quickly, splashing water on his face and changing his shirt. He packed a few belongings in an old sack and headed out to meet his friends. They got together just as the festival was going full swing. John sent his younger brother to tell Megan he would be arriving soon. As his brother scampered off, John and his friends celebrated with a few pints from the kegs.

Unfortunately for John, Mr. Kelley had found out about their plan from his younger daughter, who herself was infatuated with John. She didn't want to see him leave, and so the night before the festival, she confessed everything to her father. As you might imagine he was livid and he beat her within an inch of her life for keeping the secret from him for so long. He felt betrayed and wanted to punish Megan and John for what they had done to him. He sent for the local law officer, who he had in his pocket, and they rounded up a group of men who would help him with the task.

John and his friends were drinking up a storm when John's father hurried over to him. His father had found out about John's plan to leave and pleaded with his son to reconsider before it was too late. They argued heatedly and then began to exchange blows. Thomas O'Malley was a strong man, but he was no match for his son and the fight lasted for only a few minutes before John stormed off, leaving his father on the ground sobbing.

It was already after nine and Megan was waiting anxiously for John's arrival. His brother said that he was on his way, but that was over an hour ago. There was a knock at her door and when she opened it, her father burst in, knocking her to the ground. He began to beat her uncontrollably, cursing her for betraying him and the family name. The leather strap struck her repeatedly and blood started covering it, turning the black of the leather into a crimson red. She cried out to her younger sister, who was standing behind their father, but her cries for mercy were ignored as she had received the same beating only the night before and could only watch as her father continued thrashing Megan. The beating lasted for a long time and when Mr. Kelley finally stopped, Megan was not moving; her body slumped in a bloody, lifeless heap. Her sister ran to her side but her father shoved her away and two men came in and took Megan's lifeless body away. They put her into a fire pit and burned her bloodied corpse until only charred bones remained.

Mr. Kelley returned to the festival and told everyone of the plot against him by John and Megan. He declared the festival over and said that no one was to speak her name ever again or there would be dire consequences. He also announced a bounty on the head of young John O'Malley, and ordered his family banished from the town forever. The crowd dispersed, chasing the O'Malley's back to their home and throwing rocks and sticks at them. John returned to town just as his family was being forced out of their house. His father told him what had happened and pleaded with him to run for his life. A mob gathered around John and began throwing stones him. He ran away from the crowd and headed off towards Thomas Kelley's house to find Megan.

All of John's thoughts focused on his only love Megan, and his emotions began to turn to rage against his uncle. He stopped at the sight of Megan's final resting place and walked over to see the burnt remains of her body still smoldering in the pit. John could not bring himself to cry, no matter how much he wanted to. The rage was intensifying and he was changing. His mind began to split into two separate halves, burying his personality and his pleasant memories deep within. His blood started to boil in his veins, and a low growl began to rise from deep inside his throat. The rage in his mind focused on one thing; he must kill Thomas Kelley.

He made his way through the woods, following a path that he and Megan had used to avoid detection over the years, and arrived at the house. He looked down and saw that his body was changing; the muscles on his arms bulging out of his skin and his hands curling into powerful fists. He climbed up the wall and into the window of Mr. Kelley's bedroom. His uncle wasn't there. He walked into the bathroom and saw his target in the tub with his housemaid sponging off his hairy back. Upon seeing its cause, the rage inside of him took over John completely and his bones stretched as he grew at an alarming rate. The growl, once low, made itself heard across the house and out into the yard. At that moment, he ceased to be John O'Malley. He became pure evil.

Demons Within

The rage flowed through his veins and his muscles flexed up and down under his skin, growing larger with each rep. His breathing became shallow and his mouth grew wide, exposing newly formed jowls and long, sharp teeth. The housemaid was the first to see him at the door and she let out a hideous scream. Mr. Kelley looked up just as John was completing his transformation into evil. He had ceased to resemble a man at all. His skin turned into a thick, matted coat of fur, and his teeth had grown into powerful fangs that were dripping black ooze onto the ground. His eyes, once green and glimmering, had also turned black.

He ran over and swiped at the housemaid to quiet her screams and his sharp nails took her head off in one swipe. Her body slumped to the floor with blood pouring from her still convulsing torso. Her head bounced once on the floor and rolled out of the room towards the stairs. Mr. Kelley rose from the tub and tried to run, but it was too late. John opened his mouth, stretched it around Mr. Kelley's head, and snapped down. There was a loud crack as his uncle's neck broke away from the rest of his body. The headless body of Mr. Kelley stood there for a moment as blood poured out of the gaping hole where its head used to be, turning the once clear bathwater into thick, crimson ooze. The bloodied body fell with a splash into the tub with the red ooze sloshing over the side and onto the floor.

There was a lot of commotion coming from downstairs. Apparently, someone had seen John running towards the house and upon hearing the housemaids' screams, called for help. A mob of people ran into the house and came across the head of the housemaid rolling towards them, leaving a trail of blood covering the stairs. A few of the people turned their heads and puked, causing the floor to become slick, while a few others ran up the stairs to the bathroom. John, feeling a wave of panic come over him, flung himself out the window to avoid the mobs wrath. They got to the bathroom and discovered the macabre scene. There was blood all over the walls and the lifeless bodies continued to ooze all over the floor. One of the people held up a torn shirt, which was the same one that John had been wearing that night.

The townsfolk were in shock by the events and searched for John everywhere, but couldn't find him. They banished his family from the town and never heard from John again. John, heartbroken from his loss and confused about the events that had just taken place went to the pier and got on the boat that was supposed to carry him and his true love to America."

I sat there silent for a moment, not quite sure of how to respond to the story he had just shared with me. From what I could gather, this John O'Malley person had somehow changed into some kind of a monster that sounded like Chaos. How was this directly relevant to my present situation? Was he merely describing how this demon had come to America? If so, I didn't really need that kind of history lesson.

"Ok," I said, "so some guy named John got pissed off at someone for killing the person he loved and killed him. By the way, nice job telling the story, it was such a tragedy. Is that all there is? Because if that's what you brought me here to tell me, I gotta say I'm not impressed."

"Oh no, my friend," he snickered, "the best is yet to come. That man, John O'Malley, was your great grandfather."

History 101

My jaw dropped and I felt my heartbeat quicken in my chest. Was he saying that my great grandfather was Chaos, the demon who was filling my every thought? My hands were growing cold and a painful stabbing began to work its way up to my chest. There was no way that he could be telling me the truth. There had to be a trick, something else he wasn't telling me. I felt heat coming from my pocket and I began to go numb.

Coming to America

I tried to breathe, but the pain in my chest intensified and my left arm went numb. I was having a heart attack, no doubt about it. I fell off the chair and hit the burnt wooden floor hard, my head smacking through the weakened wood. Thoughts were racing through my mind and I felt myself slipping away into unconsciousness.

When I opened my eyes, I was no longer in my office. I was on the deck of a boat and it was raining, down pouring actually. I got to my feet and looked for a place to get out of the raging storm. The boat was pitching from side to side and the deck was very slippery. I looked around and saw men running everywhere. They were hollering out to one another and it was difficult to hear them over the strong winds whipping over the boat.

Suddenly, a loud crackling sound pierced through the air. The men started to run towards me and I got out of the way just as a large mast came crashing down, splitting in half as it hit the side of the boat. Two men grabbed onto the ropes that were whipping out from the broken mast and tried to pull it back over onto the boat, but the deck pitched hard again and I saw the men pulled over the side and into the angry sea. Someone grabbed my shirt and I fell, sliding down some wet stairs, to the galley below deck.

I hit the floor below and landed on top of someone, who let out a muffled cry of pain. I got to my feet and turned around to help the person to their feet. It was an older woman, dressed in ragged clothing and she had dirt all over her face and her arms were covered with open sores. I helped her up and turned towards the opening just as a large wave came crashing over the side. The icy water shot into the galley and knocked me back into the wall as two men ran in front of me to close the door that led to the deck. They placed a large piece of wood into two slats on either side of the door to keep it from blowing open.

The older of the two turned to me and said, "You gave us quite a scare young man. What were you doing up on the deck? You know the captain told everyone to stay below until the storm passed." He put a blanket over my shoulders and led me down the hallway to a large area that was filled with people. They were all ragged looking and their clothes were all tattered, and their faces filthy. The smell in the room was atrocious and I fought to keep from throwing up. He led me to a bed, laid me down, and threw another blanket on top of me.

"What is this place?" I asked him, my voice shaking from the cold.

"You must have banged you head above lad," he said as he tucked the blankets tighter around me. "This storm is taking its' toll on everyone. You rest now, and no gettin up for you." He got up and walked over to a group of people huddling by a small stove. A young girl came up to me and handed me a steaming cup. I thanked her and lifted the cup to my face, drawing in a long, deep breath. It was tea. I took a few sips and the girl sat down on the bed beside me.

Coming to America

"What were you doing up there?" she asked, her voice thick with a Celtic accent, "You could have been thrown overboard.

"I saw two men pulled over the side by the waves," I said, taking another sip from the hot mug, "no one went after them."

"We've lost a lot of people in the storm already," she said. "We thought you were lost as well until papa brought you back down." Her eyes were a deep green and her bright orange hair was poking through her stocking cap. She had milky white skin and I couldn't even begin to count the freckles on her face. "Please don't go up there again. You're the only friend I have now."

"Where are we going?" I asked her.

Her eyebrows went up and she looked at me as if that was the strangest thing she had ever heard. "We're going to America, of course. We've only been on this boat for six weeks, all cramped together like fish in a barrel. Did you bang your head up there love?"

"I must have," I said, "because I don't remember anything." I looked around and some of the people were pointing at me while they were talking to each other. I couldn't make out what they were saying. For all of the people down here, it was eerily quiet.

"Well don't you worry a hair on that pretty little head of yours Johnny boy, I'll look after you and keep you out of trouble." She took the tea from my hands and laid me back down on the bed. The boat was swaying violently through the waves and I could see that many people were getting sick.

"Excuse me dear," I said, "did you just call me Johnny boy?"

"Of course silly," she laughed, "that's your name. Mr. John O'Malley. You said I could call you Johnny boy on our first night here. Don't you remember? I hope you're not catching the fever that's going around." She put her hand on my forehead and I felt the warmth of her skin.

"Excuse me for not remembering," I said, "could you tell me your name lass? I seem to have forgotten that along with everything else."

"My poor, sweet Johnny" she said as she caressed my head, "you must have the fever. I am Catherine and I will take care of you, just as you have been taking care of me." She continued caressing my head and I began to relax. "My father says that when we get to America you will be staying with us. Isn't that wonderful Johnny?"

"Oh that's good. I wondered how I 'd manage on my own." I closed my eyes and listened to the sound of the waves crashing into the side of the ship.

"Hey, wake up," a voice cried out. "Come one now, get off the floor boy."

I felt something slap my face and opened my eyes. It took a moment to realize where I was. I was back in the police station.

"Get up," the cop said, "your lawyers made your bail. You're free to go. I wouldn't make any plans on leaving town anytime soon if I were you." The sheriff pulled me to

Demons Within

my feet. "You've got a hearing tomorrow and if you don't show up, we'll come and arrest you." He was standing there staring at me through his dark glasses with his hands crossed over his chest.

"What time is the hearing?" I inquired.

"Ten sharp, "he said, "Your lawyer has the packet we gave him. You think you can stop torching things until then?" There was a definite sarcasm in his voice and as I made my way around him and headed to the door, I stopped and turned around.

"Where is my lawyer now?" I asked.

"He had an appointment and said he would meet you at the smoke shop tonight. Now if you'll kindly get out of my sight before I change my mind and keep you here, I'd appreciate it." He brushed past me, knocking me back into the wall. I shook my head in disgust and left the station.

He said he would meet me at the smoke shop. Oh yes, I almost forgot, I was supposed to get together at Tony's tonight. With all of the things that happened, I almost forgot. I checked the time on the clock at the bank. It was already five o'clock. The day was flying by. I wondered where the stupid dog took went. I wouldn't have to be concerned about it if Barney Fife had just let me calm him down in the first place. I was getting kind of hungry so I stopped at the restaurant and got a turkey club and some fries to go.

I got home just as the workers were finishing up and the place looked like no fire had ever happened. That was good because they charged enough for their services. I gave the head guy my credit card information and they packed up their tools are left. I walked around the house, assessing the work that had been done and making a mental checklist of things that I would have to replace. The only things that were ruined were the chair and the couch from water damage.

I went to the kitchen, grabbed a beer, and ate my late lunch. I wanted to get some rest before my meeting, so I went upstairs and set the alarm for seven. Sleep came surprisingly quick and before I knew it, the alarm was blaring in my ear. I turned it off and went to grab a quick shower.

When I finished, I heard loud barking coming from downstairs. I toweled myself off, threw on some pants, and went downstairs to see that my dog had returned from another adventure-filled day. I let him in and he shot right past me to his food bowl, which he inhaled in a matter of seconds. I filled the bowl again and he finished that one more quickly than the first one. I'd never seen him eat like that. Usually he took his time, grabbing a mouthful and walking around while he ate. It was as if he hadn't eaten in a week. I filled his water dish and sat down to watch him.

There was something different about the dog. It wasn't just his behavior that had changed, but his appearance had been altered somehow. His fur, which was always shiny, had taken on a dull tint, almost mangy looking. I got up and went around him to see his face. His eyes were bulging out of his head as he continued to drink from his dish. He looked almost maddened and I was getting a little nervous so I called out to him, but he ignored me, concentrating on the task he was undertaking. He finished the water in the bowl and perked up his ears, looking towards the stairs, lifted his head, and howled. The sound sent shivers all over my body. He sounded like a coyote. He stopped howling and ran upstairs towards the bedroom and I followed behind, leaving enough room between us in case he turned on me for some reason. He went into the bedroom, jumped on the bed, and began to dig at the mattress.

I called for him to stop but he continued anyway, his actions becoming more intense. I continued to scold him from the doorway as fluff from the mattress began to fly out, covering the floor in puffy piles. I walked slowly to the other side of the bed to see what was causing him to go crazy like that. I didn't want to upset him any more than he already was so I was careful to move quietly. He began to chew at the mattress as he dug, spitting the filling out onto the floor. I got to the other side and called out his name, clapping my hands together each time I spoke. There was no stopping him from destroying my bed.

Suddenly he stopped digging and looked at me. I could see something in his eyes, a look of sadness, and he slowly backed away from the hole he created and laid down whimpering. I continued to watch him closely unsure of what he was going to do next. His whimpering grew more pronounced and slowly worked into a growling bark. He stood up on the bed and his barking continued, getting louder each time. I was scared. He walked over until he was right next to me and continued his maddening bark. I wondered what the hell he was doing.

I put out my hand to him, hoping he wouldn't bite it off, and called for him to stop. Suddenly, a high pitched whining sound pierced through the room. The dogs barking stopped as the whine's volume grew louder until it was almost unbearable. I put my hands over my ears to shield them from the onslaught of sound, but it was no use. The whining continued and my dog backed away from me and lay down next to the hole in the bed. The noise seemed to be coming from me somehow and I noticed a bulge in my pocket so I reached inside and pulled out the key. The whine, no longer muffled by the insulation of my pocket, grew louder and began shaking the room with its sonic pitch.

A lamp fell off the table, crashing onto the floor and shattering into many pieces and all of the light bulbs began to explode. It sounded like a fierce gun battle was taking place. I dropped the key and grabbed one of the pillows from the bed to cover my head. No sooner had I done that then the high-pitched whine stopped. I removed the pillow from my head and looked at the dog who was still lying next to the hole he had dug so fervently. I called out to him and he responded, coming over to me and sitting down at my feet. I reached down to pat him and he looked to the mattress, whimpering softly.

I picked up the key from the floor and looked at the figurine dangling from its strap. The mouth on the demon had gotten bigger, and its eyes were bulging out even further from its head. How had this little thing created such a loud, piercing sound? Well, at least the dog was normal again and not the maddened beast he was just a moment ago. He was still whimpering at the bed, so I went to see if I could determine what was upsetting him.

Demons Within

The mattress could not be repaired, the dog had made sure of that, and the hole went all the way to the box spring. There was fluff and foam strewn all over the room. I got onto the bed and explored the area around the hole. Something was inside the mattress, something hard. There was no light, as the noise had shattered all of the bulbs, so I had to feel around blindly. I grabbed the item from the mattress, pulled it out, and saw that it was a book. I got off the bed, went to the window, and opened the shades. The moonlight came in through the window and shined on the book. I looked down and saw what had been driving the dog so mad; it was the book of Chaos. How did it get inside the mattress?

I sat down on the bed and the dog jumped up, placing his head on my lap. I held the book still for a few minutes, not wanting to let go of it for fear it would disappear again. I wasn't going to let it out of my sight, even for a second. I still had a meeting tonight at Fat Tony's and I had to take the book with me. Maybe somebody there could help me shed light on the book's true meaning. I only hoped that it wouldn't end up becoming something that I would regret.

A Very Motley Crew

I cleaned up some of the mess from the ruined bed as best I could. Tomorrow I needed to get a new bed, that is, if there was a tomorrow. I went to the closet, pulled out a small carry on bag, and put the book safely inside. Fat Tony didn't give me an exact time for the meeting, so I decided to head over. The dog's leash was gone, so I fashioned a rope around his collar. If he took off again, he would really have to work hard to do get out of the knot I made.

It was dark outside and the wind had picked up significantly. I zipped up my jacket, hunched my shoulders, and set out for my meeting at Fat Tony's Smoke Shop. I knew Tony would be there, probably with his fat, smelly cousin. Tony told me that the owner of the now closed shop would be there as well. I hoped that was the case, as I felt no one but he could help me out. Cigar man would probably be there as well as the sheriff told me that my 'lawyer' would be meeting me there. Was he connected to the man that owned the shop? I hoped not, for if he was, I had no chance of getting the help I needed. I wondered how the two of them would react when they were both face to face with me as there would be no way to hide their true intentions.

I walked along with my head down to shield myself from the blast of the wind. All around me, leaves blew across the road in a twisted dance, spinning together first on the ground and then, slowly building up their speed and intensity, they would shoot into the air exploding away from each other before they returned to the ground and sought out new partners for the next round. The sky was cloudy and many of the dark clouds made their way around the light of the harvest moon.

I pulled the bag close to my body to both keep it from blowing away and to give me an extra layer of warmth. The dog didn't like being out in this kind of weather and was fighting my every step. There were a few people hurrying to their homes from their cars, papers flying from their hands as they ran. The air smelled like a storm was brewing and I quickened my pace to the shop, the dog trailing farther behind with each step. A group of people came out of the restaurant and I spotted someone that looked familiar. The dog began to whimper and I stopped to see the man getting into his car. It was the man from the horror shop. I ran over to his car as the sky opened up, releasing a torrent of rain. I called out to him, but the wind and thunder drowned out my voice. He turned on his headlights and sped off, leaving a spray of water in his wake. I waved my arm, frantically trying to get his attention, but it was no use. I watched as his taillights disappeared into the night.

"Hey," someone called out, "get out of the rain. You're going to catch you death of cold."

I turned and saw the woman who ran the restaurant running towards me holding an umbrella. I ran to meet her and we made our way into the restaurant.

"What are you doing in the middle of the road?" she asked.

"I was trying to catch the man in the car that just left." I said. "Do you know him?"

A Very Motley Crew

"Yes, he's a professor at a college up here." She replied. "He comes here every now and then, but it's been a while since I've seen him." She took off my coat and sat me down at a nearby table. "I'll get you a nice hot cup of coffee." She said. "Don't you move now, I'll be right back."

I shook off the chill in my bones and the dog shook the water off his drenched fur. The spray covered my shirt and I had to put my hands up to keep it from getting into my face. The woman returned with the coffee, as promised, and sat down across from me. I thanked her for the warm beverage and took a long sip from the cup.

"Why were you trying to catch him?" She asked.

"I have met him once before and need to ask him some questions," I replied. "Tell me, what does he teach?"

"He's a professor of history," she said, "from what I gather he deals with theology mostly, good versus evil."

That explains his knowledge of demons, but it still doesn't tell me on which side his loyalties lie. His car wasn't heading towards Fat Tony's so either he wasn't planning on attending the get together, or it wasn't yet time for it to happen. I looked down at the dog and saw that he had gone to sleep at my feet. His fur still had a dull appearance even now when it was wet. I hoped he wasn't getting sick, but based on all he'd been through it wouldn't surprise me.

"You don't happen to know where the professor was going, do you?" I asked, hoping that she could shed some light.

"He normally gets together with a few people on Thursday nights," she said.

"Fat Tony's? Is that where he goes?" There was a pleading in my voice.

"Fat who?" she asked, "I've never heard of such a place."

"There's a cigar store," I fumbled in my pocket and pulled out the card, showing it to her, "this one. Fat Tony's'. It's just up the road a little ways from here."

"That card is for an attorney," she pointed out, "not a Fat Tony."

I pulled the card back to me and looked at it, unbelieving what I saw. This had to be the card I got from the shop. As I looked, the ink on the card began to bleed, staining the tips of my fingers. I put the card down and grabbed a napkin to clean my hands. The woman got up and excused herself and I watched as she hurried behind the counter and whispered into her husband's ear as she pointed in my direction. The man picked up the phone and I heard him ask to speak to the police. I got up, grabbed the card and the bag, and ran out of the restaurant, ruining yet another place where I felt safe.

The rain was pouring down and every step I took, water splashed up to my chest. The dog was running alongside of me, keeping pace now as if sensing my panic and we ran around the first corner and ducked underneath an overhanging awning to get out of the rain. Why had they called the police? I bent down and put my hands on my knees to catch my breath. The dog was nervously pacing around me, and I soon

Demons Within

became entangled in the rope that I was using to keep control of him. I heard a siren in the distance growing closer as I struggled to free myself from the rope. I didn't want to have another run-in so soon with the sheriff. I twisted myself free and ran towards where Fat Tony's was supposed to be.

I approached the store as the siren was growing louder, its menacing scream piercing through my head. Fat Tony's stood just where it had been before. How could that be? The woman in the restaurant hadn't heard of it before and at the mention of its name, she had summoned for the police. The lights in the shop were on and I could hear music coming from inside. The rain was driving against me, forcing me into the doorway. I saw the glow of the police lights approaching and reached for the doorknob. Locked. I jiggled it rapidly but it still did not budge. Panic began to grow inside my head and I pounded on the door, screaming to be let in. The sirens were louder now, their whine piercing through my skull. The dog was getting frantic from the noise and struggled to pull free from the rope.

No one came to the door to answer my pleas, so I ran around to the side of the building. The sirens were even closer and the lights were shining through the darkness in the alleyway. I looked around for a place to hide and spotted a door on the side of the building. I ran over and slammed my body into it, hoping that it would yield to the force of my weight. The door was not as strong as the one in front and it flung open just as the bulk of my weight struck it and I crashed through, falling to the floor. The door slammed against some metal shelving causing a loud, metallic ping, as the items on the top two shelves tipped over and fell towards where I lay. I watched as large metal box fell rapidly towards my head and struggled to regain my footing. Too late. The box struck the back of my head with the force of a bullet, and threw me back down to the cold, hard cement floor. A shot of lightning forced its way through my entire body and I felt my mind slipping away. My head hit the cement floor with a loud crack and everything around me went silent.

I felt myself falling downwards and, my arms reached out to grab onto something to stop my descent. I hit the ground with a thud and rolled onto my side. I was spinning uncontrollably and then suddenly came to an abrupt stop. I opened my eyes and found myself staring into the eyes of an old man. He had a look of panic on his face and I could smell the fear coming out of his pores. He picked me up and carried me over to a group of people cowering in a corner. A few of them reached out for me and I soon found myself wrapped in their collective warmth.

I fought to free myself from their grip when I saw something floating towards me. As soon as I saw her, the fear left my body and I began to feel more at ease. She knelt down, placing her soft hand on my cheek and I immediately felt her warmth coursing through my veins. I thought she was surely an angel of mercy sent to save me from the throngs of people holding me down among them. Her deep, green eyes looked sorrowfully into mine and she spoke softly as she continued caressing my face.

"Johnny, don't fret now," she said. "Everything is good."

Tears formed in the corners of my eyes and she immediately wiped them away with her soft hand.

A Very Motley Crew

"The dream is over, my love, and you are safe. Please be still so we can tend to your wounds."

A strong pair of hands lifted me up and placed me on a bed. People gathered around and began to talk in their secret tongues. The floor swayed beneath me and I heard the sound of crashing water outside. I realized that I was back on the ship. It was coming back to me quickly. An old woman came up and put a cold towel on my head. I felt my body burning up and was having difficulty breathing.

The angel sat down on the bed and stoked my hair as she held up a steaming cup to my lips and I sipped its hot liquid. The taste was sour and I spit it out.

"Johnny, please be still," she said, "you must take this to lower your fever." I looked into her sad eyes and realized that she had been crying for sometime. I took the steaming cup from her hands and drank it down, the bitterness making its way down my throat causing the muscles on my neck to contract as I swallowed. I finished the cup and handed it back to her. Slowly, the people who had gathered around us began to leave and it was soon just the two of us on the bed.

"How long was I out for this time?" I asked, not sure that I wanted to hear the answer.

"It has been almost a month since you fell ill and your night screams have gotten worse," she sadly replied. "Before you came back to me, you were shouting the name Megan. Do you remember that Johnny?"

Her face was a mixture of sadness and concern. She had aged a little since the last time I saw her; her hair longer and her clothes no longer seemed to fit her well. I thought for a moment about the name she said I had screamed out. Megan. I almost forgot her in my fevered state. I felt a wave of sadness come over me as tears continued to stream down my face. An old man walked over and whispered into Catherine's ear. She turned and nodded her head to him and got up from the bed.

"It's time for your prayers Johnny," she said.

The old man stepped in front of Catherine and held up an old book over my head. I looked into his eyes but because of the darkness, could not see their color. The man started speaking a language I had not heard before as he placed the book on my chest and opened it. I felt a great pressure building up in my head and the book was getting heavier. The man turned the page as moonlight began to pour through the small window above my head. The light reflected off the page and for a moment, I was able to see the old mans eyes. They were black; a deep brooding black with no life coming from them. The man caught my gaze and stared through me as I lay on the bed. My body began shivering as the old man placed his hand on my leg. It burned. I screamed out in pain and two men rushed over, grabbed my arms, and held them down as the old man continued to read from the book. His words made no sense to me but as he read them, I felt the pressure in my chest and head increase tenfold.

The book began to glow a hazy green and illuminated the room, exposing every dark corner. I looked around at the faces of the people who were cowering in the corners and saw that they were afraid. Everyone was huddled together, clutching each other.

The women were shielding the eyes of the children and looking away from the glow that had spread to cover them all.

The old man placed his hand on my head and continued to speak in tongues. His hand grew until it covered my entire head. I looked into his eyes and saw that the blackness had gotten deeper, and the eyes themselves protruded from their sockets. His grip on my head tightened and a jolt of electricity shot from his hands, shooting through my brain and down to my chest. The book raised itself off my chest and started to spin, its once hazy glow becoming clearer and more intense. The men who were holding down my arms released their grip and ran to the corner of the room where they quickly disappeared into the cowering crowd of onlookers.

I turned my gaze back to the old man and saw that he was floating in the air alongside the book. I watched with horror as his face began to bubble, the skin peeling off and revealing the twitching muscles underneath. His mouth twisted in an unnatural way until it had wrapped around his head. A button flew past my head as his chest burst through the fabric of his shirt, revealing a thick coat of matted hair. The undecipherable words continued to come from the creatures gaping mouth that was dripping with dark, black ooze. I struggled to my feet and cowered in the corner, my legs tucked underneath my arms. The creature floated towards me and I began to make out what it was saying.

"Enter now and forever stay, for the demon in you will rule the day. As long as your blood continues to flow, the demon you created will continue to grow."

My chest burned as it spoke the words and I saw Catherine in the corner of the room tear herself away from the grip of the crowd around her and run towards the beast.

"No, don't touch him Johnny," she yelled, "he needs you to survive. Fight him!"

I got to my feet and the creature kept up his verse, getting closer to me each time he finished the second line of the chant. I looked under the bed and saw that the green light was not shining there so I dove for the space just as the creature reached for me with his curled, bloodied hand. I slid to the safety of the darkness under the bed, but the creature managed to grab onto my foot. A wave of coldness shot through my body as its grip tightened and began to pull me from my safe place and I saw Catherine jump over the bed at the creature. I screamed for her to stop, but it was too late.

The creature pulled me from the bed and I looked up to see it closing its mouth around Catherine's head. The coldness had caused my legs to go numb, so I pulled myself up onto the bed with the sheets. I reached out for Catherine, grabbed her ankle, and pulled with all my strength to keep her from its jaws. The creature looked down at me and laughed, giving me a knowing wink. He dove at me and as I screamed out for help, it flung itself into me.

"Holy shit," a voice cried out, "get over here, you gotta see this."

My head was pounding. I opened my eyes and tried to locate the voice. Everything was blurry and the light was too bright, burning my retina. I closed my eyes again and the voice returned,

"Joey, bring a towel," he said in disgust, "there's blood all over the floor. Jesus H. Christ buddy you o.k.? Give me your hand."

I reached out to the voice and he quickly pulled me to my feet. My head snapped back and then lurched forward as the man picked me up by my waist. The force of the motion was too much and I opened my mouth and released a stream of puke down his back.

"Oh man, that's nasty," he said and threw me down on a small couch. I bounced off the cushion and puked again, that time I was the one who ended up being covered. I opened my eyes and looked up to see a blurry figure walking towards me and I could smell the familiar scent of stale cigar smoke.

"Tony?" I asked, "Is that you?"

"Relax kid," he said, "you took a hell of a spill. Here, put this on your head so you don't bleed all over my sofa." He threw an old, smelly bar towel at me and I pressed it to the sore spot on my head.

"What happened?" I asked. I felt panicked as I remembered running from the restaurant, the pulsing lights getting closer with each step. "Where are the police who were chasing me?"

"Ain't no cops here son." Tony replied. He took his shirt off and threw it to the side. "You know, that shirt was silk. I can't clean puke and blood out of it, you stupid shit."

"I'm sorry about your shirt," I said, "how did I end up bleeding on the floor?"

"You came bustin through the door like you were Elliot Ness or something. Joey jumped behind the shelves and was about half a second away from shooting you. You should try knocking next time, save yourself a lot of trouble."

I saw that I was in what appeared to be the storeroom of the cigar shop. Tony was standing in front of me in all his weighted glory with a damp, chewed cigar stub hanging from his lips. There were shelves full of cigars and various other smoking paraphernalia all over the room and I saw Tony's cousin Joey the trash man step from behind a row of shelves in the back, brandishing a gun in his right hand. He must have just come from work as I could smell him from the sofa I was sitting on.

"I see you're still gettin into your share of trouble pal." Joey said as he tucked the gun into the waist of his ever-tightening pants. "You're lucky I didn't stick one in your chest."

"Where's my dog?" I asked

"Little bastard bit me when I went to pick you up," Tony said, "I had to fight him off me with a broom. He's fine now, in the smoke room. I gave him some water and locked him in there 'till we could see if you were o.k."

"He's fine," a voice said from the doorway, "Tony, Joey, give me a few minutes alone will you?"

"Whatever you say boss," Joey said." We'll be in there finishing our discussion."

Demons Within

The figure stepped from the doorway and I saw that it was the professor.

"O.K. John," he said, "we need to talk."

Vulcan Mind Meld

The professor came over and sat down next to me. He looked even more ragged than I remembered; his hair was falling out in chunks and his skin seemed to hang off his bones. He let out a noticeable sigh as he sat down, placing his hand on my knee. I felt the coldness of his touch through my pants and shivered. The air around us seemed to get cooler as well. The professors' breathing was shallow and he winced in pain with each breath that he took. My head was still throbbing and blood was dripping down my face from the gash. I pressed the towel harder to the wound, hoping it would stop the flow from getting into my eyes.

This man had put the fear of Chaos into me with his harsh warnings and imposing demeanor and now he was nothing more than a shell that was once a man. He tightened his grip on my leg and motioned to the door.

"Tony has been a great help," he said, "but I fear that he is now in over his head."

"Where have you been?" I asked, "You were supposed to meet me at my house. I waited but you never came. Instead, I had other company."

"I saw it all," the professor said, "but you opened the door before the agreed time. I told you that he would do whatever it took to stop you."

"No," I replied, "You said that Chaos would do whatever it took to stop me. The demon wasn't the one at my door."

"Don't be so sure. Do you really know anything about Chaos? No you don't. The demon comes in many forms and you should always be wary of that fact when you try to gain answers to your questions."

"Are you saying that the man who has been tormenting me is Chaos?" I was getting very frustrated with this whole affair. I got up and started to pace the room, glancing at the professor with a certain measure of hatred and disgust. He needed to come clean and I wasn't going to leave here until he did. I went over and picked up my duffle bag, extracting the book from it, and returned to the couch.

"So you still have the book." He said. "I thought it was taken from you."

"So did I," I replied, "but my dog found it. It wasn't where I put it though, but instead buried deep inside my mattress."

"Keep it safe. It will be very important to you soon."

"I need to know what is going on." I said. "Tell me about Chaos. Anything you tell me can help."

"What have you learned since we last spoke?" He asked.

I told him of my dreams of the fire; running from Chaos' shack in the woods; and dying. I also told him the story that the Cigar man told me at my house. I took my time to make sure that I wasn't leaving anything out because I didn't want to hear the same things I already knew. It took a lot longer than I thought but I finally caught him up until the point of my crashing into the store where we both now sat.

"You have leaned a lot," he said, "but do not forget that the tale you heard was spoken by someone you cannot trust."

"If you don't mind, I'll be the judge of trust from this point forward. You did not live up to your end of the bargain so any trust I had in you has long since gone."

"The presence kept me away that night, but I was there. I gave you Tony's card to get you here. It took all of my strength to get into your head and retrieve a piece of a dream that you could identify without giving yourself away. I put the card in the cap and recruited the dog to see that you got it. I haven't been able to do much since then, so Tony has had to handle some of my affairs.

I will try to tell you as much as I safely can about Chaos. Chaos appeared in this world long ago during a plague took countless souls all over the world. The oppression of the people, as well as the squalid conditions that existed around the world at the time, fanned the flames that Chaos used to lick the world clean of those he deemed unworthy. As the plague continued to grow, Chaos used the panic and fear to spread his seed to all the corners of the earth. People began to fear him as a god who was inflicting his wrath on those who did not give him the proper amount of tribute. They constructed large temples to honor him and many of the leaders of the time used the people's fear of him to gain absolute power over them.

Many people fled the large cities, searching for a safe haven away from the oppression of their 'chosen' leaders. A few of these leaders went on to conquer many lands in the name of this 'god', and the people that were conquered suffered greatly at their hands. The leaders often sacrificed young children of both believers and non-believers in an attempt to appease Chaos. This process was the result of fear itself, and made Chaos even more powerful. However, as his sphere of influence grew he began to see signs of resistance among those he sought to control.

He knew of a particularly powerful resistance leader named Judge whose movement against the powerful rulers of the time was gaining momentum in one of the provinces. Chaos thought that he could turn Judge to his side and gain even more followers. The thought of being among those who feared him excited him. Finally, he would be able to feel what the people felt when his name was mentioned. Until then, he had only seen the leaders act in his name. Now, he would feel their fear as he walked among them and see for himself the panic in their eyes as they begged for their pitiful little lives.

Chaos greatly underestimated the power that Judge had in his heart and soul. He was a very strong willed man who always stood up to those who sought to oppress him or his family. Judge was also missing something that was required for Chaos to survive; fear. Judge never feared for himself or others and his strength came from his faith that the days of oppression would end as son as the people rose up to face their masters. He had already killed the governor of his province when he came to collect Judge's sister for sacrifice. His village cheered on as Judge plunged a sphere into the governors' chest, ripping out his heart. Judge took the still beating heart over to a fire and held it up for all to see. Then he said, "If evil such as this can die, then there is hope for all to live free."

He threw the heart into the fire and it exploded in a burst of crimson, raining down on everyone in the village. The spattered blood of the tyrant, as well as the faith emanating from Judge, sunk into the skin of those who watched and killed the seed that was inside of them. The people gathered around and lifted him on their shoulders as they paraded through their newly freed town.

The joy of the townspeople spread through the remote villages of the province and soon, there was a feeling of hope felt by many more people throughout the land. People rose up against their oppressors with a renewed sense of being and regained control over many of the cities. The great leaders, once holding so much power over the common people, began to fall as their armies crumbled against the mass of people rising against them.

Chaos watched with great anger as the events transpired and set out to stem the tide of uprisings. He summoned all of himself from around the world and came together for the first time, as a whole. His newly combined power made the earth beneath him shake and the skies filled with thick, dark clouds with streaks of lightning shooting between them. Chaos felt the power coursing through him and released violent wind on the great sea. The sea took the wind and formed great waves that grew to hundreds of feet while traveling at speeds that would make Apollo jealous. The waves shot over the shores and came crashing down on the great cities, drowning out the terrified populations and destroying the very temples built to honor him. The raging winds continued on their destructive paths, creating violent tornadoes that tore through kingdoms, sucking up everything in their path, and leaving total devastation in their wake. The ground in some places opened up and swallowed entire cities, leaving only the tales of those who survived as proof that they actually existed. The forces continued to wreak havoc on the earth for many years until the earth was finally still.

Chaos tried in vain to rein in the destructive forces, as they were quickly getting out of control, but by the time he did the devastation was too great to bear. Seeing all of his temples destroyed and his great leaders drown by the force of the waves, Chaos felt devastated and weak. All of his loyal followers and those who feared him were gone, leaving only those who were against him and had no fear. The people of Judges village joined together in prayer and their loud voices carried with the wind to every village and person that remained. Slowly, others joined in the prayer until it carried to all the corners of the earth, wiping out the very fear that Chaos fed on to survive.

Chaos, devastated by what he had done and weakened by the lack of fear left in the world, struggled to reclaim some small portion of what he once was. He found an old, deaf man on a high mountain who hadn't heard the prayers carried by the wind and concentrated all of his remaining power into him. His power, although weakened, was still stronger than a normal person was and the force on the man proved too great. As soon as Chaos entered the man, he fell from his perch on the high mountain. The mans body crashed through the earth with such a great force that Chaos ended up back in Hell with the devil holding court. He begged to be released back into the world, but this was no longer the time of evil. The faith of the people above kept all of the demons at bay and the world was at peace for a thousand years.

Chaos is pure evil, but certain things are required in order for him to show himself. There has to be a deep level of rage and hatred in the person that he takes, for Chaos feeds on this emotion more than any other. There also has to be a seed of evil inside of the person that he possesses. He has been known, on rare occasions, to take those who themselves harbor no hatred towards others but by situations of circumstance are present where these feelings prevail. He feeds on fear and panic, as these feelings make even the strongest willed people weak and susceptible.

Chaos was not without hope. The seeds that he planted in many of those who lived above him still survived and it would only be a matter of time until one of them took root. When that happened, he could once again return to the world but in a much smaller role than he had before. Instead of ruling over all people and events, he would only rule over one person. He would have to influence others to his way if he wanted to spread out. This is a much slower process, but one he takes to with great vigor. One of those seeds did take root in form of John O'Malley. John's feelings of rage towards Mr. Kelley helped the seed inside him grow and before he knew what was happening, Chaos had taken control of his body.

John's rage built up over many years through events all around him. He came from a poor family with no hope of ending their cycle of poverty. His uncle was a tyrant who would beat him just for fun. He also had a love that could never be fulfilled with his uncle's daughter Megan. When his uncle killed Megan, it proved to be too much and John's soul filled with rage. That rage is what opened the door again for Chaos to enter this world, as the seed that passed to him over the course of many generations took root and grew until John was powerless to stop it.

Now you know the entire history of Chaos. I hope this helps you in your quest."

I sat still for some time, absorbing what the professor had told me, not believing that the demon chasing me was capable of all those things. I stood no chance of defeating him now, or ever. I was not cut out for this task.

"So," I said, "what can I do to stop him? I am only one person and not that strong."

"You have everything you need to expose him within your reach. Now it is up to you to put the pieces together." He got up and started walking to the door. His bones were dry and cracked with each step. I felt a great deal of sadness for the old man. Seeing him in this condition, I knew he wouldn't be around for much longer.

"Wait," I said, "how do you know all of this?"

"I know everything, and nothing. Believe me if you want to overcome him. Doubt me if you want to die."

Demons Within

"I want to believe you, but this sounds impossible." I picked up the book and held it out for him. "Tell me about this book. How can it help me expose the demon?"

"Use your eyes," he said, "they will show you what you need to see if you want to see it. I cannot tell you anymore now, I can feel my strength slipping away and I need to rest. Keep the book safe and the key close; they are your only hope."

I watched as the old man turned and walked out of the room. I was left with only the old book and the key. I needed to put these to work somehow against Chaos. I put the book back into the bag and held it to my chest as I laid down to rest. The dog came trotting over from the room and jumped on the couch. It felt good to have him back again. I closed my eyes and fell asleep, not knowing that I would never sleep again.

I was on the ground, still unable to feel my legs. I had save Catherine from the jaws of this demon, but at what cost? I saw the thing laugh and release its grip from Catherine. It winked at me, I'm sure of it, and then dove right at my head. Why was I still here? Surely, in my weakened state and at this distance, it would have no problem overtaking and killing me. Maybe killing me isn't what it wanted. I felt some strength returning to my legs, so I pulled myself to my feet and surveyed the room. The demon-thing was no where to be seen.

Catherine was cowering in the corner, her eyes filled with fear. I reached out to pull her to the safety of my arms but she resisted, pulling her hand from mine and looking away.

"Catherine," I said, "everything is fine now. Nothing is going to hurt you. Come to me and I will keep you safe."

She didn't make a move. I looked up and saw all of the others in the room were staring at me the same way, with fear. There were muffled prayers coming from the back of the group and a few of the women in front had passed out from the stress of the events. I made my way over to them, but two large men moved in my way. They were the same two men who restrained me on the bed when the old man began to chant. They put their hands on my shoulders and pushed me back into the wall. I felt the fear in them as they looked back over their shoulders to the group cowering in the shadows.

"Why is everyone afraid of me?" I said. "You have nothing to fear, the demon is gone."

"You are the demon boy!" The large man in front of me shouted. "We saw you release the demon from your bed and take down the old man when he was trying to help you. We saw your eyes as he was ripped apart, his guts spilling out of his body and covering the floor. They were glowing brighter with each scream he released. He begged for his life, but you twisted him and we heard his neck snap. We saw you force your evil on poor Catherine who was going to your aid. You wanted to take her the same way you took the old man, but you stopped. We saw you take the demon back into yourself with one breath and cast the room back into darkness."

"I did nothing of the sort," I said, "Catherine, tell them. Tell them how I saved you. Tell them how the old man changed and floated around the room. Please Catherine, help me!"

Catherine got up and walked over to the men. She placed her hands on their shoulders and they turned to her. I felt a warmth envelope me and saw Catherine's hands glowing. The fear went out of the men and they parted, allowing Catherine to come up and face me. Tears were streaming down my face and I felt them burn my cheeks. Catherine lifted her hand and touched them, drying them instantly.

"Calm now, my love," she said, "they cannot harm you."

The warmth coming from her began to fill the room and I saw the fear leave the eyes of the people cowering against the far wall. The mumbled prayers became louder and I heard the words changing as the people came closer to see. Catherine moved closer and placed her mouth to my ear.

"I feel you inside of me," she whispered, softly so no one else could hear. "Already it is growing and I am no longer afraid. Something great will happen soon, you'll see."

She reached out and took my hand, placing it on her belly. I felt the heat coming from her and looked into her eyes. The color was changing from the deep green that I had fallen in love with to a much deeper color. Her pupils were widening and I watched as the transformation continued through various other shades of green until they were black. This should have been the end, but the black continued to darken until it was darker than the night itself. The heat from her belly grew warmer during this change as well, and it began to burn through my skin. I pulled my hand away from her and her eyes quickly changed back to their original color.

"How did you do that?" I asked.

"It wasn't me, it was you." She said. "You created this and now you are changing me to your image so that I will make a more suitable bride."

The crowd had reached us and was now reaching out for Catherine's warmth. She closed her eyes and dropped her head. A bright white made its way from her and covered the people in warmth, causing some of them to cry with happiness. I looked down at the hand that was on her belly and saw that the heat had left a mark in the middle of my palm. I raised it to my face so I could see it more clearly. The marks shape was changing as I watched, its edges becoming more defined and the center changing from bright red to a much deeper crimson. I touched my finger to it and felt the heat slowly fading until it was cold, so much so that I started to shiver.

I looked back up at Catherine and saw that she had made her way through the crowd of people and was sitting on the bed where I had spent so much time over the last few months. The crowd parted and I saw that their eyes had all turned black. I walked over to Catherine and sat down on the bed beside her. She reached out and placed her hand on my knee, griping it slightly. She turned and looked into my eyes and I could feel her changing more with each passing moment. The warmth continued to come from her and her skin took on an ever so slight tint of green.

"What's happening to you?" I asked.

"You put yourself into me. I don't know how, maybe it was from your mind. However it was done, it can't be reversed. We both just need to accept our newly given feelings and live on together."

"I don't feel any differently." I said. "The only thing that's changed is my fever's gone."

Demons Within

"You are the one that changed me. The change has always been inside you, I can feel that now. I don't know what it means, but I'm sure that we will find out before too long."

She took her hand off my knee and got up from the bed. I felt overwhelmed and needed to lie down. She pulled the blanket over my shoulders and kissed me gently on the forehead. I closed my eyes just as she said, "I love you Johnny."

I woke up and saw that I was back on the couch in Tony's shop. I got up and rubbed my neck, which was stiff from the way that I slept. The dog was asleep on the floor and he woke up as soon as I called his name. I walked over to the smoke room but found it empty. I checked the front of the store and there was no one was there either. I wondered how long I was asleep so I went over to the dirty front window and looked outside. The sun still hadn't risen so I guessed that only an hour or so had passed since I had laid down for my nap. The dream was still fresh in my mind, as was the story the professor told me about Chaos. I still had many questions, but there was no one here who could answer them.

I couldn't go back to the resort, or even show myself in town, as the police were probably still looking for me. I didn't have anywhere to go that was safe. My head was beginning to throb from all the thoughts racing through it so I went back to the couch in the backroom and sat down. I had no where to go and only the dog to keep me sane. This wasn't going to work. I had to either find a way to get safely back to the resort or find another place to hide.

I looked around the room and my eyes came across the metal box on the floor that had knocked me out. The dog ran over to the box and put his paw on it. The impact had bent the metal of the lid and I could see there was something inside. I got up from the couch, my head still throbbing, and went over to check it out. The dog backed away as I approached and I grabbed the box from the floor and returned to my seat on the couch. My hands were shaking and my headache was getting worse. I struggled to keep a grip on the box, but it slipped away and fell to the floor. The lid opened the rest of the way and a small cylinder rolled out of the box, coming to rest beside the dog's paw. He barked once and lay down beside it, covering it with his paw. I reached down and took it from him, holding it up to my face to see it more clearly.

There was a thick, clear liquid in the cylinder and it had small black flecks floating inside of it. I moved the cylinder back and forth and watched as the liquid slowly rolled from one side to the other. I put the cylinder down on the couch and picked the metal box back up from the floor. There were a few other items inside so I tipped it over and let them fall into my lap. There were a few small sewing tools and a small thimble of thread. There was also an old newspaper clipping that had browned with age. I picked it up and opened it to see what it said.

It was an old headline from the local paper dating back to 1921. The bold text at the top read, 'CHURCH BURNS, HUNDREDS FEARED DEAD'. I looked down at the story and discovered that there has been a mysterious illness sweeping through the town and doctors couldn't figure out the cause. Many people had already died and the local pastor was calling on people to join together and pray for a cure. The story went on to describe what steps the local officials had taken in an attempt to find the cause of all of the deaths. People were panicking and many had gone to the church to pray. Apparently, someone saw lightning strike the church during a storm and flames quickly engulfed the building. People heard the screams of those trapped inside but the heat was too great for them to get near to help. The fire raged on for hours, the flames growing hotter by the minute, until the church burned to the ground.

The thought of all those people burned alive made me sick to my stomach. I put the clipping down and put my head between my legs to take some deep breaths. The dog was whimpering and pawing at my leg. I looked up and saw that he was holding the cylinder in his mouth. The liquid, once clear, was now crimson red. I took the cylinder from the dogs' mouth and held it up to the light. The black flecks inside were beginning to grow together into a single object. I turned it over in my hands and the liquid turned from crimson slowly back to clear. The flecks now joined, it began to change its form, taking on a distinct shape. I watched as the strange process continued in the cylinder, wondering what the result would yield. The blackness completed its transformation and the level of the liquid in the cylinder began to drop. There was no opening in the cylinder so I didn't know where it was going until I held it closer to my face. The liquid was being absorbed into the newly formed shape, causing it to grow larger, until it absorbed everything in the cylinder leaving no empty space. I put the cylinder back on the floor and watched as it began to throb like a heart, growing and shrinking with a steady rhythm.

The dog backed away from the cylinder, his ears cocked up, and started to howl. I got up from the couch and moved to a safer difference to watch the events transpire. The cylinder began to bounce off the floor with each thump of the object inside, causing the metal of the cylinder to release a loud ping each time it flexed. The dog continued to howl and I watched as the object continued to grow, causing the sides of the cylinder to bulge out. The cylinder fell onto its side and started to roll towards me, still jumping when the object inside flexed. I backed away from it until I reached the far wall. The cylinder continued on its course until it reached my feet. It stopped and popped one last time, coming to rest in its upwards position.

I stood still for a few more minutes in case it had something else in store. The dog stopped howling and walked over to the bag. He barked and scratched at it, digging at the zipper. Slowly, I made my way around the cylinder and went to see what was bothering the dog this time. I opened the bag and saw that the keychain had grown to twice its normal size. I reached down and picked it up. It was much heavier than before and I actually had a hard time lifting it out of the bag. The features of the figure on the end of the chain had grown more pronounced and I could make out more details on it. The skin of the demon was covered with a thick coating of fur and when I rubbed it between my fingers, it almost felt alive. The teeth of the demon were definitely sharper than before and there was a liquid dripping off them. I could also make out a tongue that was black and covered with tiny, white marks. I rubbed my finger along its length and felt the slickness of the ooze dripping from the marks.

I out the chain back into the bag and took out the book. The picture on the front was taking on the same characteristics of the keychain, every detail more pronounced and it seemed to be bulging off the cover, like a pop up. I noticed that the book was also pulsing, just like the object in the cylinder. I felt a presence in the room and looked away from the book to see what was causing this feeling. A shadow made its way through the doorway and I found myself looking again at Cigar Man.

Battle Royale

"What's up kid?" he asked.

There was always the same beginning to our meetings, but I never knew how each one would end. I was very weak from the loss of blood from my head as well as mentally drained from my most recent experience. If this visit turned out to be anything like the last one, I felt I surely wouldn't survive. My mind was not capable of processing any more information and I felt the muscles in my body screaming out for relief. I sat down on the couch and watched Cigar man perform the same ritual that he always performed whenever he appeared. He lit his stogie with the same method, watching as the smoke curled up into the air.

"What the hell do you want now?" I asked.

"Whoa," he said, "easy there buddy. There's no need for hostility here. I came to get what's mine."

He spoke with the same authoritative tone that he used on me before. I had a feeling this was going to be a bad meeting. He took a few long hauls from his stogie and walked over to the cylinder on the floor.

"I see you found it. Good. Now we can move on without further delay."

"I don't know what it is that I found," I said, "and I also still don't know what you are looking for. The last time we were together, you pulled me back to my burnt down house to give me a half-assed history lesson."

I got to my feet and my hatred for him quickly returned, causing my pulse to quicken and my hands to clench into tight fists. I heard my heartbeat in my ears and concentrated my stare directly into his eyes. He returned my stare and removed his sunglasses, revealing his dark, black eyes. My gaze intensified and I felt a power coming from deep in my chest. My heartbeat quickened and I felt the adrenalin coursing through my veins. My body temperature began steadily rising and I felt the heat making its way out of my pores. The lights in the room seemed to dim as I felt a surge of energy shoot through my body.

Cigar Man must have noticed something change in me because I began to pick up a feeling coming from deep inside his soul. Never before had I experienced someone else's emotions as clearly as I was now. I looked into his eyes and felt something familiar. Only this time, the feeling wasn't coming from my head, it was coming from his. I watched as his black eyes, once so ominous and overpowering, flicker briefly to a lighter shade of gray. I saw into his soul at that moment, and what I saw made the energy flowing through me grow more powerful. Deep inside this dark mans soul, I felt fear.

I needed to take advantage of this momentary shift in power somehow before he regained control of his wandering emotions. I summoned all of my strength into my hand and shot forward to strike him down. The blow landed squarely on his mouth and it hit with a loud bang that shook the walls around us. The room exploded in a brilliant, white light and both of us were thrown to the floor from the force of the blow. The ceiling separated and large chunks of it rained down on our heads. I put my arms up just as the largest piece came crashing down over me, pinning me to the floor. I looked at Cigar Man and saw him fall back into the wall, tearing through the plaster and shielding his head from the falling debris. The room continued to shake and the walls were collapsing around me. I had to get free before the falling debris killed me. The piece of ceiling on top of me was quite large and it took a great deal of effort to free myself. I scattered from under it as another, even larger piece crashed down, shattering it into a thousand pieces.

Cigar Man was in a more perilous situation. The force of my punch had not only pushed him through the interior wall, but through the hard, brick exterior wall as well. I ran over to the hole and saw that the world outside had undergone drastic changes since I entered the shop. The sun was up, but the sky wasn't as it should be. Instead of a clear, blue sky there was one with a greenish tint. The clouds in the sky were different as well. Instead of the white puffiness normally associated with clouds, they were black; a deeper black than I have ever seen. The landscape was changed as well. The trees, once tall and proud, now bent down and scraped their branches on the ground below. Even the ground itself was different. The streets split apart from the ground and I could see what appeared to be blood on the underside of the asphalt. The buildings had stretched out into unnatural shapes, twisting into each other like pretzels, and the cigar shop we were in had grown twenty stories or more.

Cigar Man dangled from the edge of the shop, holding on with only the tips of his fingers. His legs were flailing uselessly below him and he struggled to grab onto the still growing building with his other hand. The building began to twist as it grew, causing me to fall back from my view of the changing world. I grabbed onto the floor and tried to pull myself back to the wall, but the room had already turned 180 degrees. I fell through what was once the ceiling and into the attic, landing on the ceiling, my foot crashing through to the world outside. I could hear the sound of the bricks tearing themselves away from the building and crashing into the ground below. The room continued its violent turn and soon I was dangling upside down, suspended by my foot, from the ceiling of the attic.

I looked towards the opening in the wall of the storeroom and saw a hand reach in from outside. I watched as Cigar Man pulled himself into the room and dusted off his clothes. I saw the book bag on the floor at the same time as he did. He made his way towards it and reached down to pick it up. I couldn't let him get that bag, but I was trapped. I twisted my body back and forth in an attempt to free myself. Pieces of the ceiling began to break free and fall off, crashing around the man below. He looked up and our eyes met as I continued to struggle to get free. A smile curled up from the side of his mouth and he picked up the bag and headed back towards the hole.

I continued twisting around, yelling for him to stop, and my foot finally slipped from the hole. I fell head first towards the floor and turned to my side to avoid what would have been a life-ending blow to the head. I hit the floor and continued down, causing the floor to swell around the room. The floor swelled up under his feet and threw him back towards me, the bag flying free from his hands as he fell. I bounced back up as if on a trampoline and grabbed the bag in mid-air. I looked down and saw the man bouncing back up off the floor so I spun my body around, extending my arm to my side, and caught him on the side of the head with the bag. The force of that hit was even greater than when I hit him before and the room blew apart, forcing the walls around us to disintegrate.

The blow pushed him back with great force, but his foot slipped through the strap of the bag and I was pulled with him out of the building at bullet speed. I looked down and saw the landscape rushing by, all of its features blurring together, as we sped across the sky. The force of our speed pulled the skin away from my body and I felt myself ripping apart. I opened my mouth to scream and it stretched out, causing my lips to flap violently and my tongue began to retreat into my throat. The wind stripped away all the water from my eyes and I felt its force shoving them back into my brain. We picked up speed and my skin turned to rubber, stretching me out until I was nothing more than a long, thin string hurtling through the skies.

I looked at Cigar Man as he was putting his hands over his head and he began to scream. I strained to see what he was protecting himself from and I saw a large wall ahead of us approaching quickly. The wall grew larger and he curled himself into a ball, lowering his head and tucking his legs up under his arms. I strained to pull my legs up but it was too late. We hit the wall at full force and crashed through it, the world beyond showing itself to us for the first time. My body snapped back together as I hit the ground. I was still going at an incredible rate of speed and a long trench of disturbed earth cut into the newly found land behind me. I slid for a few hundred yards before finally coming to a stop.

My eyes, nose, and mouth were full of dirt and I slowly got to my feet, coughing up big chinks of earth. The air around me was thick and I found it difficult to breathe it into my lungs. I turned around and saw the earth that I slid through closing up and within a minute, there was no sign that it was ever disturbed. In the distance, I saw Cigar Man getting to his feet, staggering as he did. My head was heavy and I looked around for the bag. It was up ahead, halfway between him and me. The land was flat and I thought I could cover the distance in no time at all. I started to run for the bag, breathing in more of the thick air as I ran, and saw that he was running as well. His legs were longer than mine were so he was covering the distance with half the strides I was using. I kicked my legs into high gear and sped towards the bag. The ground under me felt like rubber and gave me an added bounce with each step I took. I got to the spot where the bag was at the same time as he did. We both reached for it, but the ground opened up and swallowed the bag, leaving only dirt for us to grab.

We both stood back up and stared at each other in disbelief. I looked around and noticed something strange. There were no trees, no bushes, no grass, and no people. The sky was clear of all clouds and instead of being blue; it had a deep green tint. I looked past him into the distance and there was nothing to see there as well, no mountains rising up from the earth, no buildings where people would live, no birds in the shy, and no roads to travel on the ground. The only thing I could see was dirt. Miles and miles of lifeless dirt. Where was this place?

I turned my attention back to Cigar Man. I could see that there was a level of concern rising in him, and that he could sense that something wasn't right as well. He was looking around as I was, taking in the lack of scenery and asking himself the same questions. I noticed that his hands were shaking and he had started to sweat.

"What is this place?" I asked. "I've never seen anything like it before."

"You may not have seen it before," he said, "but you know it quite well. We are inside of your mind."

I watched as he began the pace nervously around me. How could we be inside of my mind? The mere thought of it sent a shiver down my spine. If we were indeed inside my mind, then where were all of the thoughts? I would think that they would be visible somehow, in either words or pictures, maybe even in lightening shooting from one lobe to the other. Cigar Man grabbed onto my arm and I felt his panic go through me.

"We've got to get out of here." He said. "We can't last very long once they come."

"Once who comes?" I asked. "What is it you are so afraid of?"

"I can usually go in and out of here as I please but now I find myself powerless to control what's going on around here." His voice was starting to crack as he spoke.

"If we are in my mind, then why is it empty?"

"I don't know," he said, "you have been so intent on discovering the secrets of that book that now you have no other thoughts inside of you. Once the book disappeared, your mind must've gone with it." He stopped pacing and looked directly into my eyes." Tell me you still have the key. Tell me you didn't leave it in the bag."

"I don't have anything on me," I said, "everything was in the bag. What is so damn important about that key?"

"The key is the answer to everything. Without the key, you have no way of controlling Chaos' power."

"How can I control his power?" I asked. "I can't even control my own."

"Wait a minute, you haven't read the book?" He asked.

"No," I said, "I never got the chance. I was supposed to read it the night you showed up at my house and took it away."

"Why would I take it away?" He asked. "You created me to keep its secrets safe."

I felt my stomach begin to turn as he spoke those last words and an acrid taste made its way to my throat. He said that I created him. That wasn't possible. I have been running from him as long as I can remember. He has always been there when something bad was happening to me so there's no way that I made him. This must be one of his tricks to get the book again. Only this time, I don't see anyway of finding out what that trick is or how to expose it. He must have pulled me here just like when he pulled me back to my house from the police station. There was only one problem with that theory. He seems genuinely afraid to be here and I can feel his emotions changing to fear.

I was still not totally convinced of this fear, however, and I decided to test him as best I could. "If I created you," I said, "then why have you been causing me so much pain?"

"I have not been the cause of your pain," he said. "You have only to look as far as your own demons to see that to be true. I have been there to keep them at bay."

"That doesn't make any sense," I said. "If that were the case, then you would have protected me from the dreams instead of creating them to keep my fear flowing. I know that you are Chaos and the professor warned me that you would do anything and everything in your power to stop me from finding that out."

He shook his head and turned his back to me, surveying the endless landscape of emptiness around us. He was quiet for a long time and I thought he was thinking up another great story to throw me off the path of truth. When he finally turned around, I saw the fear gone from his eyes and his cold stare returned, making my blood run cold. He raises his hands up and they began to glow with a slow, pulsing rhythm.

"I want you to think of something," he said, "something that you fear. Don't say it out loud, but once you think of it bury it deep down inside of your soul." He started to walk around me, keeping his hands extended outward, palms up, as he did so. I watched the pulsing glow grow faster as my mind raced thinking about what he said. I felt the air around me get cooler and out of nowhere, a strong wind blew through the barren land, kicking up dirt as it raced through. The dirt swirled up into the air and began to cluster together, forming some kind of shape. The wind intensified and more dirt added itself to the ever-growing shape that was beginning to take on a familiar look. The outline grew more detailed and I could make out distinct features in the center of the dirt mass. It grew taller, almost touching the far reaches of the sky above, and its consistency began changing. It was no longer dirt in front of me, but a more solid mass. The dirt grew together into long strands of hair coming from the center of the mass and looking up; I saw the familiar black stare of the one thing that scared me the most. I was looking directly into the eyes of Chaos himself.

All of his features were now clear and I saw the dark, black ooze begin to drip from his long teeth. I wanted to run but my legs, as they had on so many other occasions, were frozen in place. I continued to watch as Chaos' body heaved up and down as he took deep breaths of the surrounding air.

"Bury your thoughts," Cigar Man screamed. "Bury them deep down inside and lock them down."

The wind around us became stronger and I fell back onto the hard earth. I looked up at Chaos and saw that he was bending down, his mouth opening wider with each inch he grew closer to my head. I wanted to close my eyes and wish him away, but something was forcing them to stay open; something from deep inside of me. Chaos' face began to change, his features becoming less fearsome. His eyes, once black, were now green and his mouth took on a more human appearance. I could now make out a face emerging from the changing scene. Cheekbones emerged from the once thick mat of fur, and the fur itself was receding back into a newly formed skin. My jaw began to drop as I realized what it was that I was witnessing, and the fear that had for so long ruled my emotions changed to a feeling of sheer horror.

I was seeing something that I had refused to see before, no matter how many times it had shown itself to me. I felt my heart sped up and my breathing became very shallow as I fought to suppress the truth from coming to the surface of my mind. The transformation was complete and I looked to Cigar Man.

"Look up and see the truth." He said.

I raised my head and looked into the eyes of the demon, the same demon that tormented me throughout my life. When I looked into his eyes I began to cry, as did he. The thing that I feared the most was Chaos. I forced that thought deep into my soul and locked it down. But there was another thing that I feared, probably more than the demon himself. And this thought had overtaken the guards that were hiding my fears from the light and brought it to the surface to be judged. The thing that I feared most was the truth. It was this truth that I alone had hidden from the light and built many walls up to protect it. It was this very truth that made me create Cigar Man to guard it from those who sought to capture it and harness its great power. Now, this truth would change me forever.

I looked into the eyes of Chaos, and saw myself.

"Be wary of those who act in your best interest."

Anonymous

"The quest for truth is not one to be taken lightly."

The Book of Truth

Truth Shall Set You Free

Now that the truth lay before me, I could no longer stay in my state of denial. I had to face the facts, and the facts were that I was the one causing everything to happen. How could I have kept this suppressed for so long? My life was the one thing I thought I knew and now it was just another mystery for me to solve. I lacked both the strength and the will needed to accomplish this overwhelming task. Now I find myself trapped with this new knowledge and apparently stuck inside my own mind, with only the company of an imagined character to keep me from going insane.

Cigar Man vanished the demon figure from my new world with a wave of his hands, or maybe I did it since we're one and the same, and placed his hands on my shoulders. I felt his pain at not being able to do the job that I created him to do. His facial expression was no longer intimidating and I felt a twinge of pity for him.

"Now you know," he said, "and only you have what's needed to get us out of here alive."

"I don't know what to do." I said. "It's all too much for me to handle."

"I'm sorry it had to come to this, but you left me no other choice. When the bag disappeared I had nothing else to use to shield you from the truth."

"I still don't fully understand everything." I said. "If you were the one meant to protect me from this truth, then why did the professor warn me to stay away?"

"I hate to tell you this, but he had a different agenda than I did. He may have passed himself off as a friend to you, but believe me he meant only to harm you."

"But he told me about Chaos. Why would he do that if he was against me?"

"What he told you was false," He said. "He tried to convince you that there were outside forces working against you, myself included, when actually you had control of the forces the whole time. By telling you this, he hoped to weaken you with fear to the point where he could take control of your mind and harness the evil to work for him. I was trying to keep the truth buried in your subconscious mind but he was intent on bringing it to the surface. I fought him in your dreams and tried to keep the secret safe, but you were already making connections."

"So there is nothing else to worry about except for my own thoughts?" I asked. "This seems a little too simple."

"Your thoughts aren't the only thing standing in you way." He said. "The professor is still strong and since you have lost both the book and the key, it's going to be almost impossible to stand alone against him. However, there is still hope. The bag is in your mind and now you need to find it before its too late."

Truth Shall Set You Free

"If he is truly against me," I said, "and if the book is what's needed to stop him, why did he give it to me ion the first place?"

"The book contains stories about Chaos." He said. "But it goes into more of a detailed history. The professor got control of the book long ago and changed it. The book is supposed to chronicle Chaos and all of those affected by his power. The professor has changed certain facts about Chaos, including his lineage over the last hundred years or so. If you read the book with him, he would have pointed out that Chaos passed through you but was now living as someone else. That would've made you more fearful, since you had no way of knowing that it was false."

"So you're saying that he meant to gain control of me by making my level of fear rise, causing Chaos to take over and then he would take Chaos. But something still doesn't make sense. Why didn't he just keep using the dreams to gain control?"

"I was created to keep the truth in you safe from all who sought to grab the power for their own agendas. When I interrupted his dreams, he had no other choice but to try a different approach."

"Who is he anyway, and why does he need this power so badly?" I said.

"The professor made a mistake that I thought you might pick up on. In your last dream, he revealed that Chaos entered an old man in a failed attempt to stay in the world. What he didn't tell you was that HE was the man that Chaos passed through. The old man felt the power of Chaos as he passed into his body and as he fell, he tried to hold on to every bit of that power that he could. It was too much for him to handle so he had to let it go. When Chaos crashed into hell, the devil sent the man back to the world to live forever alone as punishment for trying to control his demon. Since that day, he has spent every waking moment trying to get back the power that he once held as his own.

When Chaos returned to the world through John O'Malley, who was your great grandfather, the professor somehow sensed his presence and tried in vain to regain the power. He has come close on many occasions, but never as close as he is right now."

"How did I become Chaos then?" I said. "I never knew John O'Malley."

"John had a seed deep inside him that had been passed on through many generations. This seed was a sleeper, as there was never any rage for it to latch on and grow. He passed the seed to his wife, Megan, and she passed it to her two children. They both carried the seeds and passed them on. This process continued and now here we are with you as its keeper."

"O.K.," I said, "but that still doesn't explain how the seed became active. According to the stories you've told me, there has to be some seriously deep seeded rage for the seed to take root. I can't recall ever feeling that level of rage."

"The rage didn't come directly from you," he said. "The first time I showed myself to you was at your grandfathers' side when he was dying. By the time the cancer affected him to the point you saw, he was filled with rage. He wanted to live more than anything and no one could help him come to terms with the inevitable.

Demons Within

When you entered the room the seed in him had already reached full maturity, but it couldn't take over because his body was already too weakened by the cancer. When you saw him lying on the bed, your feelings changed. Your hatred of death grew to the point of rage and Chaos detected this. He jumped from your grandfather into you at that moment. When you left the room, you felt yourself losing control. It was at that point that Chaos had a firm grip on your soul and has since been working to overpower your mind."

I stood there and processed this information, remembering that day in the hospital more clearly with each moment that passed. The wind returned to where we were and a loud screech echoed through the emptiness. The memory came rushing back to me and I felt overwhelmed by its power. The sky above us began to explode in a brilliant show of lights, all the colors bursting into one another, creating beautiful patterns that rained down over us. The wind picked up and soon the colorful patterns blew across the sky, causing the once dark and ominous view to glow warmly down on us.

I watched this display with my new ally and felt my heart grow inside my chest. There was a feeling of love in the air, more intense and focused than I had felt before. The patterns above us took on distinct shapes and I was able to make out portraits of people I loved in their brightness. I saw my grandfather as a young man, taking his new bride into their new home, and I felt a tear leap from my eye to join the scene above. I watched as the tear made its way toward the scene and then saw it explode and its remnants rained down over our heads. The lights continued to create wonderful patterns that captivated all of my attention and I continued to weep as the scenes updated themselves.

I turned to Cigar Man with tears in my eyes and saw that his expression hadn't changed at all since the show started. I walked over to him and put my hand on his shoulder. He pulled away quickly, leaving me confused, and walked away.

"Isn't this wonderful?" I asked. "Every thought I have shows up in the lights. I haven't felt this good for a long time."

He turned back toward me and I saw his expression change. It wasn't one of joy as I had expected, but rather anger. Why would he be mad at such a beautiful sight?

"What's the problem?" I asked, walking closer to where he stood.

"This isn't you doing this." He said. "If you were creating these memories, I wouldn't be here right now. I only appear during bad times. This is the work of someone else and I wouldn't get too caught up in it if I were you."

"But I can feel it here," I said, pointing to my heart. "So it has to be coming from me."

"As long as you have dark thoughts in your mind," he said, "I exist. I'm going to look for the bag. I suggest you do as well or we'll never get back to reality."

He turned and walked into the horizon with the brilliant light show still raining down to the earth around him. I watched for a few more minutes as the captivating scenes changed to my own life and then I felt what he was talking about. A chill ran over me as I saw my birth; more specifically, the birth that happened right after mine. I saw my mother lying on a bed, struggling to push out, while my father held me with concern in his eyes. A nurse was bending over her, trying to calm her down, while a doctor continued to yell for her to push. The monitors were beeping loudly and I couldn't hear anything over them. My mother gave one final push and fell back onto the bed, drained from her experience.

The doctor grabbed the baby and rushed it over to a tented table. I saw my father screaming, but the noise of the alarms was making it impossible to make out what he was saying. The doctor worked feverishly on the newborn but apparently, it was too late. He took off his gloves and walked over to my mothers' bed and I could see the pain in his eyes; I could actually feel his pain in my own heart. He spoke and I saw my mother scream out to him. My father, who was still holding me in his arms, started shaking his head, saying no over and over, as he slid down the wall.

I felt my heart break then, and the lights changed and took on a much darker tone. The nurse took me from my father and placed me in a small crib beside my mother's bed. My father bent over her and wept on her shoulder. I could feel his tears soaking through my shirt and I fell to the ground and wept with him. I felt myself changing, almost splitting in half, and I realized what I had just seen. I was not alone when I was born. Another boy should have been part of my family; another person for me to know and love; another person to know how I felt. The revelation crushed my emotions and I felt my rage for death building back up again. Why didn't I know about this before? My parents should have told me. That might have explained a lot of the feelings that I always had in my life, the feelings of solitude and depression specifically. I placed my head in my hands and continued to weep uncontrollably.

I felt a hand on my shoulder and looked up to see Cigar Man bending down, his eyes still not showing any emotion whatsoever.

"Get up," he said, "we have to get going now while we still have time."

He helped me to my feet and we walked together to search for the bag, the scenes above us disappearing, and the sky returning to the same lifeless green it had been before.

"It will all be over soon," he said. "Just keep your focus on the key."

Dimebag

We walked for hours together in the baron land that was my mind. He kept his arm around my shoulder to keep me from falling down in despair. Along the way, we talked about many different things. I knew that he was aware of them all, as he was just a figment of my imagination, but he listened anyway. The air thinned out and was no longer as difficult to breathe. I noticed that the ground was more solid as well, and we covered a great distance in a very short period. As we talked, he showed me that I still had some control over my mind, and encouraged me to focus all of my thoughts on the bag. He said that when I was ready to see it, it would appear.

We came across a valley with no visible way to cross. I looked down its length and couldn't see a place where the land joined together. Cigar Man told me to take my concentration off the bag for a moment and visualize a rope. I closed my eyes and struggled with this task for a few minutes before finally seeing the rope before my eyes. He told me to visualize the rope stretching out to the other side of the valley and joining the two pieces of land together. It took a lot of my strength, but I was able to do it. We tied the rope to a tree stump that was cropping up from the ground and checked to be sure that it was stable.

"This is going to take a lot of effort," he said. "I need to be sure that you are up for this challenge. Let's rest for a while so you can regain your strength. While we do that, I need you to stay focused on the bag. We will soon be entering your subconscious mind and I gotta tell you, it's not going to be a pretty sight."

"What's waiting for us there?" I asked.

"Chaos is there," he said, "and he knows we're coming."

I lay down and closed my eyes to rest for the battle that I was sure waited for us on the other side. My newfound friend gave me some hope that I could actually be successful and this would all soon be over. I fell into a deep sleep with the dreams continuing to lurk in the dark corners of my mind, waiting for me to weaken so they could once again wreak havoc with my mental state.

During my sleep, my friend couldn't keep all the dreams away and one of them made its way through the barrier he constructed to show itself to me, but only in small fragments that I couldn't fully piece together.

I saw my brother, or someone who resembled me in every detail, coming home from the hospital after his birth. I watched as they brought him into the house to a waiting crowd of well-wishers. My grandparents were there and their faces lit up at the sight of the newest family member. My father passed the newborn to them and they took him away into the other room. I was seeing the scene from my fathers' eyes, and my vision turned to face my mother, who was sitting in a wheelchair looking dazed. My father spoke to her, but the sound was muted so I couldn't hear what he said. She nodded and he helped her from the chair and together they made their way up the winding staircase to the bedroom.

Dimebag

My father tucked her into the bed and kissed her forehead before heading down to join the waiting people in the living room. He walked in and I could finally hear the sounds of the people in the house. They were all surrounding the baby that my aunt was holding in her arms, doing all the things people normally do to a newborn. My grandparents looked up and saw my father standing alone in the doorway. I was still seeing this from his perspective and I felt a great sadness in him. My grandparents walked over to him and sat him down on the couch between them.

"What's wrong son?" his father asked, "Where's Deb?"

"I had to put her to bed," I said. "She's still on a lot of medication from the hospital."

My grandmother put her hand on my leg and said, "What did the doctor say?"

"He said that she will eventually get better, but right now she needs a lot of support. She didn't expect to lose one of the babies and she's really shaken up."

The scene in front of me turned to a blur and a new one appeared out of nowhere. We were in a school and it looked like a kindergarten class. There were kids running around and I was seeing it from their level. This wasn't a memory of my kindergarten class; I knew this because I had excellent memories of that year. The teacher was in the middle of the room and asked all the kids to find their seats. There was a lot of confusion as the small bodies clumsily bumped into each other trying to follow the teachers' orders.

I found myself at a table with five other kids who I knew very well. My best friend Todd was sitting directly across from me, talking excitedly to another of my friends Kenny. They were both having a great time talking to each other and I wanted to join in on their fun.

"Hi Todd," I said, "What are you guys talking about?"

He looked at me like I had two heads and said, "I don't know you, so mind your own business."

I felt crushed by his rejection and then someone tapped me on the shoulder. I turned around and saw a geeky little kid with thick glasses smiling at me.

"Are you still coming over to spend the night Paul?"

"My name's not Paul." I said. "I'm Johnny."

"Of course you're Paul," the geeky kid said, "we've only been best friends for three years. I think I know your name by now, geez."

The scene changed again and I saw myself in a college dorm room. There was a knock at the door and it opened, revealing a cute petite coed.

"Hi Paul," she said, "Are you ready?"

"Am I ready for what?" I asked.

Demons Within

"Don't be silly, you know that we have rehearsal tonight. Don't try to back out now, my daddy paid the minister today and Jay already picked up your tux so there's no way you're getting out of this. By the way, I got the test results back and it's true, I'm pregnant!"

The scene changed again and soon I was in a hospital room. There was a woman in front of me screaming out in pain and a doctor was bent over between her legs. I walked over to the woman and she grabbed onto my hand, squeezing it hard until I thought that my fingers would snap off.

"It's almost time Paul," she said, "I can feel him turning now inside me. I love you so much."

"It's time now Kelley," the doctor said, "Give me one more good push."

I watched as she bit down on her lip, which was already chapped and bleeding, and pushed. The doctor reached down and before I knew it, there was a baby screaming in his arms.

"Congratulations," he said to us, "you have a healthy, baby boy."

I woke up screaming and saw that I was back in front of the large valley in my mind. Cigar Man was leaning against the tree stump enjoying a few puffs of his favorite vice. He looked at me and smirked. I detected something coming from him, some kind of feeling, but I couldn't quite make it out. He got up and came over to sit down.

"Good sleep?" He asked.

"Not really," I said, "I had a strange dream."

"Sometimes what we dream is actually the way things should be." He said. There was a noticeable attitude in his voice towards me and I couldn't figure out the reason for it. If he was something that I conjured up, I didn't think he should speak to me this way.

"Is there something wrong?" I asked.

"Let's get going," he said, "we've got a long haul ahead of us and we've already lost too much time." With that said he got to his feet and pulled me up. My arm popped and I thought it was going to come out of the socket from the force he used.

"Take it easy," I said. "Why are you being so rough?"

"We only have a little time left to find the bag," he said, "and you broke your concentration during your sleep. I'm not fooling around anymore; we need to move, now."

We walked over to the precipice and I looked down. It was a few thousand feet to the bottom and he expected me to balance on a rope all the way across to the other side. This was crazy.

Dimebag

"How about I think up a better way across," I said. "I don't think that the rope is the best way."

"We don't have time for that," he said. "By the time you figure out how to use your own mind, we'll be out of time and Chaos will win."

He was definitely not the same person anymore and I began to fear him as I had on so many other occasions.

"Concentrate on the bag," he yelled, "the rest will take care of itself." He went over and stepped on the rope. I saw it shake as he took his first few steps towards the other side of the valley. "Let's move, kid"

I went over to the rope and put my foot on it tentatively. The rope shook, but not as much as when he first stepped on it. I put my arms out to my side, just as they taught me in gym class, and stepped forward with my other foot. I felt my stomach muscles tighten as I tried to keep my balance on the unstable rope. I looked ahead and saw that he was already fifty or so steps away. I took a few deep breaths and closed my eyes to take my next step. It became easier for me with practice and before long I was a pro; moving across with all of the confidence of a circus tightrope walker.

When I was about three quarters of the way across, I opened my eyes and what I saw almost made me lose my balance. Up ahead, rising as high as I could see, there was a great mountain. This was unlike any mountain I have ever seen before and more closely resembled a volcano, as there was fire shooting out of its peak, raining down ash to cover the ground below. The shape of the mountain wasn't what you would think. Instead of a mass of land gradually rising to a peak, the mass twisted into itself; creating holes in its' center that were filled with a black ooze that dripped down the sides. There were many peaks in the twisted mountain and all of them seemed to be spewing a mixture of fire and tick, black ooze.

I paused for a moment to regain my composure and balance and Cigar Man turned to me and said, "Keep your mind on the bag."

I decided to keep my eyes open as I wasn't sure what would be appearing next or what kind of danger was waiting for me when I got to the other side. A wind blew up from the valley below and the rope began to swing back and forth, as I struggled to balance myself. I was walking slower because of the wind and it took considerably more time to cover the remaining distance to the other side. I got within four steps of reaching the land and then there was a loud explosion from the top of the mountain. I looked up and saw a plume of flames erupt from the mountain and then fire and ooze began to fall all around me.

The wind grew more powerful and I felt my leg slip from its tender grip on the rope. A large blob of ooze covered in flames fell from the top of the mountain and crashed into the rope. The fire burned through the rope and it broke, sending me over the side in panic. I reached out to grab the rope as it was falling back towards the safety of the land ahead and managed to grab the tip of it with my fingers as I fell. I gripped down with all my strength to hold on, but the momentum of my weight swung the rope quickly to the side of the land, and I crashed into it, causing me to

Demons Within

lose my grip on the small piece of rope. I watched it swing away from me and I began to fall towards to my certain death below.

Cigar Man watched this happen and shouted out for me. "Concentrate on the land!" He yelled. "Look at the mountain and visualize it underneath you!"

I struggled to keep my body from twisting in the air as I heard him shout from the safety of the land above. I looked at the peak and then closed my eyes, memorizing every detail about its features. I took that picture in my head and began to turn it around, causing its twisted shape to take on a more traditional appearance. I took a plume of fire and ooze that was shooting from one of the many openings and merged it together into the mountain. I reached out my hands to grab it and pulled it towards me with all my strength. The newly formed piece of land stretched out from the looming mountaintop and soon it stretched all the way to the bottom of the valley. I changed my grip and stretched it upwards towards me and saw the land around it start to grow up from the valley floor, forming a small hill at first, and then growing taller and wider until it was the size of a medium sized mountain. I let go of the land in my head and smashed it down with my hand. The peak of the newly formed mountain flattened on impact and the force of my blow formed a plateau.

I felt my body hit something hard and I opened my eyes and saw the rope dangling from the land a few hundred feet over my head. I was safe, for now, and I got to my feet. I saw that I was standing on solid ground so I walked over to the side and looked down. Far below, I could see the floor of the valley that almost claimed my life. I didn't understand how this happened, but I was in no mood to question my good fortune. I stepped away from the side and looked back up to the rope. I could see Cigar Man looking down at me over the side and it looked like he was trying to say something. I strained to hear it, but the wind was still violently blowing and I couldn't make out any other sound.

I stood there and thought about what I had just done. I did indeed have some control over this place and now I just needed to think of a way out of my present situation. I decided to concentrate on the rope swinging in the wind above. If I created it, I could also change it. I focused all my thoughts on the very end of the rope and closed my eyes, willing it to me. The rope straightened out and stretched away from the side of the cliff. I saw it stretching in my head and concentrated even harder to get it all the way down to where I was waiting. I felt something hit my head and I opened my eyes to see the rope dangling in front of my face. I had one it, but the process drained any remaining energy left in my body. I fell to the ground, to weak to stand any longer.

I looked up and saw Cigar Man descending the rope. He must have sensed my lack of strength and was now coming to my aid. He repelled the cliff with all of the finesse of a veteran mountaineer and before long he was on the plateau. I reached out for him, but my arms were too weak. He hoisted me over his shoulder and began the long climb up to my subconscious mind. We reached the top and he put me down. My strength was all gone now and I could no longer keep my eyes open. Just before they closed, I saw him place his hand over my head and say, "Truth."

Flying High

I found myself floating over the mountain that was the entrance to my subconscious mind, looking down into its vast secrets, and I was amazed at the sheer volume of information hidden inside. The landscape was drastically different compared to the outside with large trees that had huge pieces of fruit hanging from their branches, their weight causing them to droop to the ground. I swooped down to examine one of these fruits and first noticed the size. The fruit resembled a pear, but not in the normal sense of a pear, as it was well over ten feet tall. The skin of the fruit was a very bright green and there seemed to be light emanating from its center, glowing first blindingly bright, then dimming to the point of darkness. The fruit was also emitting a constant hum that sounded like a condenser fan running from and air conditioner.

I walked around the tree and saw an endless row of glowing fruits as far as my eyes could see, each one following the same pattern of emitting light; bright to dark. Looking down, I saw a sloped hillside with what appeared to be even more fruit. However, these fruits weren't glowing like the others, they were all dark. They must have fallen from one of the trees and many were badly bruised. I walked carefully down the slope; the soil on the ground was very fragile, and looked closely at one of the fallen ones. There was a sound coming from it, but not the same constant hum as the healthy ones. It was more like the crackling sputter of a radio that lost its signal. All of the fallen fruits seemed to be putting out the same sound. I walked among the ranks of the fallen and soon I came across another field, but unlike the endless field of trees, this one was flat.

There were wooden stakes jutting out of the ground with slips of paper attached to them, gently blowing in the breeze. All around me there were rows and rows of these stakes, each row with a different colored piece of paper attached. I walked to the closest one and stretched out the paper to read what it said. 'Ideas'. I pulled up the stake from the ground and saw what looked to be a carrot dangling from the end, its roots were long, and a lot of soil erupted from the ground as I pulled. I held the carrot closer to my face and heard the same hum coming from it as the pears were emitting. The carrot didn't glow like the pears but rather pulsed in the rhythm of a beating heart.

I placed the 'Idea" carrot back into the ground, taking care to return the soil back to its original condition, and proceeded to the next row of stakes. The color of the paper was a greenish blue and I stretched it out. 'Hopes' it read. I pulled it up as I had the carrot, and saw a radish at the end of the stake. The radish looked sick; its roots were beginning to shrivel up. I touched one of the roots with my fingers and it crumbled before me, falling to the ground. I picked up another one of the stakes in the row and saw another radish in the same condition, its once bright color faded to a dull white. I put them down, not replanting them as they were already dead, and went to another row.

I grabbed one of the papers from the stake and saw that the words read 'childhood'. I pulled up the stake, with a lot of effort, and saw a good looking, healthy potato swinging from the end of the stake. I turned the potato around and couldn't find any imperfections whatsoever. I listened for the hum, but there was none. The potato was neither emitting any light nor moving in any way. I held it up higher and noticed that there was no dirt on its skin. Perplexed, I touched it and a hollow sound came from the otherwise perfect plant. I ran my hand along its skin and it felt smooth, almost ceramic. I took the potato over to a rock and slammed it down. It shattered like glass, breaking apart and revealing the emptiness inside. The potato was not real. I wondered who would plant fake potatoes in the ground. And what about the paper on the stake? If this was indeed my mind, then was this saying that my childhood was fake like the potato? If that was the case, then what exactly about my childhood was a fake? Was the potato merely a single memory that wasn't real, somehow planted here by something else? I went back to the row and pulled up a few more stakes. They all had ceramic potatoes attached to them.

This was getting stranger by the minute. I put the potatoes down and left the field, not wanting to see what else was planted there.

I walked back through the field of pear trees, noticing that more fruit was falling from their branches as I passed through, and headed up a hill. I reached the top and looked out over the vast fields that each held different pieces of my mind. In the distance, I could make out a building of some kind. It looked to be a farmhouse, with a low picket fence all around it. I saw a barn behind the house and there were animals going in and out f the large door. There was also a man, or something, riding around on a tractor. I strained to see more clearly and it appeared that he was going in circles. As long as I was here, I should go check it out.

I started back down the small hill and passed through a field of corn that grew to the limits of the sky above. It was difficult to get through the corn maze and soon I found myself treading over the same ground. I tried a different route, but I ended up in the same spot every time. The green sky above was growing darker and I feared that I would be stuck in this field forever. I felt a hand on my shoulder and turned around to see Cigar Man standing behind me, looking extremely aggravated.

"Time to get up," he said and snapped his fingers.

I woke up and saw that we were back at the entrance to my subconscious.

"I hope you didn't lose your focus on the bag." He said. "We're running low on time here."

"I saw some pretty strange things," I said. "I think I know where the bag is. I saw what looked like a farmhouse with someone riding a tractor around in circles, but when I tried to get there, I got lost in a corn maze."

"You were pretty deep inside your subconscious," he said. "Its going to take us a long time to get there at the rate we're traveling. We should head out. Stay as close to me as you can and keep focusing on the bag. If we get separated once we enter, there's no way I can find you."

"You found me in the maze," I said.

Demons Within

"That was a dream, this is real. Let's go." He walked over to the entrance and slid a key out of his pocket. "This is the same key I gave you to find the book," he said. "It opens the gate to the darker, inner reaches of your mind." He put the key in the gate and turned it. The gate slid open slowly and a thick fog crept towards us, spreading out to cover the ground at our feet and wrapping around my ankles. "Stay close," he said, "Chaos is awake and knows we're coming for him." We crossed the threshold of the gate and he turned to close it quickly. "Don't want to let this shit get out, you know." He said. "It could really mess up your day." The gate slammed shut and we were inside, for better or worse.

I hadn't seen this part during my dream and I felt very timid walking though the dark entrance of my own mind. I looked up and saw the peak of the mountain that gave us so much trouble to begin with. It was no longer spewing fire, but instead pouring out thick blobs of the eerie, black ooze. The sky inside was no longer green, and I watched it change to a crimson red as we walked deeper into the woods ahead. The trees were dark and loomed ominously overhead, their branches reaching down with evil intent, and their bark growing like a vein filling with blood.

There were noises coming from the darkness, like animals running from bush to bush to gain a better view of the people who dared to tread on this sacred place. The sky completed its transformation and the crimson red began to rain down over us.

"Keep close," he said. "If we get separated, there is no hope. Concentrate on the bag."

We fought through the overgrowth and soon came upon a stream running through our path. The stream ran red like the sky and it seemed to be boiling, bubbling up deeper crimson from its bed. We went to the edge and stopped, looking for a way across. It was about fifteen feet to the other side and I didn't see anything we could use to make our crossing easier.

"We need to cross here," he said. "If we don't, we'll lose our way."

"Maybe I should just conjure up another rope," I said. "That worked last time."

"You don't control your subconscious mind," he said. "From this point on, we're on our own. Stay close to me and only look to the other side. Don't look at anything in the stream."

We stepped into the bubbling stream and I noticed that it ran cold. It was fairly deep and before long, our heads were the only things visible. I concentrated on the bag and stared at the waiting shore on the other side as we waded through the stream. Something started to pull on my ankle and soon it was hard to walk. It seemed to be pulling me away from the shoreline. I struggled against both the things pulling my legs and the increasing flow of the stream that had doubled its speed since we stepped in.

"I'm having a hard time walking," I screamed out to him.

"Concentrate on the bag and don't look into the stream," he said.

The force of the stream grew to the strength of rapids and the flow began to shoot over my head. I continued to struggle forward and had to use my arms to keep myself from going under. The things that were pulling on my legs began to bite and the pain shot from my ankles up to my head. My lungs strained to breathe in the air that had grown acrid, and I took on many mouthfuls of the thick, bubbling blood that kept pushing me deeper into the stream. I spat out the blood and it hit the surface of the stream and turned back to shoot into my eyes.

The cold blood blinded my vision and I felt my body going under the increasingly growing stream. I kicked at the things that were pulling me back and they granted me a temporary reprieve from their maddening force. I broke the surface of the stream and took in a deep breath of the acrid air whipping across its surface. I saw that the stream pushed me way off my course and I had to fight against the flow just to get back to the center. Cigar Man reached the shoreline and pulled himself out of the stream. I called out to him, but the blood flows smashed into my face and drown out my plea.

I saw something coming towards me in the flow and I attempted to swim around it. The object sped its approach and grabbed onto me, pulling me under with one swift motion. My body twisted around violently under the stream of blood and I felt my strength leaving my body. I tried to kick myself free from the thing, but the kicking only made it more determined to have its way with me. I opened my eyes to confront my attacker and met its cold stare. It was shark like in appearance, but much more vicious. Its rows of teeth seemed to have a life of their own, and each one curled around my leg and pulled me deeper into its mouth. I reached out to strike at it with my hands, but the creatures' tail whipped in front of it and slapped them away.

Its eyes grew with excitement as it chomped down further up my legs. I twisted my frame violently from side to side, but his grip tightened each time I moved. I looked to the bed of the stream and saw a rod jutting up from the earth. I reached for it, stretching out as far as I was able, and ripped it from its resting place. I took the rod in both hands and jabbed it directly between the creatures' eyes. The rod struck him and pierced its skin, sinking deep into its head. The creature shuddered and then exploded, sending me shooting up to the surface. I broke through the surface and gasped in a lungful of air. I was way off course now and all I wanted to do was get out of the stream.

I swam harder than I ever had before and reached the shoreline. I grabbed onto it and, with every ounce of strength I could muster, pulled myself free from the stream. I rolled onto my back and began to cough out the lungful of blood I had taken in. The crimson sky rained down on me and I felt the coolness of the rain run down my face. I took in a few more breaths and got to my feet. I looked back to the other side of the stream and saw that the trees seemed to have grown out more since we left. Their branches now fully reached the ground and they were growing towards the edge of the stream.

I turned around and what I saw astonished me. There was a young boy sitting on a rock looking at me with curious eyes. He was dressed in a white shirt and tie with short pants and black shoes. He was holding one of those paddles with the rubber ball attached and played with it while he watched me regain my footing. He had a look of sadness in his eyes and his face and arms were covered with purple bruises. I started towards him and he jumped down off the rock and ducked behind it, cowering in fear.

"It's O.K.," I said, "I'm not going to hurt you. I took a few tentative steps towards the boy, my palms outstretched to him as I walked. The boy cowered down more as I approached and then he threw his toy at me and ran into the woods. I started after him and soon I was deep inside the woods. The landscape gave no indication which way he ran, so I had to rely on instinct. I followed a path through the trees and came upon a clearing in the woods. The boy was sitting in the center of the clearing, his head down in his hands, and was crying. I walked to him slowly, not wanting to scare him off again, and sat down beside him. I put my hand on his shoulder and he cringed back away from me, curing into a fetal position.

"I'm not going to hurt you," I said. "Why are you upset?"

He raised his head from his hands and looked into my eyes. I could feel the pain and fear coming from deep inside him. I put my hands out and turned them over, exposing my palms.

"See," I said, "I'm not hiding anything from you. What's your name?"

"My name is Paul," he said.

"Nice to meet you Paul, I'm John."

"I know who you are," he replied, "you're the reason I'm here."

"Have we met before Paul?" I asked

"No," he said, "but you know me very well."

I looked at him, perplexed. I had no memory of him, so how could I know him well? I reached into my pocket and pulled out a handful of candy. Where had that come from? I reached out and offered some to Paul. He took a piece and put it in his mouth, eyeing me cautiously as he did. It was then that I remembered where I had seen him. He was the kid in my dreams with my parents. But why was he here in my subconscious? And why was he all bruised and beaten?

"Tell me what happened to you Paul."

He looked away from me and I heard him sobbing. I reached out to console him, but he jumped to his feet to avoid my touch.

"It's O.K. Paul," I said, "I'm your friend."

"You're not my friend. You're the one who did this to me."

I felt a wave of anger come over Paul and he clenched his fists at his side.

"Go away," he said. "Never come here again."

"Tell me what happened and I'll go away, I promise."

Flying High

He turned around and stared into my eyes and I felt his rage directing itself at me. I got to my feet and walked over to him, still raising my hands over my head so he could see I meant him no harm.

"I can't tell you," he said. "I can only show you. Then you need to leave, o.k.?"

"That's a deal Paul," I said. He reached out and took my hand and led me out of the clearing.

Vegan Vegas

Paul led me through the dense woods with the expertise of someone who had traveled this path many times before. Along the way, we passed through a few sections where the ground was almost impassible. There was one section in particular where the roots of the trees grew out of the ground and into each other, creating tall obstacles that we needed to climb in order to continue on our path. Paul was an excellent climber and scaled the roots with the dexterity of a gymnast. It had been a long time since I had to climb a tree and there was no way that I could keep up with this little bundle of energy.

After one particularly tall root, I called out to Paul so we could take a break. He made his way back to me and together we sat on top of the outcropping roots and looked out into the distance together. I felt a connection to Paul, something I couldn't quite get a handle on. I was sure that he had a lot of information but found myself struggling to find a way to ask him. Paul must have sensed my quandary and decided to speak first.

"You're scared aren't you?" He asked.

"Yea," I replied, "maybe a little bit." He looked at me and I knew I couldn't hide the truth from him. He pointed to me and laughed, but I didn't feel any joy coming from him.

"You should be more than a little afraid," he said. "If you're not, then you'll never find what you're looking for." He jumped off the root we were sitting on and ran up to the tree that it created. "I know a secret," he said. "Do you want to hear it?"

"Yes," I said, "tell me what it is."

"You're gonna die," he laughed and scampered to another root.

"Everyone dies Paul. There's not much I can do to change that."

"Yes there is," he said. "But you won't make it in time. I've seen it happen."

I jumped off the root and went over to him. He was dancing around the tree singing to himself. "You're gonna diiiie, you won't live no moooore, Chaos is waiting to settle the scooore."

I stopped in my tracks at the sound of that name. "Paul," I said, "what do you know about Chaos?"

He continued his dance and kept on singing, "You're gonna diiiie, Chaos will wiiiin, he will expose you for your mortal siiiin."

I wasn't going to get through to him this way so I decided to change tactics. "Paul, have you ever been to the garden with the seeds in the ground?" Paul stopped dancing and looked at me; his face showing an expression of surprise at the mention of the garden. He stepped away from the tree, came over to me, and scowled.

"How do you know about my garden?" he demanded. "No one knows about that, especially you!"

"I was there," I said. "Tell me about the potatoes. Why did they break so easily?"

I felt Paul's anger grow and he started to stomp around. "Why did you go there? You're not supposed to see." He picked up a stick and threw it at my head. I ducked as the stick whizzed by, just missing its intended target. Paul was mad that he missed and picked up another stick and hurled it at my head. I wasn't quick enough and the stick hit the side of my head, piercing the skin. I put my hand to where the stick hit and there was a small trickle of blood beginning to come from the wound. I got to my feet and went after him, but he quickly retreated up the tree.

"That wasn't very nice Paul," I said. "I didn't do anything to hurt you."

"You're not supposed to see," he replied, and started throwing some acorns from the tree down at me. I put my hand over my head to shield it from his fitful wrath and decided that enough was enough. I climbed up the tree as acorns continued to rain down at me and soon I reached the branch where he was sitting. He tried to get away, but I grabbed his ankle and forced him to sit back down.

"I don't want to hurt you," I said, "but I will if you keep this up for much longer." Paul's eyes widened at the threat and he tucked his body back into a fetal position and began to cry. I released my hold on him and he pushed himself closer to the tree. "I won't hurt you Paul, I promise. Just don't throw anything else o.k.?" He raised his head and looked to see if I was sincere. "I promise I won't go back to your garden. I just want to know what it is. Can you tell me that much please?"

He leaned against the tree and sniffled, wiping the snot away from his nose with his arm. "O.K.," he said. "I'll tell you, but you promise you won't go back there?"

"If you tell me what I need to know, I promise."

He got to his feet and jumped down from the branch. I followed, preferring to climb down instead of jump. Paul sat down on the ground and motioned for me to join him, which I did. He looked like a kid who got caught doing something wrong and was now waiting for his parents to dole out his punishment.

"That is my secret place," he said. "I go there sometimes when I need to get away." His eyes were full of emotion and I could see the tears starting to return. "Now that you know where it is, I can't go back there."

"Why can't you go back Paul?" I asked.

"It won't be safe anymore," he replied. "He'll wreck it more now that he knows how to get in safely. The birds used to keep him out but now he has a way around them."   " Who'll wreck it Paul?" I asked, not sure that I wanted to hear the answer.

"Chaos," he said. "He's gonna come back and wreck it all and I'll have no place to go." This place was getting stranger by the minute. I didn't remember seeing any birds when I was there. Paul did know Chaos though and maybe he could tell me where he was, or maybe he knew about the bag. Either way, I needed to get some more information from this kid before he decided to shut up for good.

"Tell me about the birds Paul," I said. "Chaos seems too big to let a few birds get in his way."

"He hates the birds," Paul said. "They peck at his eyes and eat his skin. Chaos gets hungry and goes to eat the pears, but the birds have their nests in the trees and they chase him away." He looked down at the ground and his voice became softer. I had to lean forward to hear what he was saying. "When the birds fight him, some of the pears fall off the trees and die. If he keeps it up, there won't be anymore pears left and the garden will die."

I remembered the pear trees he was speaking of; their giant fruits glowed brightly from those trees. That explains why the ones on the side of the hill didn't glow. They were probably connected to the rest of the garden through the roots. What about the fields of veggies though? How did they play into the scheme of things here?

"How often does Chaos come to take the pears Paul?" I asked.

"All the time," he replied. "The birds lose a lot of their numbers during the battles with Chaos and that makes it easier for him to get the pears. I get sad when the pears die. And scared too."

I felt his fear growing inside and put my hand on his shoulder to reassure him. This time he didn't pull away, but curled up under my arm. His fear passed to me, but I found the strength to fend it off for a time. We sat there for a while not saying much of anything and I felt the connection between us growing stronger. After some time passed, I confronted Paul with a few more questions that needed answers.

"Paul," I said, "I know this is hard for you, but I need to know about the potatoes in the garden. Please tell me why they weren't real. This is really important so think about it before you answer."

He was very quiet for a while and I could see him struggling with is thoughts. I knew he wanted to tell me the truth, but I felt the conflict in him as he was weighing his loyalties. I gave him a few minutes to come to terms with the question and as I went to repeat it, he answered.

"There used to be wonderful potatoes in my garden," he said. "I had the best garden ever. But then Chaos showed up and things started dying. I kept watering and feeding them, but he changed the sun so they wouldn't grow anymore. I saved a few of them but the rest died. After that, he left me alone for awhile. I made a mold of one of the potatoes I saved and created some more I could plant where the others died. I filled back all the holes so no one would know the difference. After I was done with the potatoes, I went to take care of the radishes. They were in really bad shape and some of them were dying like the potatoes did. I did everything I could to save them and now it's up to Chaos whether they live or die."

Things were starting to clear up now and I took a few minutes to process what Paul just said. The potatoes that were labeled childhood were all gone and he replaced them with fake ones. He did say that he saved a few of them and now they were hidden away. I would need to get a look at these, as I was sure that they would go a long way to understanding. The radishes that were marked 'hopes' were safe for now, but a few of them didn't make it. I saw the roots myself so I knew this to be true. The pears were a new development and if I wanted to stop Chaos, I had to know fully how they affected me. According to Paul, I didn't have much more time until there were no more pears. He seemed to have the same feeling that Cigar Man had when it came to time here, that it was quickly running out.

"The carrots seem to be doing very well," I said to Paul. "What's keeping them safe from Chaos?"

"They grow more and more every minute," he said, "and I can't keep up with them. I don't think Chaos likes carrots to much. He's never even tried to take any."

That information was key. The carrots were labeled 'ideas' and Paul said that they were always growing. Perhaps this was just the kind of information I needed. If I kept ideas growing, maybe they could shield the rest of the garden from Chaos. There was only one problem, ideas grew underground and there was only so much land for them to use. No, I needed to concentrate my efforts on saving the pears. Chaos, for some reason, liked those most of all. If I could find a way to keep them on the trees, then nothing else would die.

"Paul, why do you think Chaos likes the pears so much?" I asked.

"That's easy," he said, "they control everything else and they're sweet. I like the way they glow and hum. It's very relaxing. Maybe that's why the birds like it there so much."

What can you tell me about the birds?" I asked. Paul got back to his feet and started skipping around.

"I'm bored," he said. "You ask too many questions. I want to go now. You still want to know what happened to me right" I felt his feelings change to concern. He thought I would leave him. This feeling was very strong in him. I wonder if he's had someone leave him before.

"O.K. Paul," I said, "we'll go. However, this time slow down a little. I can't keep up with you."

"Deal," he said, and we were off again on the strange trip through my inner mind.

We went through one more section of woods with the tree roots sticking far out of the ground and then we came to another clearing. The grass was lush and Paul took off his shoes to run through it. He looked like he was having a lot of fun, so I too removed my shoes. The ground was cool and the tall grass tickled my toes. The green sky was not as ominous here and if it weren't for its color, it would be normal. I caught up to Paul as he was catching his breath.

"Where are we going?" I asked him. "How much farther until we arrive?"

Demons Within

"We need to make a stop first," he said. "We're almost there. If you look hard, you can see it."

I looked in the direction he was pointing and could make out the outline of a house. It was a familiar house, but I didn't remember where I saw it before. We took off towards the house and it grew larger as we approached. The ground beneath us, once cool and refreshing, turned rocky and unyielding. I stopped to put back on my shoes as Paul continued to sprint towards the house. I caught up to him at the fence surrounding the house and then realized where I had seen it before. It was the farmhouse from the garden. I took a step back and saw the familiar barn in the back, just as it had been in the dream. Paul opened the door and motioned me inside.

As soon as I crossed the threshold, the house took on a different feel. I knew this house even better than just from a dream. My family lived in this house in back when I was younger. The last time I was here I was only five years old, but the memories of that time came rushing back to me as if it was only yesterday. Paul ran upstairs and told me he'd be down in a minute. I took that opportunity to explore the rest of the house. I walked into the kitchen and saw that it hadn't changed from what I remembered. There was an old, small table with three chairs against the far wall, and the legs of the chairs had wheels on the ends. I remembered rolling around the kitchen when my mother used to bake, and the smells of that time began to fill the room.

I walked through the kitchen and peered through the serving hole in the wall to the dining room. It was the same in there as well. My mother always kept that room in immaculate condition and we only used it on special occasions. I ran from there to the main living room. All of the furniture was the same; my fathers' old recliner sat against the wall, still needing repairs; the old, stiff yellow couch stood against the opposite wall with the same familiar butt indents on its cushions. I walked over to the fireplace and checked out the items on the mantle. The old clock ticked reliably, noting the time to be two o'clock on the dot. The clock cranked its gears and the bells started ringing. The sound filled the room and I waited for the sound that always followed. The grandfather clock in the foyer always ran a minute or two behind this clock and when the bells finished, it took control of the air, chiming proudly.

I looked along the rows of knickknacks that my mother kept on the mantle and saw the pictures. In the center was my parents wedding photo standing tall above the rest. There were a few smaller photos of their parents arranged neatly in front of it. There was my great grandfathers' photo, clouded over by the poor lenses of the time. Then I saw what I was looking for; the picture of my first day at school. I picked it up, held it closer, and saw that something wasn't right. My parents were there, as I remembered, but I wasn't in the picture. They were leaning down over a young kid, but it wasn't me that their attention focused on; it was Paul. I dropped the picture and it hit the floor, shattering the glass. I heard a shrill cry coming from behind me and turned to see its source. Standing in the doorway with his fists raised and his mouth hung open in a scream was Paul.

"Noooooooooo," he screamed, and ran over to pick up the fallen picture. He grabbed the picture and started to pick up the pieces of broken glass from the floor. I bent over to help him, but he shoved me away angrily. I fell over and went to get up, but he shoved me down again screaming, "Get out of here!"

"I'm sorry about the picture Paul," I said. "I didn't mean to drop it, honestly."

"You get out of here now," he said. "You ruined everything now, just go." He plopped to the floor and started crying as he attempted to piece the glass frame back together. I stood up, looked down at him, and started to cry. I tried to control the flow of emotions forcing their way to the front, but it was no use. I put my head in my hands and wept as I went out the door.

When I walked out of the house, the air grew immediately colder. I raised my head from my hands and looked into the sky. Gone was the pleasant green that Paul and I had run through the cool grass underneath, replaced now with a darker, angrier sky that was filling with even darker clouds. I heard the distant rumbling of thunder as I walked to the back of the house towards the barn. The thunder grew closer and soon it was directly overhead, booming loud enough to shake the ground at my feet. I picked up my pace as the ground continued to shake from the thundering clouds above and soon I was at the door to the barn. I fumbled for the latch and eventually it unhinged. The wind blew in from the sky violently and caused the door to fling open and bang into the side of the barn. I stepped into the barn and the door slammed shut, catching the latch.

It took a few minutes for my eyes to become accustomed to the lack of light in the barn, the only source coming from an exhaust hole cut into the wall above. I heard some rustling coming from the darkness in front of me and slowly made my way to the wall. The rustling sound grew louder and I felt my fear returning. I didn't know what was in here, but now that the door was locked, I would just have to wait and hope for the best. I slid carefully along the wooden wall, feeling my way with my hands, and felt many splinters piercing their way through the skin on my palms. The rustling stopped and then I heard something else, like a sniffling sound. Whatever was rustling around was now trying to catch my scent. I placed my hand over my mouth and slowed my breathing in a feeble attempt to hide my whereabouts. I kept to the wall and continued to use it as my guide as the sniffling sound got closer. I could smell the thing in front of me, it was very close now, and my breathing quickened. A loud bark echoed through the barn and I felt the thing pounce on me, knocking me to the ground.

I hit the soft earth and raised my hands to protect my head. The thing started licking my arms and I could smell its breath. It smelled like peanut butter. I opened my eyes and saw my attacker. It was my dog Rusty from when I was a kid. He saw my eyes open and barked happily, backing away so I could get to my feet. I got up and he jumped up for me to pet his ears. He was very happy to see me and his long tail started to whip my legs. I calmed him down while I wondered what he was doing in the barn. My eyes were now used to the light and I walked around the barn to see what else was waiting for me to find.

Rusty ran ahead of me to the back of the barn and started barking excitedly. I hurried back to meet him, but tripped over a small trunk in the middle of the barn. I robbed my ankle and could feel the welt already beginning to form. When my foot hit the trunk, it popped open its lid. I bent down and looked inside. The trunks' contents consisted of mostly dusty looking photo albums. I reached down and opened the nearest one. The pictures inside were of scenes from my life. They weren't pictures in the normal sense of the word, and as I examined them more closely, they began to move. Each picture not only contained a scene, but also the event associated with it as well. The first picture I saw was Christmas morning. I was grabbing a present from under the tree and my parents were looking on with great excitement in their eyes. I watched with excitement as the picture showed me the events unfold. It was like watching a home movie. I flipped through the book and saw that every Christmas from my life was contained in this single book, each picture representing a different year.

I put the book down and picked up the next one. I dusted off the cover and it read, 'Birthdays'. Opening the book, it read just like the Christmas one and I watched myself blow out the candles at my third birthday party as the dog jumped on the table to take the first piece of cake. The remaining books also had labels on them describing different events in my life. There was a separate book for each level of schooling: elementary, secondary, college. I found it amazing that these albums existed. The dog barked at me and I went over to see what was exciting him so much. Behind an old tractor, I saw some of the items I thought I lost in the fire at my house. My baseball cards were all here along with all my Red Sox paraphernalia. Boy, I was glad the dog got my attention and I was able to see all of these things.

That's when a ton of questions showered over me. Why were these items locked up in the barn? Why were the things that happened to me placed neatly into albums and locked away in a trunk? Why was Paul in the pictures on the mantle with my parents? Why wasn't I in those very same pictures? I felt very dizzy and sat down on the trunk. Rusty came over and placed his head on my lap. This trip to my childhood home hadn't answered many questions, and the discovery of the items in the barn only created more. The wind outside picked up and the walls of the barn began to shake from the force. I heard a cackling laugh coming from the loft of the barn. It was a very evil laugh.

I walked over to the ladder that led to the loft and shook it to see if it was secure. It was, so I decided to climb up and see who or what was laughing down at me. I reached the top of the ladder and looked around the loft. The laugh seemed to be coming from behind a bale of hay against the wall. I pulled myself up and slowly walked towards the hay, the laughter growing louder as I got closer. I reached the haystack and slid silently around the corner to confront the heckler hidden in the dark corner. I paused just before turning the corner fully, drawing in a few deep breaths to calm my nerves before I took on this latest challenge. I counted off, one...two...three, and then jumped behind the haystack and screamed to scare whatever was lurking there.

My scream failed to scare the person, as he just sat there looking at me with a demented stare. I saw a younger version of myself sitting in the corner, stroking what looked like a pear, while he laughed with the tone of someone who had lost his

Vegan Vegas

mind. I shook off my initial shock and walked slowly towards him, my hands above my head to show no harm.

"It's o.k." I said, "no one here is going to hurt you." He looked back down and continued to stroke the pear as if it were a new puppy. I crept closer still, using calming gestures in an attempt to keep him calm. "Why are you locked in the barn?" I asked. He stopped stroking the pear and looked up. I could see great sadness in his eyes and he looked at me with pity.

"They said they'd be right back," he said. "We were in the field and they came and started taking the pears off the tree. We told them to stop, but they took us and all of our things and locked us in here." He held up the pear and extended it out. "This is the last one. I keep it alive by talking to it and telling it that soon I'll put it back in the tree so it can grow as big as the other ones were."

Thats Just Nasty

The pear was still glowing a bit, flickering on and off, but not with the same intensity as the ones I had seen before. One good note, it was still humming which meant that it wasn't dead yet. I sat down beside the scared boy and touched the pear. As soon as I touched it, the glow intensified and started to pulse brightly. The hum also grew in volume and before long its sound drowned all others n the room. I could here the dog starting to bark from beneath us, the sound obviously didn't agree with his ears. I took the pear from the boy and held it up high. The light coming from the fruit shot up to the ceiling of the barn, filling the room with an eerie, green glow. The fruits hum started pulsing along with the light and I felt it work its way through my body.

The scared boy got up and watched the light shooting across the barn and I could feel his level of excitement growing. I looked at the fruit in my hand and watched as it grew larger right before my eyes. A concentrated beam of light shot from the center of the fruit and hit the ceiling above. I looked up and saw a scene beginning to take shape in the light. I saw myself in the light battling with Chaos.

The scene grew and soon I found myself a part of it; the scene causing the barn to disappear. I was watching the battle from the prospective of on onlooker, gazing down from above the destruction. The fight was happening in a large field and I saw many bodies strewn across its bloodied ground. There seemed to be two major groups fighting each other with Chaos leading the charge against my group. The combatants were dressed in medieval attire, body armor and swords with people on horses wielding large, bloody axes and long, gleaming swords, and they were charging at each other with blood curdling screams.

The bodies that had fallen were twisted and bloodied. I saw a few that were still living; their screams and moans lost by the overwhelming sounds of the battle. The armies of Chaos consisted of diseased looking people with lifeless eyes. They appeared to be controlled by the demon himself. Chaos would point in a certain direction and a pack of them would blindly go to fight to their deaths. My armies were outnumbered ten to one, but fighting with the ferociousness of a determined cause. The tide of the battle seemed to be turning in favor of my armies and the undead turned tail and started back over the hill from where they had charged.

I focused in on myself; sitting on top of a horse with my sword raised towards the retreating army, and saw that I was reciting from a book held in my hand. As I quoted from the book, my dead soldiers rose up from there place of death and turned to give chase to the retreating forces. The newly arisen soldiers were moving slowly towards the retreating army, as they had to stop to retrieve a limb or two that had been torn from their bodies.

The armies of Chaos disappeared over the top of the hill and my armies were quickly beginning to overtake some of the wounded. The skies thundered and blood rained down over the battlefield causing it to become slick. As my army climbed the hill, they started slipping over the bloodied ground and each other and soon they were all entangled in a large heap, each struggling to regain their footing and get to the top of the hill. A loud cry made its way from the other side of the hill and then I saw Chaos leading his armies back over the top to overtake my fallen soldiers. My soldiers fought fiercely, but they were no match for the wave of forces coming over the hill. Those who could regain some kind of footing saw that it was a lost cause and quickly turned tail to retreat.

The scene disappeared and soon I found myself back in the barn with the scared boy standing at my side. The pear's glow returned to its previous state and the hum coming from inside it quieted until it was barely audible. I turned to the boy and handed the pear back to him. He shook his head and said, "No, you're the one who should keep it safe. I can't fight him like you. Take it so he won't find it when he comes back."

I lowered my hand and put the pear on the haystack. "What do you know about Paul?" I asked. "You know, the boy who lives in the house."

He cowered down and said, "Paul has been here as long as I have. I use to live in that house until Chaos came and put me in here. Paul came to the house, took all of my things and packed them into boxes, and put them in here with me. He said that if I was good, he would let me live for a while."

"Do you know where he came from?" I asked.

"I don't know," he replied, "but I've always known he was here. Until recently, I only felt him but now I can't feel anything. He left my memories but to me, they're only pictures that have no meaning."

"Were you there when he planted the seeds in the field?" I asked.

"That's my field," he said. "I planted everything in there. Everything was growing really well until he started replacing things."

I remembered that Paul said that Chaos changed the sun so things wouldn't grow anymore. He said that he replaced them so no one would know the difference. "Paul said that Chaos started killing everything and he was trying to save them. He seemed really sad when the potatoes died and planted more to replace them."

"Chaos didn't kill the potatoes," he said. "They're all in the box with the pictures. I'm sorry, but I'm very tired now and I want to go to sleep."

"Try to stay awake for as long as you can," I said. "I'll come back for you, I promise." I held up the pear over his head with both hands and squeezed it as hard as I could. A trickle of juice made its way from one of the pores and dripped down onto the boy. He lifted his head and opened his mouth to take in the sweet nectar. "This should help keep you awake and safe for a while. Whatever you do, don't let anyone take the potatoes out of the barn. Bury them deep in the ground if you have to." I put the pear back in my pocket and turned to leave.

"Please don't forget me," he said. "You're the only other one who knows I'm here."

"Don't worry," I said, "nothing can make me forget myself, no matter how hard it tries."

I walked to the barn door and it opened before I could try to release the lock. As I walked out of the barn, Rusty barked and ran out ahead of me.

"Take good car of Rusty," the young me said. The door to the barn slammed shut and I followed the dog along the path that I hoped would lead to regaining my sanity.

The path the dog had chosen led us back to the field of dying vegetables. I looked across and saw that the rows of carrots had started to grow over the others in the field. The dog didn't intend to go through the field, but instead up the hill and into a lush valley of flowers below. I followed as close as I could, but my two legs were no match for the four of the dog. I got to the edge of the flowered field and saw him racing through it, barking happily. There were many different breeds of flowers here and they all seemed to be thriving in this strange environment. The smells all blended together, creating a fragrance that had a very hypnotic effect. I walked through the flowers and felt my head get dizzy, the pollen worked its way through my lungs, and soon it was difficult to breathe. I staggered to the ground and fell into a deep, relaxed sleep.

No dreams made their way into my head during my sleep, but I felt my body being pulled along the field. All of the wonderful scents of the various flowers continued to permeate my thoughts and senses and I found my level of happiness growing. My head was a blur of thoughts and they were all of great importance in my life. The memories seemed to merge into each other until the only thing that remained was a single feeling: joy. I didn't want this feeling to end but soon my sleep was rudely interrupted by the sound of the dog barking at my feet.

I opened my eyes and saw that he had dragged me through the field and we were now on its edge. The landscape took on an entirely different look and the happiness that had only recently encompassed my whole self quickly retreated into my mind until the only thing left was a feeling of sorrow and loss. I got to my feet and looked around at my newest surroundings. The flowers were gone, replaced by weeds and brown, dying grass. The trees that I could see were dying as well; their limbs gray and brittle. The roots of the trees jutted from the round and I could see that they were reaching to the sky, begging for relief. Corpses of birds that had fallen from the sky covered the ground and I could see that something had been feeding on their guts. There had to be hundreds of dead birds, maybe even thousands.

I walked along the trail of death and came across another sight that made my stomach turn. There were body parts scattered all over the ground. They looked like they had been torn from their hosts' bodies and crushed deep into the ground. I saw a leg sticking out of the ground with some of its pelvic bone still attached, dangling from a piece of muscle. I bent over and puked, my last meal spreading itself on the bloody ground creating a putrid pool of colors that somehow fit the scene perfectly.

Looking up from the puddle I created, I saw Rusty sitting with his back to me, ears cocked. Something in the dead field was scaring him, as he had begun to whine nervously. I lifted my head up fully and peered out over the field. Overgrown grass and weeds spread out over the entire landscape. At the very edge of the growth, I could see a small clearing with what appeared to be a boat resting in the center of a small hill. This was definitely out of place. The dog continues to whine and bark in the direction of the clearing and I decided to go check it out.

The dead grass was brittle and cracked at our feet as we made our way through the field. Along the way, I saw a few more bodies strewn across the ground, though not as many as I had seen at the edge of the flowers. It's as though these people were running from something; something that scared them to death. The bodies here were whole, not torn apart as before, but something about them wasn't natural. The bodies were on the ground with their heads raised to the sky. There arms were raised over their heads as if shielding them from something coming at them from above. The mouths of the dead were wide, there screams forever displayed for all to see. Walking through them, I saw that the birds hadn't picked at all of them yet as some still had eyes in their heads. Their eyes were even more disturbing than their open mouths. They were frozen open in the widest possible position. I didn't really want to see anymore, but I had to find out what happened here.

I walked over to the corpse of one of the fallen that still was blessed with its eyes. Its skin was dissolving away from the bones and hung loosely, letting the wind tear it away. Its face was more intact than its body, somewhat, and I saw that it was covered with seeping wounds and boils. Whatever killed it didn't do it quickly. This poor bastard probably suffered for a few minutes until the life was literally scared out of him. I peered into his eyes, which were a deep black, and saw something stuck in the center of the pupils. I reached out to touch it and discovered that it didn't rub away. It was coming from inside the eye, almost like a reflection in a mirror that didn't disappear. I squatted down to get a closer look at the reflection.

What I saw in that dead persons eyes made me almost as frightened as he was when it attacked. I saw a winged beast swooping down from the sky with it's' mouth open wide. The beast seemed to be breathing something into himself as he grew closer to the ground. I couldn't make out the full picture from this angle so I decided to do something that under normal circumstance I would have considered atrocious. I reached into the dead mans skull and pulled his eye from its socket, a loud slurping sound accompanying my action.

I held the eye closer to my face and I could feel its nerves wrapping them-selves around my hand. I looked deep into the blackness of the pupil and tried to make out the whole scene. The eyes came to life and I was granted the opportunity to see and feel what this dead soul did just before he died.

I saw through the dead mans' eyes as he ran through the dead field away from the screams of his fallen comrades. I could hear the sounds of flesh being torn away from bone and the repulsive noise of loud cracking as those same bones were snapped away from their bodies. My heart rate sped up to match that of the scared young man as he screamed and ran from his impending fate. A few others bumped into him as they rushed past and he was thrown to the ground next to a severed leg. He screamed out and turned away from the repulsive limb as a loud, wailing squeal shot into his ears from above. I looked up with the man and saw the beast rise up from the field, his jowls filled with blood and bits of shattered bone. The beast took in a deep breath, creating a great force of suction that almost pulled us from the ground. I saw through the mans' eyes as he raised his hands over his head as the beast flew down to where he had fallen.

The beasts' inward breath caused everything around us to uproot and shot into the sky towards its mouth. I saw limbs fly up but they were immediately spat out of the mouth of the beast. The man on the ground continued to scream and watched with horror as the very souls of his fallen brethren were sucked into the beast above. They didn't go willingly, but were instead torn from their masters in the most violent way. The beast turned his sights on the fallen man and I felt a ray of heat envelop the ground around us. The man wailed out in pain as his skin began to boil, causing it to drip off his bones. He opened his mouth wider and the beast flew into hit and I felt the mans soul being ripped from his chest. His body began to convulse and writhe in pain as the beast wanted to get every bit of the mans soul before moving on to the next victim. I felt nauseous and before I knew it, a stream of puke shot from my mouth into the sky. The man puked also, but his was not from revulsion. He was puking the beast free to rein his terror on another unsuspecting soul. I watched the beast fly from the now dead mans mouth and swoop into the air with a shrill cry of victory. The dead mans eyes were now still, and the beast soon moved out of his range of sight. Although I could no longer feel the man alive inside me, I could still hear the screams of those who watched this happen and were now becoming victims themselves.

My conscious self returned and I was now staring back at the reflection of the scene in the eye. I lowered my hand, dropped the eye to the ground, and watched as it rolled lopsidedly down the path. I had just witnessed a horrific battle scene from the eyes of a now dead man and realized what it meant. This man was one of my soldiers in the battle against Chaos. He must have been one of those who were able to free themselves from the bloody ground of the hill and was retreating when he was struck down.

I got up and saw the dog ahead of me on the trail. He barked and chased himself in a circle, and then he ran up the trail out of sight.

The dog was running at full speed towards the clearing and I had to pause a few times to catch me breath along the way. At my last pause before entering the clearing, I saw the dog stop just before he stepped into the new grass of the clearing and lay down. Finally, I could take a well-needed rest and absorb all of the new things I had learned since entering the strange and macabre world of my own mind. I found a rock that looked butt friendly and sat down to reflect.

So many things were going on at once that I didn't think I would make it through the rest of the trip. So far, I had actually entered my own mind, traveled back to my childhood home only to discover that someone named Paul had replaced me, saw my memories replaced and my hopes dying, met myself stroking a pear, died in a battle with Chaos, and now I was following a dog that died thirty years ago. Last but not least, I lost the person I had come here with; the only other person to know how to get out of here in one piece. He did tell me to stay close, but the blood stream wasn't my fault. Besides, it was his fault that I was in here in the first place. If he had just told me the truth from the beginning, I wouldn't have attacked him and we wouldn't be trapped here.

Well, there was no use fretting over events that I couldn't change. I felt that I was getting closer to something, but finding out what that something was before it was too late continued to torment my thoughts. I know that I couldn't change anything in my subconscious mind, but maybe there was a way to force my rational mind into it in order to help unravel this mystery. To do that, I needed to find Cigar Man again. Surely he knew more about my mind than I did, as he was a product of it, and would know everything that it was capable of doing.

I got up off the rock, which actually wasn't butt friendly at all, and headed over to the dog. He didn't move as I approached the edge of the clearing and as I stepped over him, he grabbed onto my pant leg and growled.

"Whoa," I said, "easy there fella. You led me here so let's go."

The dog obviously disagreed with my plan to enter the clearing and pulled my pant leg more viciously, causing it to tear. I continued to chastise him as I tried to free my leg from his grasp, but he continued to pull. I heard the seam of my pants ripping up my leg and started to kick my leg harder before he tore them off my legs. I managed to free my leg, but the dog had won the battle. A large piece of fabric from my pants hung from his mouth, its edges ragged and soaked with drool. He shook the piece in his mouth and the slobber rained out of it over my head. Apparently, he didn't like the flavor too much and spat it out. I scolded him just like I did when he was alive, and reached down to retrieve his ill-gotten souvenir.

I picked the piece off the ground and shook it over his mouth to scold him when I noticed something strange. The fabric of the material had changed from its original state and instead of holding a piece of cotton chinos it felt like I was holding a piece of slick rubber. I rubbed the fabric in my hand and felt the rubbery texture turn to a slimy material that started to run down my arm. I jerked my hand up and released it just as the transformation of the material was complete. The slick ooze fell to the ground with a splat and spread out, creating a black circle on the ground.

I watched the circle grow until it was the size of a manhole cover. The dog barked and started to chase his tail around again. The sounds around us grew eerily quiet and I felt the air thicken until it was the consistency of heavy syrup. The dogs' actions slowed as he fought against the resistance of the thickening air and I felt its weight pushing me more solidly against the ground. I lifted my arm and could actually see the air moving around it, creating thick ripples in its wake. The air was turning into a thick liquid and each movement created ripples through the muck. The dogs' movement stopped and he started to float up. I could see the panicked look in his eyes as his body turned in the soupy air. I stood perfectly still and then felt my body lifting off the solid ground and into the air.

The soup was growing thicker and I was getting farther from the familiar safety of the ground. I struggled to move but it was like swimming through mud. I shot out my arms and legs and tried to swim back towards the ground. Each stroke took a lot of strength and it took six or seven repetitions to make any downward progress at all. The dog must've had the same idea and his little legs were paddling like crazy to get him back to safety. We both struggled against the increasing pressure around us and eventually I could touch the edge of the ground with the tips of my fingers. I tried to grip the ground to pull myself down with no success when I noticed the black circle had continued to grow.

I used what little leverage I had with my fingers on the ground to push myself towards the hole, each move more difficult than the last. It seemed to take forever, but soon I was at its edge. The force in the air began to crush all of its weight against me and I was soon flattened back to the ground, my arms still holding onto the edge of the hole. My ears began to fill with liquid as the pressure increased, the pain becoming unbearable. I lifted my head with immense difficulty and saw the back half of Rusty sticking out of the hole. The pressure had trapped his legs to the ground and now it was forcing them deeper into it, creating an indentation in the surface. I grabbed onto the edge of the hole and pulled myself along the surface of the ground feeling my chest burrow through the unyielding soil. My head broke the surface of the hole and I looked down into its darkness, not really wanting to see what was there, but the increasing pressure left me no other choice.

The pressure continued to force my body into the ground and I could no longer hold my head above the hole. I took a deep breath, closed my eyes, and threw my head into the hole in an attempt to find safety from the pressure that meant to crush me to death. I broke through the hole's surface and immediately noticed that there was no pressure or resistance to my actions there. My upper body was free to move at will, but my legs were still being crushed from above. I gripped onto the side of the hole and pulled myself into it with all my strength. My legs slid painfully along

Demons Within

the surface of the ground as they moved slowly into the hole to rejoin the rest of my body. The pressure seemed to be pulling them back and soon a tug of war match broke out between us, I gained and inch, it took it back.

My strength was almost exhausted and my grip on the edge of the hole soon gave out. The force began to pull my body from the safety of the hole and I struggled to regain at least a partial grip. I was almost completely out when something reached up from inside the hole and pulled me back away from the force outside. There was a brief struggle, as both sides wanted to win the tug battle, and then I felt the pressure release its grip on my legs. The force inside the hole pulled me through in a single motion just as the air crashed into the ground above; creating a violent shockwave that blasted into the hole and dragged me along for a bumpy ride.

My body twisted violently from side to side as the force of the shockwave propelled me forward through the darkness of the hole. I felt my skin stretch out and begin to tear away from my bones as I continued to hurtle through the air. My hair stood on end and started to rip from my scalp, which was excruciatingly painful. I screamed out in pain and when I opened my mouth, my tongue was pulled away from my face and stretched out deep into the darkness ahead. My clothes were torn from my body and soon I was naked and stretched out in the darkness, still hurtling towards an unknown fate.

The force of the shockwave began to diminish and soon my naked bodies decent into the hole slowed, allowing my skin to return to its normal position and my tongue to come back to its home. I still couldn't see anything in the blackness, but I could make out a sound that was making its way up from the bottom of the hole. It was soft at first, but soon grew louder as I continued to fall towards its source. It was a slurping sound like water being sucked down a drain. The sounds volume grew louder and soon became deafening, and I felt myself once again being pulled down against my will. The force pulled me down in a circle, each revolution growing smaller and smaller, and the slurping noise grew louder and louder, as I was pulled farther down into the darkness. My body went around faster and I could feel the g-forces pulling my skin back from my face, flapping in the air. The slurping sound penetrated my bones and they began to shake from its force, as I was sucked into the drain with a burp.

I emerged from the drain and saw that there was light on the other side. I flipped my body around as I continued to fall, and I saw the ground approaching rapidly. I tried to put my hands in front of my face, but I was going way too fast and hit the ground before I could react. My naked body slammed into the ground and my mouth was instantly filled with dirt. I turned my head to cough it out and felt the pain finally catch up to my body. I couldn't move my legs and thought I had broken my back. My arms were sore but movable, so I braced down and pushed myself onto my side.

I looked around at the green, glowing landscape and saw that I had landed right in the middle of the vegetable field by my old house. There was a sharp pain in my back, like something was poking into me, so I reached back and grabbed it, pulling it away so I could see what it was. It was a wooden stake from one of the plants. I opened the paper attached to the end and saw that it read 'childhood'. I had landed right on the row of potatoes. I rolled over, looked down at the disturbed ground, and saw the potatoes sticking out of the ground. I scanned the row and saw that all of the potatoes were sticking out of the ground, the soil around them piled up as if someone had recently been gardening here. When I left here before, none of the ceramic potatoes were uprooted, except for the one I had shattered. I reached over to the nearest stake and pulled it up, revealing a dirty potato in the ground. The ceramic potatoes before weren't the slightest bit dirty and even shined when I saw them last. I grabbed the potato and held it up to the green light in the sky. This one felt real, not glassy like the others. I held it to my nose and sniffed, the smell of a real potato permeated my sinuses. I dusted off the dirt and felt the rough skin of the veggie with my hands. This was real.

My legs hurt badly so I had to pull myself along the ground with my arms. I checked each potato along the way. They were all real, not ceramic like before. Something had removed the fake ones and replaced them with these since I had been here last. The only one who could've done that was the young boy in the barn. I told him to hide the memories so no one would find them until I returned. He must've figured that no one would check here for them. Poor bastard. I hoped he was safe and that Paul or Chaos hadn't seen what he was doing. They would surely inflict their wrath on him in a horrible way.

 The pear. Oh no, he had given it to me to keep safe and now it was gone along with the rest of my clothes. Great. I lost the bag, the book, the key, and now the pear with my clothes. There's no way that I could continue, especially with pain that was racking my body. I pulled myself over and saw that there was a larger hole dug into the ground at the end of the row of potatoes. Large piles of dirt were strewn all over the ground around it and there was more dirt being thrown up from the hole. Someone was still digging there. I tried to call out, but the muscles in my throat hadn't yet recovered from the fall. I pulled myself up and crawled over to the hole as dirt continued to fling into the air and fall into the mounds.

I reached the edge of the nearest mound and saw something sticking out of the dirt. I clawed my way up to where it was buried and pulled it out. It was the pear. The glow was weak and the hum had begun to go static, but at least it was safe again. I held the pear close to my chest and willed it to be healthy again. I could feel my hands getting warm as I squeezed the fruit tightly in my grip, and concentrated all of my thoughts into its center. The crackling static grew louder as my hands pressed new life into the dying fruit. I closed my eyes, squeezed down harder on the pear, and felt the juices inside begin to drip down my arm. My skin soaked in the juices like a sponge and soon they were coursing through my veins, healing my wounds and energizing my soul. I opened my eyes and saw the fruits glow brighten in a healthy pulsing as the static noise gave way to a constant hum.

The pear grew in my hands and soon doubled in size. The juices from the fruit finished their travels through my body and then began to seep out of my pores, drenching the ground beneath me in a sticky, sweet pool. My legs were no longer filled with pain and I got to my feet, still pressing hard on the pear, until all of its juices had exited my body. I felt like a new man, although still quite naked, and put

Demons Within

the pear down in the center of the pool of juices on the ground. I watched the pear soak its healing nectar back inside of it until none remained, then something amazing happened. The ground underneath the pear began to change. New growth sprouted from seeds buried deep within, long since considered dead, and shot into the sky. The new growth grew tall and began to fork off into branches that flowered within seconds after being created. The roots of the tree spread out over the field and soon reached their dying brothers in the woods. They grabbed onto the roots of the other trees and began to throb, breathing new life into the dying trees. I watched with wonder and amazement as the flowers grew into fruits, small at first, but then growing larger and glowing brighter until they reached maturity. The newly formed pears started to hum in unison and their sounds echoed through the fields, even penetrating the dark, dense forest beyond the low-lying hills. The other trees in the field had started to regain some of the life they had before and soon they too were flowering.

I was still astounded by what I had just witnessed when I was hit in the head by a flying piece of rock kicked up out of the still growing hole. I walked up the large mound of dirt and peered down to see if the boy was the one doing all of the digging. I saw that the boy wasn't the one doing the digging but rather Rusty was, and he was going at it in a frenzied way. I called out to him but he didn't respond, preferring instead to dig deeper and faster. I jumped into the hole with the dog and looked into his frenzied eyes. He didn't even seem to be aware of my presence. It was like he was possessed by the need to dig as if his very life was in danger if he did not. I decided to join him, naked or not, and soon we had gone many more feet into the soft earth.

The green sky above us opened up and rain poured down from its clouds, turning the soil to mud and beginning to flood the hole that we were digging. The dog didn't let this faze him one bit and continued on his quest to reach whatever was buried here. We dug for a while more until the dog abruptly stopped and let out a steady stream of barks. I looked into the flooded hole to see what he saw but the mud made that task virtually impossible. I reached down into the muck with both hands and felt something there. I grabbed it and pulled it to the surface. I couldn't tell what it was because of the mud that was caked to its sides. I took the object and climbed up the slippery side of the hole until I was finally at the top.

The rain was cold on my naked skin and I was shivering uncontrollably. I heaved the bag over the side of the hole and pulled myself up. A pair of legs covered in black pants and black boots greeted me. I lifted my head up to see who was standing there and saw Cigar Man peering down at me over his dark glasses. His face was motionless and his stare colder then the rain falling down on my skin. He reached down and picked the muddy object off the ground. The mud started to fall off the sides of the object and I could finally see what it was the dog was trying so hard to unearth. It was the missing duffle bag. Cigar Man lifted the bag up and unzipped it to check if the contents were still intact.

"Yep," he said, "it's all here. Thanks for finding it for me." He zipped the bag back up and flung it over his shoulder. "Enjoy your stay, if only for a little while." He raised his foot and then lowered it to my head, pushing down on me until I slid into the puddle at the bottom of the hole.

Nirvana No More

I splashed into the cold water and my legs quickly sunk into the wet soil until I stopped hip deep in the mud. I looked up and saw him relight his cigar that had gotten wet from the rain. He looked down one final time at me and flicked his still lit match into the hole. It landed in the muddle, hissing as it extinguished.

Your Call is Important to US

My misplaced trust in Cigar Man had landed me naked and vulnerable in this hole and I was even farther away from understanding now than I was before we entered the strange land of my subconscious mind. I should've known that he was untrustworthy from the start but his story was very convincing at the time. I wanted to kick myself for trusting him with my life. Now that I knew he hadn't meant to help me in the first place, I was stuck with another problem to figure out. Was I actually trapped in my own mind, or was this just another dream that I would soon wake from with even more questions?

The rain was cold on my naked skin and the coldness began to work its way to my bones, causing me to shake as I looked for a way out of this damn hole. Rusty was still in the hole and his fur was matted to his skin from all of the rain. I looked up and saw Cigar Man sitting on the dirt at the edge of the hole. He was now holding the pear, turning it in his hands to examine it more closely. I could hear the pears hum but noticed that it was no longer glowing as it had been. He looked down at me, holding the pear out at arms length.

"Where did you get this?" He asked with a great deal of anger in his voice. "I thought there were no more of these."

Even if this was only a dream, I didn't want him to find out that I had visited the barn, as I was very concerned about the boys' welfare. I was sure that he knew about the existence of the boy but since we had become separated, he might not know everything that I had found out. A little lie on my part might just get him to release some more information.

"There are plenty more where that came from," I said. "I was just on my way back to the field when you arrived."

"That field is dead," he said, "I killed the last tree myself. Tell me where you got this or I'll make you regret it."

He rose up from where he was sitting and peered down the hole. I saw his face begin to fill with rage and his features contort in an evil twist as his eyes grew wider, forcing his brow to curve downward like two black snakes, until they joined at the top of his nose. His muscles began to bulge underneath his skin and ripple throughout his body as he twitched and convulsed with a renewed feeling of strength and power. He lifted his arms up in the air, still holding the pear that had healed my wounds, and closed his hands around the glowing fruit.

The crimson sky boomed thunderously as he tightened his grip on the pear, trying to squeeze the last of its life away. The ground under my feet began to shake violently, causing my naked body to fall back into the cold, muddy water with the dog. The rumbling continued and large pieces of earth began to tear away from the side of the hole and rain down on top of us, threatening to bury us alive. The dog started to dig a tunnel into the side of the hole to escape as large pieces of rock and tree roots began to pierce through the mud and close the hole more quickly.

Cigar Man seemed oblivious to the changing landscape around us, preferring instead to focus all of his energies and attention on destroying the last pear and me in the process. Looking up from the hole, I saw a trickle of juice work its way out of his hands and run down his arm as he strained his muscles to crush down on the pear. The juice flowed down from his arm until it reached the ground at his feet. As soon as it hit the soil there was another great rumble of sound as a giant root shot out from the side of the hole and into my chest, pinning me into the side of the muddy wall.

The giant root continued to grow, forcing me deeper into the wall of mud, as the sky thundered above. I grabbed onto the powerful root and tried to wiggle myself free, but the root had wrapped itself around my torso making escape impossible. The hole began to grow, pulling down everything that was in its path including Cigar Man, who fell into the muddy water still gripping the pear in his hands. He splashed into the cold water as another giant root shot from one of the walls and grabbed onto him, trapping him underneath the waters surface. He struggled against the force of the root, twisting his body back and forth, as it wrapped itself around him and pushed him deeper into the muck.

I saw that he was still holding the pear in his hands and wondered why he hadn't released it to better help himself get free. The muddy water around him began to bubble up as the root worked its way around his chest like a python squeezing the life from its prey. He thrashed his legs out into the water, creating a muddy shower that rained over my face, but still he refused to release the pear so he could get free. I braced my arms against the growing root and pushed down, hoping that the mud covering my body would act as a lubricant and allow me to slip out from its grasp. It worked. I pulled myself up through the root, its splinters tearing at my skin, and back out into the center of the hole.

I saw Rusty still digging into the side of the hole as I splashed through the cold water towards where Cigar Man was trapped. I could see the pear glowing through the muddy water and I called out to him to release it so I could help him escape. His head broke through the surface and I could see from the look in his eyes that he did not intend to let me have the pear willingly. The forceful rain pounded against my skin as I dove into the muck to retrieve the pear from his grasp. Diving deep into the water I couldn't see through the muck, so I had to rely on my sense of touch as I worked my way to where he was struggling. I felt out with my fingers until I grabbed onto his hands clenched tightly around the pear. His grip was viselike and I had to pry it apart one finger at a time. I felt the root growing around his arms and his body began to convulse from the lack of air in his lungs. I pulled his hands apart and the pear floated free up to the surface.

I broke through the surface of the mud and gulped in a large lungful of air. The pear was floating on the far side of the muddy hole so I had to swim over to retrieve it. I hadn't gone more than two feet when I felt his hand grab my ankle and begin to pull me back underneath the muddy water. I kicked out with my other leg until he finally released his grip and swam quickly towards the pear on the other side.

Demons Within

As soon as I reached it, the rain stopped and the sky began to change back from crimson to green. The thunderous skies grew quiet once more and the ground no longer shook underneath my feet. I took the pear and held it up to the sky and it began to glow, though this time differently than before. The bright green glow that was familiar to me was replaced by a deep, orange hue and it filled the sky above with its brilliance.

The familiar hum of the pear began to pulse high and low, as it called out to the root holding Cigar Man under the water. I watched the root release him from his grave and slowly sink back into the side of the hole. He broke through the surface of the water and immediately gasped for air, taking in too much at once, and coughing out muddy water from his lungs. He was no longer wearing his hat and although he was covered in mud, there was something different about him. Gone were the chiseled features of his face, replaced by softer curves and a cleft chin. His eyes were different as well, no longer cold and black, with no feeling coming from them, but green in color with a softer look around their edges.

He shook his head and I swear that I saw blonde hair beneath the mud that was flying off him. I turned to where the dog had been digging and saw that he was no longer there; a large tunnel in the side of the wall marked his last known position. I lowered my arm and the pears glow filled the hole where the both of us were standing, covered head to toe in mud. The bright orange hue pierced through the mud and it began to fall away from our bodies, splashing into the cold water at our feet. I looked back toward Cigar Man and saw him whole, as the last of the mud fell off his clothes, and I was shocked by what he had become. Gone was the imposing figure dressed in black that I feared as much as Chaos himself; the man who penetrated my every dream and waking moment, the man who tried to bury me in this muddy hole. Standing in front of me now was not a man but a boy, and an angry one at that.

He glared at me as he brushed the remaining mud from his sleeves and I could feel his hatred toward me growing more with every second that passed. I tossed the pear between my hands and walked towards him, a scowl beginning to form on my face as I got closer.

"Hello Paul, I said. " You want to tell me the truth now?"

He rushed towards me, his legs splashing up large arches of water in his wake, and reached out for my head. I held the pear out towards him and the glow became a focused beam of light that shot into his chest, stopping him in his tracks.

"You don't know the power of what you're holding," he said. "Give it to me now before it takes you over."

"Not a chance," I replied. "I agree that I don't fully understand what power this holds, but I do know that it holds power over you." I walked closer to Paul and squeezed down on the pear, forcing it to absorb my anger as I had absorbed its juices. The beam of light coming from the pear changed to red as it took on more of my anger and hatred. "You tried to kill me," I said. "You claimed to be a friend and now your true colors are revealed."

Paul fell to his knees in the cold, muddy water and I put the pear right up to his head. "You don't want to do that," he said. "The truth you seek is going to be your downfall. You haven't even read the book. How can you possibly expect to handle the truth without even so much as a clue as to what it means?"

"I know that you are responsible for everything that I have been going through," I said. "I know about the barn now, and what you did to me. I saw the fields where you took over my memories and replaced them with false ones. I saw the scared boy hidden in the corner and he told me about the connection between you and Chaos."

"Lies," Paul said. "That boy couldn't possibly have told you anything. I put him there so he would be safe from you, so you wouldn't hurt him anymore."

"I've had enough of your lies," I said, and put the pear right in the middle of his forehead. The rage coursed through my veins and into the pear, causing its orange hue to grow into a deeper red until it was the color of blood. I wanted to kill him now, crush his head in my hands like he crushed the pear, until his blood ran down my arms and soaked into my skin, absorbing his power and his life.

I was so focused on killing him that I didn't see him reaching down into the muddy water until it was too late. He pulled up the bag that had fallen into the hole with everything else and flung it at the side of my head. The blow knocked me down into the muddy water and allowed him to regain his footing. The pear was thrown from my grasp and into the muddy water at his feet. I looked up and saw Paul open the bag and pull out the book from inside.

"You idiot," he said. "I should have been the one who lived, not you. You don't deserve to have Chaos' power for yourself." He held the book up and started chanting something that I had heard before in a dream.

"Enter now and forever stay, for the demon in you will rule the day. As long as your blood continues to flow, the demon you created will continue to grow."

I watched Paul as he chanted these words while holding the book up to the sky and saw the change in him beginning to take place. His body floated up into the air and I saw his skin begin to bubble, as if something was trying to break through the surface and enter this perception of reality.

"Wait," I said. "I don't understand. What do you mean you should've lived instead of me? Why would I want Chaos' power?"

His skin started to peel away from his face, revealing the muscles underneath and his mouth began to twist in an unnatural way until it had wrapped itself around his head. He chanted the words again and soon he was speaking in tongues, as his chest grew through the fabric of his shirt, revealing a thick coat of matted hair. A dark, black ooze started dripping from Paul's stretched and twisted lips as his eyes began to bulge from their sockets and change from green to black.

"You know more than you think," he said. "Do you remember that dream you had when everything wasn't quite right? You saw life as it should have been, my life. Those were my memories, my wife, and my son being born. You took all of that away from me but now it's my turn. Now that I have the book, your seed is mine and I will finally become as it was meant."

I knew he was transforming into Chaos and this place was way too small for us to do battle. I got up and headed for the tunnel as Paul, my brother, continued the evil chant.

"As long as your blood continues to flow, the demon you created will continue to grow."

I ran through the narrow tunnel and looked back as Paul completed his transformation into the beast that I would soon battle for control over my sanity. The pear. I forgot the damn pear. I knew that I needed it for some reason, but turning around now seemed like the wrong idea. The beast was almost to the edge of the tunnel now and I could smell his rancid breath around my head. I heard a loud howl and turned around to see Rusty running towards me from the other side of the tunnel. He was running at full speed and he shot past me right into the path of Paul, who had now completely become Chaos. The dogs sudden presence must have startled the demon, and he pulled back just as he was about to enter the tunnel.

Rusty shot out and lunged up at Chaos' face, his fangs bared and his claws extended from his paws. Chaos reeled backwards as Rusty struck his neck and his jaws clamped down on the demon with the force of a pit bull. A stream of green and black fluid shot out of the demons neck at the spot of the bite and he reeled back, howling in pain. It was now or never for me to make my move. I shot out into the hole to get the pear as Rusty continued to bite and claw at the demon, causing more ooze to shoot out of his veins and rain down on the surrounding landscape. The demon who was my brother howled out, grabbed poor Rusty by the neck, and threw him into the wall. The dog let out a loud yelp as his spine broke on impact with the wall with a loud snap. His lifeless body slid down into the water and he was gone. Poor Rusty. He risked his life so that I could escape. I had to move quickly so his act wouldn't be for nothing. I got the pear and turned back towards the tunnel with Chaos now turning his attention back my way. He let out a loud howl and grabbed my foot, trapping me in the hole with him.

So close. The demon had me and I fought frantically with everything I had to try to escape his grasp. His breath created a cloud that enveloped me in its stench and I felt his other misshapen hand grab further up my leg as he pulled himself into the tunnel. The ooze seeping out of his pores mixed with my sweat to create a dense fog that soon filled the hole and I couldn't see. I crawled on my belly, clawing at the ground with my arms, and felt the demons weight come down on my back, trapping me where I lay.

I was trapped. Chaos lifted his head back and released another loud howl that shook the walls of the tunnel around us, causing large chunks of earth and rock to fall down around my head. I felt the ooze that was dripping from his jowls hit the back of my neck and I thought the end was here. He had won. He started to chant something that I couldn't quite make out and then something happened. The pear began to sing. Not with words, but with the sound of a harpsichord, filling the air around us with its sweet tunes.

Your Call is Important to US

The glow intensified and its brightness cut through the thick fog until I could see light at the end of the tunnel. Chaos put his hand up around my neck and wrapped around it, sending a cold chill throughout my body. The pear started pulsing as the sweet sounds grew louder until they drown out the howls coming from the beast on my back. The demon was putting all of his weight on my neck and his fingers struck gold, closing off my windpipe. I gasped for air and could feel the blood growing hotter in my head as I kicked out at him, trying to get free.

The light from the pear grew brighter than the sun and I reached back and struck it at Chaos. A large wave of juice came rushing out of the fruit and crashed into his hand, soaking into his skin and mixing with his blood. He howled out as the juice worked its way through his veins, causing his once cold, black blood to boil. He released his grip on my neck and I felt his weight suddenly off my back. I struggled to my feet and turned around to see him putting his hands around his head, which had swelled to twice its normal size and was throbbing between his fingers. His eyes, that were once deep black with evil, were now filing up with the juice, and its orange color was drowning out the blackness and seeping from the corners. The juice ran down his face, creating a trail of scorched skin that bubbled up and peeled away, revealing a newer, more burnt layer beneath.

He fell to his knees and his matted hair began to fall off in clumps, creating large piles on the ground around him. His head continued to grow and more of the black ooze was forcing its way out of his ever-growing pores to escape the burning juice that was flowing through him. He opened his mouth and screamed out, but the ooze gurgled up from his throat and muffled his cries until a steady stream came pouring out of his mouth.

The walls around us kept shaking and large chunks of rock crashed down on his head, splitting it wide open to reveal his jellied brain filling with the juice. He looked up at me as the last of his fur fell from his body, revealing his naked skin covered in sores that were seeping with a mix of juice and ooze. His imposing frame grew smaller until it was that of a normal child curling up in a fetal position with his legs tucked under his arms and his thumb in his mouth, looking up at me with trepidation and fear. His skin turned to a pale white and his muscles shrank down until they were merely resting on his bones. The shaking stopped and he lowered his head, allowing his jellied brain to plop out onto the ground, hissing and smoking as it met the soil.

I watched the creature, who was my brother, as his body returned to a fetal state, curled on the ground, waiting to be born. The clumps of hair that were piled around him turned to a fine powder and slowly blew away in the breeze until they were gone, leaving only a discolored mark on the ground to let me know that they had existed there only a moment ago. I walked over to my brother, taking care not to step in the pool of jellied brains, and crouched down beside him. He looked up and I could see myself in his eyes reflection. He reached out with his small hand and I took it in my own, wrapping it gently around his fragile skin. I felt him place something in my hand as he spoke what would be his last words to me.

"He's too powerful for me to handle," he said in a raspy whisper. "I couldn't separate myself from him when he entered my body." He slipped his hand away from mine and it fell to the ground, dying as it hit. I moved my head closer to his mouth to hear him more clearly. "Take care you don't make the same mistake I did when you take him in you. He will promise you everything but it's a lie."

I picked him up and held his tiny body in my arms as I felt a tear streak from my eye. It worked its way down my face and dripped onto Paul's open head, soaking into his thin skin. The tear soaked up all of the juice that remained in him and then fell to the ground, soaking into the pool of jellied brain. There was a momentary flash of light from the pool and then it too was gone, leaving a small hole in the ground as the only evidence that it had ever existed. I took Paul's limp body and placed it on the ground where the pool had been.

"I am now a part of you," he said. His eyes closed and a strong wind shot through the hole, sweeping up his frail bones and carrying them off to their final resting place.

I stood there in silence for a moment and wept for the loss of a brother that I had never known. I opened my hands to see what he had placed there before he died. It was a small key. I went back through the hole to retrieve the bag, placed the book and the key inside and headed back through the tunnel towards the light on the other side.

Fine

The light pouring through the end of the tunnel was a brilliant white, clear and pure in every way imaginable. A warm breeze wrapped itself around me, penetrating the coldness that until now had soaked through my nakedness and chilled my bones to the marrow. My face took in the warmth graciously and although I was naked, I no longer felt cold. I continued towards the opening, the light growing brighter with each step I took, until it blinded my vision and I had to turn my back to save my retina from burning out. I walked with backwards steps through the rest of the tunnel until the heat proved too much for the skin on my weakened back.

I put the bag down for a moment; my arm muscles strained from its weight, and scooped up a handful of damp earth. I rubbed the cool mud over my skin to sooth the burning feeling and it blocked the heat very well. I scooped up a few more handfuls and rubbed the cool mud all over my face, chest, and legs to shield them from the heat of the light. I picked up the bag and turned once again to the light, but it was still too bright for my eyes and I closed them quickly before I lost my sight for good.

The opening was the only way out of the tunnel, as I couldn't go back the other way for fear of what was waiting for me there. From what I had been told, Chaos was still alive even though his latest host, my brother, had died by my hands. Now I've killed him twice. He should've just told me the truth from the beginning. I would have been able to handle the fact that I had a brother that died at birth. There was no need for him to try to take over my mind and drive out all of my memories. Unless the seeds strength, which he had gotten such a brief taste of before he died, held that much power over him that he was left with no other choice. Maybe it was that powerful feeling that caused his spirit to hold onto my mind even though his body was dying. He didn't want to give it up.

So much was now coming together in my mind. If that were true, then that explained everything that I had been experiencing lately; the dreams, the visions, and the clues. They were all trying to tell me about Paul's memories and even of his very existence. Not all of the questions I had were answered though. There was still the matter of where I was now, locked away in my own mind. And now alone since Paul was gone. There had to be something else that I wasn't seeing here. Something was still holding me prisoner until I could discover why I was here.

I sat down on the cool ground and assessed my situation. I was in my head, trapped for some unknown reason, with only a bag that held a book about Chaos and two keys; one that was given to me by a brother I never knew I had who wanted to destroy me by replacing my memories with his own. The professor, who said that I shouldn't trust Cigar Man, or Paul, in the first place, gave the other key to me along with the book. It was all too confusing for me to understand fully. I now knew that I was truly alone in my fight against my own demon, and that I couldn't get back into reality until he was defeated.

Therein laid the problem, because in order to defeat Chaos and escape the trappings of my own mind, I had to take on and defeat myself, since I was Chaos. If I wasn't without hope before, I was now. There was no way that I could see to get out of this and be the same person that I was before. Something was bound to change, and probably not for the better.

Suicidal thoughts began to fill my head and soon I heard deep howls coming from the darker side of the tunnel. A thick fog, not unlike the one that had appeared before, began to waft up from the shadows and the muddy ground began to harden under my toes. There was a change happening in my mind, looping through my thoughts and portraying itself darkly around me, and I didn't like where it was going. Although the land around me bent at the will of my thoughts, I no longer felt in control.

Something slithered past my leg, rubbing up against the bag, and shot up the wall with a hiss right beside my head. Roots from the trees above began to creep into the hole and slither along its walls, limbs twining together in an evil dance as they made their way to the ground where I was sitting. I got to my feet, turned back towards the light on the other side of the tunnel, and saw that it was fading. A rancid smell shot through the fog and into my nose, causing me to gag involuntarily as it sunk into my lungs.

My mind was blank, all of my thoughts gone replaced only by emptiness. I had no memory of where I was or how I had gotten there. I knew only two things; dark was bad, light was good. I picked up the bag and squinted as I ran towards the fading light that I hoped was safe from the dark part that was creeping ever closer. The howls coming from the dark grew louder and took on a more ominous tone. I felt I was trapped in a house of horrors as the ground I was running on twisted and bent beneath my feet. I lost my balance several times on the way to the light and had to brace myself on the moving walls. One time my hand hit the wall and the earth yielded, allowing my hand to sink deep inside of it, before closing down on my elbow and trapping me before I could reach the light.

I put my foot out on the wall and braced as I pulled my arm out of the trap. It came free too easily and I was thrown back to the ground, the bag flying out of my hand and into the dark fog. The light was within reach now, but I didn't want to leave the bag for whatever was coming. I screamed out and dove into the dark, arms extended to grab the bag, and was sucked into a hole that was growing from the place where my brother had died.

The hole wasn't that deep and I crashed to the bottom, breaking my arm in two places. I rolled onto my back, clutching my arm in pain, and saw the dark fog rolling over where I had fallen. The bag was no more than two feet from where I landed so I reached over and grabbed the handle, pulling it closer to my body, and got to my feet. The fog was growing thicker, quickly absorbing the light that was coming from the other side, and I only had one good arm to get out of the hole before all the light was gone. I heaved the bag over the top and pulled myself up while bracing my toes on a few small rocks that were poling though the dirt. The ground gave way as fast as I could climb and by the time I got out of the hole, there was only a sliver of light coming from where there had once been light as bright as the sun.

I got to my feet and ran through the rancid fog, holding the bag in the crook of my arm as I used my hand to cover my mouth, towards the fading light at the end of the tunnel. The ground changed as I ran and soon it was covered with a sea of snakes raising up their heads and striking at my legs to prevent me from reaching my goal.

Twenty yards to the end, my legs started sinking into the snakes as I ran causing my pace to slow considerably. I sloshed through them, swatting the bag at the ones who got too close to my face, and felt the sting of their poisonous venom as it shot through the veins in my legs, making them weak. Fifteen yards to go, maybe ten. I was up to my waist now and some of the brave ones were striking at my chest, their teeth sinking deep into the tender skin and releasing more of the toxins into my blood-stream. My vision began to falter as the poison took hold, slowing me down even more.

Five yards to go. Light almost all gone now. Sloshing through the snakes, legs getting cold now, head hurts too much. Sinking deeper.

A snake pops out of the pile in front of me and sinks his teeth into my nose. The teeth pierce through the nostril and the venom runs out of my nose and down my face to my lips. I lick them and my tongue soaks up the venom, numbing it. I feel it swelling in my mouth as I slosh through more and more snakes. Two yards to go. Can't see light a lot. Mind shutting down. Poison in blood. Must get to light.

I reach the edge of the opening as the poison hits my brain and I collapse onto the ground, my mind convulsing from the toxins working their way through my head. My last sight is that of the hole closing up behind me, trapping the snakes deep within it to fight another day.

I close my eyes and let the poison do its work with no resistance. Peaceful thing, death was. Real peaceful. It would come anytime now so I'll just lie here and wait. A strange mix of warm and cold air worked its way around my body, each trying to keep the other away as they seep into my skin to use the poison for their own purpose. My breathing became shallower as my lungs struggled to keep functioning against the venom. Each time I breathed, less oxygen pumped through them and my blood started to starve, killing off cells by the thousands in a futile attempt to ration its supply of the much coveted stuff.

I felt myself slipping in and out of saneness, with maddening visions filling my head, pushing out anything that even remotely resembled a happy thought. My parents flashed in front of me for a minute, filling me with warm feelings of love and happiness, but the feelings were soon banished, replaced by a scene of horror and grief. I watched as they fought to gain entry to a room that was on fire, a young boy trapped inside fighting for breath, but they couldn't get in and the boys' skin began to melt from the heat of the flames. He cried out to them and banged on the door, but the room was too far-gone. The walls exploded in flames and the boy fell to the ground, flesh burning off his bones until there was only a pile of ash.

Fine

The scene swept out as quickly as it had entered and I felt myself floating, as if being carried away by gentle winged creatures, to a place of peace. The sky around me was clear and blue, just as I remembered it from the world that I used to inhabit, with wispy clouds streaking gently across the sky on their way to heaven. Everything that I had loved in my life was appearing next to me in the clouds and I felt true peace for the first time in my life.

The winged beings carried me higher into the sky, over the peaks of mountains and the tops of clouds, until there was nothing but a clear sky as far as I could see. Up we went, higher and higher, towards the barrier that kept all of the madness contained within its grasp, and then we broke through into the freedom of space. The air should've been cold, but I felt only the warmth blanketing me from my new companions as we shot farther away from the trappings of earth.

The stars shined more brilliantly, now that all of the pollution trapped within the atmosphere no longer clouded my vision, and I could now appreciate the beauty of all of the planets that I once considered so far out of reach. We passed through the galaxy in the blink of an eye and soon we were in empty space with the lights of all of the other galaxies shining around us. We seemed to be heading for a large cluster of stars separated from all of the others by an area devoid of light and life. A shooting star streaked past me, so close that I could almost reach out and touch its brilliance with my unworthy hands, and a blast of cold air shot through the warm blanket on which I had been traveling.

The coldness forced my companions to abandon me and seek each other out for warmth and I was alone again, hurtling towards the unknown cluster of light. Gone was my feeling of peace, replaced now by anxiousness and fear. What of they were supposed to be with me when I passed into the cluster? How could I explain my presence and justify the reasons why I should be allowed access to the place of total peace? I began to panic, fearing that I had made the wrong decision in giving up my fight for life against the poisons of my own thoughts.

Hurtling through space, alone and afraid, I lost all faith in the choice I had made to end it all in order to kill off the demon in my mind. I wanted another chance to live; to fight my demon and win; to not give up and help anyone else who was thinking about giving up on them. I couldn't go now, not yet. I had to return to myself, escape from the demons grip on my sanity, and reclaim what was left of my life.

The dark space around me brightened as I approached the cluster of stars and I was astonished by their beauty. Each star twinkled and sung with its own brilliant color in a musical salute to celebrate my arrival in their presence. I passed through the barrier of the new galaxy and all the colors of the stars exploded together, creating a brilliant shower of pure white light that wrapped my body with warmth and carried my deeper inside the cluster towards the star that held them in their magnificent orbit. The feeling that I was experiencing was pure joy and although I had never before felt anything close to it, my god it was wonderful, I wanted nothing more than to return to myself, even if it meant never feeling this way again.

Stars shot past my body and danced together, their brilliant light mingling to create a portrait more stunning and beautiful than anything that mortal man should see, especially this man. This place should not have allowed humans to enter, for they would do nothing but spoil its perfection. The gravity of the main star grabbed hold and pulled me gently towards it, opening a path in the wonderful lights that were exploding all around.

I thought of my dog then, I don't know exactly why, but nevertheless I worried about who would take care of him now that I was gone. Sure, he was industrious, but he needed to be around people to be truly happy. Somebody would probably take him in, but I worried that he would get away to come looking for me and then be locked up. We had been through a lot together, that damn dog, and I wasn't ready to let him go. Not for a moment. It was pretty sad that my only reason for wanting to live was a dog, but he was the only family I really had. I had a kid, but we were young and irresponsible when he was born so we gave him up for adoption. At the time, we thought it to be for the best, but now I regretted it and wished I had never made that choice.

I wondered how he turned out, what kid of man he'd become, what his dreams and aspirations were, would he ever wonder about his real father? I cried then. I didn't cry when we gave him up, but I cried then at the thought of him. I failed in the only real responsibility that I was ever given. I failed to protect him. I failed as my own father had failed to protect me from the madness that he passed down in his genes. I failed miserably. Now I couldn't protect him from the seed that I was sure had passed to him at birth. If only I knew of this before. If only my parents had told me about Paul, I could've gotten help for my mental state. If only Paul had lived so we could form a bond and beat this together. If only.

The bright stars around me dimmed and I no longer felt the pull of the star that was carrying me along. I was floating in place, naked and alone, with nowhere to go and no one to help me get there. Alone. I thought back to the pear, my last piece of sanity, and wondered if it held any more life, or had died along with the rest of my sanity. My battle with my demon had been lost. Had I also lost the war? The place where I found myself gave no clue to the answer, only empty light masquerading as peace.

The main star was large before my eyes, but with its pull no longer guiding me I could only float alone just out of its reach. Its pull had ceased when I started thinking about my regrets, leaving me on my own to decide which path I wanted to choose was. My regrets were holding me suspended in that space, forbidding me to cross into peace until I doubted no more. If the doubts had stopped me, would concentrating on them even more actually propel me back to earth and into my body again? Did I really want to go through the hassle and pain associated with life? Or did I want to give it all up and enter peace with no regrets?

Giving up was not the way, I was sure of it. But was it already too late? I closed my eyes and let the thoughts flow freely, hoping that my regrets about life would be strong enough to pull me back into myself and give me another chance. The coldness of the space started to freeze my skin and my blood began to slow. Water from my tear ducts froze in my eyes, causing my eyelashes to turn into brittle icicles that broke off when I touched them. As my blood flow slowed, so did the amount of thoughts entering my mind. The only thing I could think off was the cold itself.

Fine

All of my memories merged into a single thought. Sadness. It was too late. I was destined to float in this purgatory just out of reach of total peace because I was undeserving of its comfort. I should never have given up on life. I should have fought for life as hard as I fought the demon within myself until I was free.

My body became still, my joints frozen in place, as I floated slowly away from the light of peace. I took one final breath and held it in for as long as I could, not wanting to release it, as I was still afraid of crossing over to the other side. The breath froze in my lungs as the last of my sanity slipped away, making its way into the dark void just beyond the nearest cluster of stars. The void absorbed my gift and a brilliant flash of light shot from its center, creating a new star that shined more brightly than anything else in the sky. The new star soon joined the other lost souls as they waited for peace to come and set them free.

Epilogue

The professor slowly made his way over to the chair, his legs no longer able to support his weight without the help of a walker, and his nurse helped him down into the cushion designed especially for him so he could sit more comfortably. The years of chasing the demon had taken their toll on him, turning him into a mere shell of what he once had been. He wished he hadn't felt the power on that mountaintop so long ago; wished he could have remained ignorant of what was happening in the world around him. He could've lived out the remainder of his small life in peace without the knowledge of what evil was planning for the world but he had chosen this path of his own free will, and now he was duty bound to stay the course until the job was finished. Only then could he pass from this world into the next and finally be at peace.

The nurse took the cane out of his hands pressed a button on the side of the chair that moved it closer to the table. The chair rumbled across the floor with a hum and his knee banged into the corner of the desk.

"Damnit Marie," he said, "I told you to fix the track on this thing."

"I'm sorry Professor," she replied. She pulled the desk towards herself and the chair completed its trip along the metal track. She reached into his shirt pocket, removed his glasses, and handed them to him. He took them from her and placed them on the bridge of his nose.

He reached across the desk and braced his hand on a large stack of papers that was teetering on the brink of falling over, grabbed a red folder that was sticking out of the stack, and pulled it from the pile. He let out a shriek as the fragile pile collapsed, covering his desk, and falling onto the floor. The nurse ran to the front of the desk and started picking up the papers as the professor cursed her from the safety of his chair.

"I told you to get the files up to date," he yelled. "How am I ever going to find anything in this mess?"

"I'm sorry, there are just so many papers," she said.

"Let them be for now and leave us alone," the professor said.

The nurse stood up with an armful of papers and hurried out of the office, papers falling from her grasp as she went. She closed the door and the professor turned back to the file.

The red folder was full of papers containing notes and observations of the most troubled patient he ever had; a man who until recently had been locked away in one of the states most run down institutions. Twenty years ago, he had been forced to have this man committed, for fear of what he could do to himself or others, and last week he received the news that the man had finally succumb to his personal demons and took his own life. For twenty years, the man had lain in a comatose state, lost in

Epilogue

his own world of madness, until waking up one day in a panicked state and throwing himself out the window, crashing into a car parked below.

The professor always thought that he could bring the man back to reality and spent countless hours every day trying to coax the man out of his self-inflicted state. Nothing that he tried, from cortical stimulation to chemical injection, even electrode therapy, would pull the man back out of his state, and the professor resigned himself to wait it out until the man finally gave up on himself.

In the early days before the man slipped from reality, the professor had many lengthy conversations with him. It was in these conversations that he learned the man was becoming, and the professor committed his entire being to freeing the man from Chaos' evil grip. He spent many long sessions, some even lasting for days at a stretch, with this man, trying to save what was left of his mind. It proved to be too little too late and the man slipped into total madness, leaving the professor physically and mentally drained.

He looked up from the file at the man who was sitting in the chair in front of him. He was a large man with chiseled features and green eyes that would have surely melted the hearts of many unsuspecting women. The meeting had been set up by an old friend of his, Tony Marachino, who had worked with the professor many times over the years in his quest to destroy Chaos.

"Excuse the mess," the professor said. "She's new and doesn't quite understand my filing system."

"That's perfectly alright," the young man in the chair replied. "Were you able to find the file?"

"I've got it right here," he said. He opened the red folder and started thumbing through its contents, mumbling thoughts to himself as the pages fell into the growing pile on his desk. He found the piece of paper he was searching for and placed the red folder on top of the spilled pile of papers on his desk. He studied the document for a few minutes before looking up at the man sitting in the chair.

"This is an old case," he said. "Are you sure you've got the name right?"

The man reached across the desk, handed the professor a business card, and returned to his seat. The professor held the card up close to his eyes to make out the faded print. Satisfied by what he saw, he tossed it back at the man.

"Well, that's the man," the professor said. "What did you say your connection was?"

"I understand you treated that man, John O'Malley, for some type of psychosis. Is that correct?"

The professor didn't answer right away, preferring instead to let the man wait while he decided if he should breach his former patients' confidentiality. The mans credentials had been properly checked out prior to this appointment. He was a detective for a police department in the city, a ten-year veteran with numerous citations for bravery and courage under fire. In his phone call to the professor, the man said that he was following up on an old lead to a murder case and just needed some background information.

The professor, always one to do all of his homework prior to any meeting, had contacted his old friend of his who still worked for that department, Tony Marachino. It turned out that Tony was the detectives' supervisor. Tony told the professor that the man was a good detective, but lately something about his personality had changed. Once extremely outgoing and energetic, he now preferred to work on his own, and he was very sensitive about asking for help.

Tony wanted the professor to probe the kid a little, find out what was going on inside his head, to see if he needed any help. The professor agreed without question, wanting to do something to get his mind off the failures of the past, not knowing that this meeting would bring back many old ghosts that he thought were long since buried.

The man looked at the professor impatiently during the silence and finally got tired of waiting.

"Professor," he said, "did you treat this man?"

The professor chose his words carefully, not wanting to divulge too much information before he found out the real reason for the detectives visit. "Yes, he was a patient of mine, but that was many years ago."

"What can you tell me about him?" The man asked. "Any information would be helpful."

The professors facial expression changed to a cold stare as he curled his brow at the man. "What does this have to do with an old case?" He asked. "I treated this man twenty years ago and as far as I can recall, there was never any instances of murder."

The man detected a trace of nervousness coming from the old man as he spoke, as if he were hiding something. He stood up and leaned over the desk until he was six inches from the professors' face. The professor met his stare and the man could see fear in his eyes; he could actually smell the fear wafting out of the old mans' pores. This was something that he had recently been gifted with, the ability to feel what other people were feeling. That gift was the driving force behind his visit to the retired psychiatrist, as well as the truth about what was happening to him now.

"Professor," he said, "I'm gonna level with you. But I want your assurance that it doesn't leave this room no matter what."

The old man sat back in his chair and pondered that question for a moment before responding. "Tell me the real reason behind your wanting information about this man and I'll consider your request."

The man sat back down in his chair and a look of despair washed over his face. He rubbed his head in his hands, pressing hard into the scalp, and then looked up to meet the professors' gaze. "I was adopted," he said, "and now that I'm about to have a kid of my own, I wanted to find out about my real father. You know, what he was like and stuff. I used my position to bypass all of the red tape you have to go through down at the records building to find out who he was. Once I had that information in hand, I set out to find him, you know, to see if we could bond or something, I dunno."

The professor remained still while the man spoke, not wanting to give away any of the emotions that were flooding through him at that moment. After all these years, the one person that he had failed was coming back to haunt him. Even worse was the fact that the man was having a child. He thought his days of chasing Chaos had finally ended. If this man was truly John's son, then he had to stop the seed from spreading further. He reached for the pitcher of water on his desk and poured himself a glass, his hands trembling with the pitchers weight causing most of the water to spill all over the papers on his desk. The young man grabbed the pitcher to steady the old mans hand and helped him top off the glass.

"Thank you," the professor said, and took a long gulp of the refreshing water. He finished and placed the glass back on the edge of the desk. "Go on, you were saying."

"Look," he said, "Lately I've been going through some pretty weird stuff and since you treated my real father, I thought you might be able to help me out. Maybe there's a connection between what he had and what's going on with me now."

"I can't release information from this personal file," the professor said, "but I can tell you that the man in question died last week. We'll never know what the true extent of his illness was, but maybe if you tell me some of the things that have been happening I can offer some guidance."

"Okay," the cop said, "but it doesn't go any further than this. Recently I've been having these weird dreams. It's kind of hard to explain, and believe me I've tried many times. I'm just going about my normal day, you know, cop stuff, and all of a sudden it's like my mind takes over and suddenly I'm a kid again, only in these dreams it's different. The memory goes along just as it should and then BAM! The world around me changes and I'm running away from this dog looking thing. Most of the time I get away, but last night he caught up to me and I saw myself in his face. I know this sounds weird but maybe it means something. I dunno."

The professor began to sweat and his hands started shaking. All of the old feelings were coming back to him in a rush and it was too much to handle in his fragile state. He turned his head away from the cop, refusing to make eye contact for fear of what he might see.

"Listen doc," the cop said, "this might sound strange but I gotta ask you. Are you feeling scared right now? Because I can smell the fear coming out of your body."

The old man jumped back in his seat upon hearing these words, his arm knocking over the glass precariously placed on the edge of the desk, sending it crashing to the wooden floor. He looked up at the cop to see what he had feared come true. The cops' eyes were turning black. His heart started racing as he realized what he had to do.

Demons Within

"You're gonna keep this between us, right doc?" the cop asked. "I know it's a little strange but it's not that big a deal."

The professor reached across his desk and pushed a button on the panel in front of him. There was a series of loud clanks as the doors and windows locked shut one at a time, trapping the man in the office with the professor. The man looked around, obviously very confused and the professor met his panicked stare.

"I'm afraid I can't allow you to leave," he said as he pushed another button on the panel. Slots opened up in the wall and a fine mist began to fill the room. The cop covered his mouth, ran to the office door, and fought to get it open. The door didn't budge. The cop took out his gun and fired several times at the latch but it would not yield. He turned his gun to the professor who was now standing behind his desk with a small mask over his face.

"I'm afraid that's not going to do you any good," he said. "This is the only way to stop you from Becoming."

The cop staggered into the wall, coughing and wheezing, as the mist filled the room and worked its way into his lungs. He pointed the gun at the professor as he slid slowly down the paneled wall. The professor grabbed his walker and made his way over to the fallen cop who could no longer move, as the effects of the mist took hold of his nervous system. He reached down and took the gun out of the cops' hands and pointed it at his head.

"I won't fail again," the professor said. He lowered the gun, looked into the cops eyes, and fired. The bullet hit the cop squarely in the middle of his forehead and he slumped lifelessly to the floor. The professor walked back over to his desk and pressed a third button on the panel that opened the windows allowing the poisonous mist to filter harmlessly into the outside air. He picked up the phone and dialed a number from memory. It only rang one time.

"Marachino," the voice said.

"It's done," replied the professor. "But there is a problem. He mentioned that he and his wife were having a child."

"That's right," Tony said. "She's due any day now."

"Go and get the wife and bring her here," the professor said. "We can't fail this time. I have neither the strength nor the will to do this again."

"Consider it done," Tony replied, and the line went dead.

He replaced the receiver back on its base and sat down in his chair, placing the gun in the drawer of his desk. He hit the intercom button and the voice of his nurs echoed through the speaker.

"Yes professor," she said.

"You can go now Marie. My next appointment is extremely sensitive and needs to be kept private."

Epilogue

He opened the bottom of his desk drawer, pulled out a bottle of gin, and poured himself a tall glass. He gulped it down quickly with most of it dribbling from the corners of his mouth. "One more to go," he said, and poured himself another glass.

About the Author

    William Hartnett lives in Bristol Rhode Island with his wife and
two sons. He has also been blessed with a lovely daughter, Allyson, who is
currently attending college. When he's not an aspiring author, he is an
avid Red sox fan and has been known to throw down a mean hand of
Texas Hold em.
    He also eats way too many Tums.

www.ingramcontent.com/pod-product-compliance
Lightning Source LLC
Chambersburg PA
CBHW030336030726
47499CB00003B/797